The Autumn of Andie

by

John V. Madormo

a sequel to
The Summer of Guinevere

The Autumn of Andie

Cover Art by *The Wild Rose Press, Inc.*

The Wild Rose Press, Inc.
PO Box 708
Adams Basin, NY 14410-0708
Visit us at www.thewildrosepress.com

Publishing History
First Vintage Rose Edition, 2020
Trade Paperback ISBN 978-1-5092-3266-6
Digital ISBN 978-1-5092-3267-3

a sequel to The Summer of Guinevere
Published in the United States of America

When my alarm went off on Monday morning, I just lay there for a few minutes. Today could end up being one of the best days of my life. On the other hand, it also had the potential of being one of my darkest days. I tried to think positively. I had spent the better part of Sunday afternoon knocking out a series of homework assignments. I had to read *Romeo and Juliet* for Mr. Drennan's class. As I read, I kept imagining myself as the ill-fated Romeo and Andie as the elusive Juliet. Maybe that was a solution to my problem, I thought. Since, like Romeo, I couldn't have the girl of my dreams, maybe ending it all was an option. But I didn't think Andie would react the way Juliet had. Andie was not about to cash in her chips for someone like me. Let's face it—she hated me. And there didn't appear to be anything I could do to change that. But I wasn't so sure Romeo's solution was the answer. Would I actually consider killing myself over a girl? I just couldn't see it.

I sat up in bed and thought about what was waiting for me at good old Anton J. Cermak College Prep today. I wondered how I would feel a few hours from now when I got home from school. Would I be rejoicing, or would I be licking my wounds? As much as I was hoping for a positive outcome, I kept obsessing on the worst-case scenario. It was making me crazy.

Praise for John V. Madormo

"*THE SUMMER OF GUINEVERE* is a compelling and captivating coming of age story about an underachieving sixteen-year-old boy named Paulie Passero in the summer of 1968. John Madormo is a powerful storyteller with an ever-changing storyline and relatable characters."

~The New England Book Critic
~*~

"This was a beautiful story told in the first person ....Although...about high school kids...I would highly recommend to any adult."

~Paranormal Romance Guild
~*~

"This book took me to a time of what I can only call innocence....Paulie...grows as a person and makes some lasting life decisions....a good story."

~Coffee Time Romance & More
~*~

"The romance was cute and I enjoyed it, but this is a hard-hitting story. ...It does show you can grow and change your situation. I highly recommend!"

~readinginthewildwood
~*~

"I have to say *THE SUMMER OF GUINEVERE* did not disappoint [and]...was everything I needed to read."

~heyitscarlyrae.com

"A remarkable slow burn reminiscent of hot summer days and the awkwardness of being a kid in love.... [It] deals with some very serious issues that were relevant in 1968 and are equally relevant now."

~Critic Meg Orton, fortheloveofmeg.co.za

Dedication

To my daughters Caroline, Christine, and Mary,
for their encouragement and support,
and for never letting me take myself too seriously.

Acknowledgements

I would like to take a moment to thank a few folks at The Wild Rose Press without whose assistance *The Autumn of Andie* would never have taken place.

Thanks to Rhonda Penders, co-founder and president of The Wild Rose Press. Nothing happens at TWRP without the blessings of the top brass. I am so very appreciative of the faith shown by Rhonda in my writing. She has been a fervent booster of *The Summer of Guinevere*, and now, *The Autumn of Andie*. I am delighted to have her unwavering support.

Another key member of the TWRP team is Lisa Dawn MacDonald, Marketing Coordinator. Lisa is my go-to gal whenever I am trying to navigate the marketing waters. Her knowledge of social media is a great resource when it comes to promoting my works. She seems as passionate about marketing my novels as she is about every other TWRP author. I couldn't ask for a better business partner.

I also need to thank R.J. Morris, Vice President, Operations Manager, and Co-Founder of The Wild Rose Press. R.J. was instrumental in choosing the cover for *The Autumn of Andie*. I would never have thought of that concept. It's perfect, as are her design talents.

And then there is my editor, Nancy Swanson. Nan is a true collaborator. She pores over every paragraph, every sentence, every word, and every punctuation mark in my writing. Her suggestions are spot-on. I wouldn't even think of disagreeing with her. She makes the editing process a truly painless experience. I am a better writer because of her.

Chapter 1

Mickey grabbed me by the shoulders. "Paulie Passero, I want the truth," he said.

"Will you please stop? I've been telling you the truth. I don't know what else I can say to make you believe me."

"I want you to admit you made up this Andie Walker business. Come clean, buddy. You'll feel better getting it off your chest. This is your best friend talking."

I laughed and plopped down on the bed. This was just another typical day for me and my best bud, Mickey Hannigan. I'd lost count how many times we had had these kinds of conversations in my room. Neither of us could believe the other guy could actually get a date with a real girl. We weren't what you would call *experienced*.

We were entering our junior year of high school with the hopes of erasing a bleak—no, make that pathetic—history with the opposite sex. Mickey had gone on two dates in his whole life. One of them you couldn't count since it was with his cousin. And the other was a disaster. He ended up puking on his date following a spin on the Tilt-a-Whirl at Kiddieland. So I guess I could see why he didn't want to believe I had a date with Andie Walker. I'd be catching up to him, and he didn't want to hear that.

"Eat your heart out, Mick," I said.

"All right, how about if I just show up at the tennis courts tomorrow and see for myself? How'd you like that?" He smirked.

I shrugged. "I could care less." I knew that would make him crazy.

"Give me a break. You don't care if I'm there? Really?"

"Just do whatever you want." I got up off the bed. "I can't believe you think I made it all up. You think I'd lie just to impress you."

Mickey's sneer soon melted into a smile. "You had me going there for a minute, partner. I almost believed this whole thing."

I stomped my foot. "Damn it, Mick. Come with me tomorrow. You'll see. But then make some excuse why you have to leave. I don't need anyone critiquing my moves."

He nodded. "It's a deal." He glanced at his watch. "Hey, I gotta get out of here. I'll see you tomorrow. What time are you *supposedly* meeting her?"

I shook my head. The Mick killed me. "Noon."

"Perfect. I'll get here about eleven. The buses don't run as often on the weekends. We'll need the extra time."

"Fine. Eleven it is."

He winked. He was toying with me now. "I'll let myself out."

"You do that." I waited at the top of the stairs until I heard the front door close. Then I fell back onto my bed and put my hands behind my head. I couldn't stop thinking of Andie. This was going to be great. I was actually going to be spending some one-on-one time with the girl of my dreams. And if I played my cards right, this could be the first of many.

I thought back to how all of this had come about. It all started with Guennie. If it hadn't been for her, I would never have had the courage to talk to Andie. Let me back up. Guennie—Guinevere Thompson—was what you might call my summer fling. All that came about when my dad asked me to accompany him to Leroy, Pennsylvania to visit his dying mother. This was the same woman who hadn't spoken word one to him for the last twenty years. You see, she disowned him when he moved from Leroy to Chicago after he and my mom got married. When he learned my grandmother had only days to live, he decided to return to his boyhood home to say goodbye. He asked me to come along to help with the six-hundred-mile drive.

While there I met the most amazing girl. She was gorgeous. And she taught me how to act around girls. We even hugged and kissed. It was heaven—until Grandma died, and it was time to head home. For a while there I was trying to figure out a way to get back to Leroy to visit her, but when she wrote a letter telling me she was going to a dance with a boy she met at school, I knew it was time to move on. It took me a few days to get over her. But the minute I saw Andie— Andrea Walker—in the hallway at school one day, I started to forget about Guennie.

My first reaction was to do nothing. I knew I'd never build up the courage to actually talk to her. That was how it had been for two years. I'd see her. I'd stare at her. I'd follow her home—not in a creepy stalker kind of way, more like an inquisitive way. I'd watch her from a distance on the tennis courts. I even sat across from her at lunch but never managed to start up a conversation. So when I saw her in the hallway the other day, I never expected anything to happen. But something did happen. I began to think about the time I had spent with Guennie and how we had talked endlessly when we were together. All at once, I realized I *could* do this. I could actually talk to girls.

And that was just what I did. We made small talk for a couple of minutes. Then I told her how I had watched her play tennis a few times. I think she was flattered I was a fan. I explained I had always wanted to learn the sport but I was kind of a klutz. That was when she made this amazing offer to meet me on the tennis courts on Saturday at noon after practice to give me a few pointers.

As I lay in bed, I kept going over what I'd say to her when we met up tomorrow. I guessed I could comment on how she looked at practice. Talk about the weather a little bit. No, that was lame. Maybe I just needed to rely on my ad-libbing abilities and go with that. Even though that strategy had failed me a million times before. But this was a new me. I could talk to girls, right? Sure. I had done it with Guennie. So before long, I hoped, I'd be talking to Andie the same way.

Then I started thinking about how I could turn one casual meeting into a string of meaningful dates. I would have to see how tomorrow went before I planned my next move. Then again, I wondered if I should try to schedule another time together. Should I ask her if she wanted to get something to eat? Yeah, that was an idea. I hopped off my bed and grabbed my wallet off the dresser. Seventeen dollars. That was plenty for lunch.

Okay, now I had a plan. I thought I could do this—as long as the Mick got lost after seeing what he came for and realizing it wasn't just a figment of my imagination.

I jumped off the bed, changed into pajamas, washed up, and brushed my teeth. I laid out a clean T-shirt, socks, underwear, and a pair of jeans. I wondered if I should shower in the morning. The last thing I wanted to do was turn her off with an attack of B.O. Before long I drifted off. This was going to be so sweet. I couldn't believe it was actually happening.

****

On a typical Saturday, I would sleep in until at least nine. But today I was up at seven-thirty. I couldn't sleep. I took a shower, got dressed, and went downstairs for breakfast. My mom was at the stove scrambling some eggs.

"Oh," she said. "I'd better make more of these." She grabbed two more eggs from the refrigerator. "Why are you up so early?"

"Is this early? I hadn't noticed."

"For a Saturday, it is. You usually don't stroll in here for breakfast till nine-thirty or ten."

My dad walked in, his eyes fixed on the newspaper he was holding.

"Why can't they find something else to write about?" he said. "I'm tired of reading about how the Chicago cops mugged those hippies. They were throwing rocks and bottles. They got what they deserved."

"Well, they did seem to go a little overboard, don't you think?" my mom said.

"Their job is to protect the citizens of this city. You

can't have some long-haired troublemakers disturbing the peace and getting away with it."

My parents were referring to the Democratic National Convention that was held here in Chicago a couple of weeks back. While the politicians were inside the hotel trying to decide on a candidate, anti-war protestors were outside clashing with police. Since a few reporters also got roughed up, the media was all over the story. The Chicago papers, as my dad discovered, were still talking about it. Some columnists were saying the city had received a black eye on account of the demonstrations and the police handling of the situation.

There was a time, not terribly long ago, when I would have been completely unfazed by a news event of this nature. But that all changed when I was in Pennsylvania with my dad. I watched the network coverage of the violence outside the convention, and I tried to imagine what it might be like to be a newspaper or TV reporter covering a story like that. It seemed fascinating. And it was really important. How else would people find out about what was going on in the world—good or bad—without reporters around to bring it into your home. One of the first things I did when I got back to school was to walk into the newspaper office and volunteer my services. They started me off with a fluff piece, but I attacked it as if it were an actual news scoop. After that, they started giving me meatier assignments. As tragic as the results of the convention were for the city, it couldn't have worked out better for me. It awakened a part of me I never knew existed. I saw myself someday with pen and paper, and reporter credentials, covering a story of national significance. I could actually see it. But you have to start somewhere. And so I'll pay my dues for the next couple of years at the Anton J. Cermak *Gazette*.

My dad set his paper down on the breakfast table and glanced at his watch. "What are you doing up so early?" he asked me.

"I've got a thing at school today."

"On a Saturday?"

"Um…yeah…it's like a research project. I'm in this group…you know…and we're meeting up to discuss our presentation."

My dad shook his head. "Well, I wish you had told me that. You've been complaining for how long about that leak in your room. I was hoping to get up on the roof and patch it up. I needed you to hold the ladder for me."

"I don't like the idea of you getting up on the roof, Peter," my mom said. "Why can't we just call somebody to do it?"

"I'll tell you why," my dad said. "Because they'll tell us we need a whole new roof. Do you know what that would cost? All I need to do is patch up a tiny hole. It's only leaking in one spot. I'll be damned if I'm going to pay hundreds of dollars for what a five-dollar can of roofing cement could do."

Had I failed to mention the fact my dad was cheap—really cheap? He had cut off my allowance on my sixteenth birthday. Since I was now old enough to work in Illinois, and since the minimum wage was a whopping one dollar and sixty cents here in 1968, I was now on my own when it came to spending money. Fortunately, I had gotten a job as a stock boy at the High-Low Foods Market a little under a year ago, and they were pretty good about supplying me with hours after school and on Saturdays. Today was one of the rare Saturdays I wasn't scheduled to show up. It had worked out perfectly.

My dad had now found his spot at the breakfast table, with the *Chicago Tribune* acting as a barrier between him and the rest of us. It was his way of letting people know he wasn't to be disturbed. I glanced at the clock on the far wall and found myself starting to feel guilty. Mickey wouldn't be here for nearly three hours. There was no reason why I couldn't help my dad with this roof business. After all, it was for my benefit. The water spot on the ceiling of my bedroom had grown larger with every rainfall.

"Dad, I don't have to meet up with these kids at school for a little while. If you need help after breakfast with the roof, I should be able to."

He peered over the top of the sports page and nodded. That was his official acknowledgement of my goodwill gesture. I wolfed down the remaining scrambled eggs and toast. I would need to change into some old clothes. I couldn't risk having Andie see me in a dirty T-shirt and jeans. She'd think I had grown up in a barn or something. Just as I was washing off my plate at the sink, the back door opened and in walked Grandpa.

"I found a good spot for my garden, Peter," he said.

"Pop, the back yard is too small to put in a garden."

"Who needs a back yard?" Grandpa said. "We can just dig up the whole thing."

There was one thing you needed to understand about my dad. He prided himself on the immaculate condition of his yard. It was as pristine as a golf course green. Not a blade of crabgrass or a dandelion in sight. The thought of digging up his pride and joy was completely unacceptable.

My dad sighed and rubbed his face. "Pop, let's talk about this in a few months. It's the fall. You're not going to be planting anything until spring. We have time to work this out."

Grandpa made a face and turned to leave. "I'll hold you to that, Pietro." He closed the door behind him.

My parents were still trying to get used to having a boarder in the house. After Grandma died a few weeks back, we had to bring Grandpa back with us. He had no other place to live. The mysterious fire, that we all knew was set by Guennie's brothers, destroyed the bar and part of Grandpa's house back in Leroy, Pennsylvania. My dad's siblings really weren't in a position to take him in, so he agreed to come and live with us. Grandpa now resides in what used to be our guest room. He and I get along great. And he's been trying to teach me how to speak Italian since he's been here. So far, all I know is *buon giorno, buona sera*, and *buona notte*—good morning, good evening, and good night. I don't know where or if I'll ever use any of those sayings, but he seems to enjoy teaching me, so I put up with it.

After a quick change, I was in the back yard holding the ladder for my dad. He had been on the roof for about twenty minutes when a can of roofing cement came whizzing past my head and hit the ground with a thud. My dad poked his head over the edge of the roof.

"You okay?"

"That thing almost hit me."

"You gotta stay awake, son. Now, bring that back

9

up to me."

I grabbed the open can and was about to head up to the roof when I thought of something—who was going to hold the ladder for me?

"Dad," I yelled, "should I get Mom or Grandpa to hold the ladder?"

"Don't be a baby. Just bring that thing up here."

We lived in a two-story home. I was about to climb up a good twenty feet into the air with no leg man at the bottom of the ladder. I couldn't believe it. I sorta kinda had a pseudo date with Andie, and I might not live to see it. I slid the handle of the roofing cement can between my teeth and began my ascent. With each rung of the ladder, I glanced down. I soon learned that was a mistake. I had heard of people who were afraid of heights, but I never thought that was me. I climbed slowly and methodically, keeping my eyes forward the entire time. When I reached the top, I took the can from my teeth and handed it to my dad.

He took it from me and didn't say anything. Now it was time to work my way down. This time I closed my eyes, which probably wasn't the smartest thing to do. I felt for each rung of the ladder as I stepped down. I was almost to the bottom when I missed a rung and slid down unexpectedly. I quickly caught myself and continued on. I had learned something about myself today, and I didn't like it. I was apparently afraid of heights, which didn't seem very manly. I decided to keep it to myself. I wasn't about to share this little tidbit with anyone else, not even Mickey.

An hour or so later I was back in my room changing into clean clothes when I heard the doorbell ring. It was ten-fifty, so it had to be Mickey. I went to the top of the stairs. I could hear him exchanging pleasantries with my mom. Then it hit me. I never told the Mick to cover for me.

"So you're a member of this group at school with Paulie?" my mom said.

Mickey paused. "What group would that be?"

"This research group for some presentation?"

I ran down the stairs before Mickey unknowingly ratted me out.

"Mick, come on up," I said. "Yeah, Mom, Mickey's in our group." I stared a hole right through him.

"Ohhhh, that group," he said. "Yeah, I'm in it. You almost ready, Paulie?"

I motioned for him to come upstairs.

"Well, it's nice seeing you again, Mrs. Passero."

"You should stay for dinner again sometime."

"I'd like that." He smiled, nodded, and ran upstairs.

It wasn't that I couldn't tell my parents I was meeting a girl. They knew about Guennie from the summer. They knew I liked girls. It was just that I didn't want them asking a lot of questions. Since this wasn't a real date, I didn't want to make it seem like it was. I mean, who tells their parents about girls you're madly in love with from a distance? It would seem creepy—and pathetic. And maybe that was my life these days, but I'd rather keep it to myself.

Chapter 2

When Mickey reached the top of the stairs, he looked at me kind of funny.

"Hey, you left me hanging down there, partner."

"I know. I'm sorry. I didn't think about it till the last minute."

"Well, I think your mom bought it. Didn't want to tell them about your lady love, huh?"

"Not until it blossoms into a bona fide love affair," I said.

Mickey rolled his eyes. "Oh, brother!"

I smiled.

He shook his head. "So are you ready for this—if this is actually happening?"

"Oh, it's happening," I said confidently. Or with as much confidence as I could muster up. "Okay, let's get out of here."

We walked the two blocks in silence to the Belmont Avenue bus stop. I think Mickey could tell I was nervous.

"I got to tell you the truth, pal," Mickey said. "I thought you'd make some excuse at the last minute to cancel this whole thing."

"Mick, how many times do I have to tell you—I'm meeting Andie Walker at the tennis courts after her practice ends. It's not an official date or anything. It's just her offering to give me a few tennis pointers."

"Oh, so now the truth comes out," he said. "I knew you'd never get a real date with her. She's out of your league."

"You really think so?"

"I know so."

As we were chatting, a pair of older ladies walked up to the bus stop. They were wearing trench coats and carrying shopping bags. One had a hair net on. The other had these warts on her temples.

Mickey leaned in and whispered. "There's Andie Walker in fifty years." He laughed.

"You're so bad." But he was probably right. Why in the heck did women age so badly anyway? These gals may have been real head-turners years ago. But look at them now. Father Time sure did a number on the fairer sex. How'd you like to wake up to one of these beauties every morning? I know, I know. You're probably thinking—but what do their husbands look like? Well, maybe it was because I was a guy, but in my opinion, men didn't age nearly as badly as women. I know there are some bald, hunched-over, crotchety old men out there who've seen better days, but they don't look as bad as their counterparts.

When the bus finally pulled up, we each dropped our forty cents in the change-taker and walked to the back of the bus—the only respectable place for people our age. Mickey glanced at his watch.

"We should just about make it," he said.

I stared forward. I didn't even hear him.

He tapped me on the shoulder. "Hey, Paulie, you nervous, pal?"

I shrugged. Of course I was nervous. I was worried

about running out of things to talk about. Thank God we were actually supposed to be doing something. Picking up a few tennis pointers should keep the conversation going for a little while, I hoped.

The bus pulled over to let someone off.

"This is Violet's stop," Mickey said. "I wonder whatever happened to her. She's not on our bus this year."

Violet. Be still my heart. Violet was this painted lady who rode our bus last year. Well, she wasn't a lady quite yet. She was probably our age, but she looked a lot older. Maybe that was because of her thick eye makeup and ratted hair. She always wore these short skirts with black nylons. We used to wait for her to get on each day. It was kind of a bummer she didn't ride with us anymore. She was only on for about twenty blocks or so. She didn't go to Cermak Prep. She went to Ridgeway. It was a much tougher school. Whenever a bunch of the Ridgeway greasers would get on our bus, I would stare at the floor. No need to make eye contact and piss them off. I once saw them stick a kid's head out one of the windows and then slam it down on his neck. Then they held it like that until they got off the bus. They usually only rode with us when their cars weren't running. Thank God.

I sighed. "Anybody who looks as good as Violet naturally has a boyfriend—with a car—who's probably driving her to school these days."

"Good point. So what are you saying exactly? That only the dogs ride buses because none of them have boyfriends to drive them?"

"Unless they drive themselves," I said. "Look at us. We have drivers' licenses, but we're still riding the bus.

What does that say about us?"

"That we're a couple of losers whose parents won't let us use the car."

"And we're too poor to have our own cars," I said.

Mickey turned to face me. "Back to business. So let's just say you *are* meeting Andie Walker today. And it goes better than you think. And you manage to work up enough courage to ask her on a *real* date. What are you going to do? Take her to the movies and out to eat on the *bus*? Real suave, man."

"Hey, I'd be happy just not to soil myself today. I haven't thought this thing out beyond that."

Mickey laughed.

"I guess I'd ask my parents if I could use the car and just pray they said *yes*."

"So who do you ask first? Your parents or Andie?"

I shook my head. "I don't know. Why do you care anyway?"

Mickey looked hurt. "Why do I care? Why do I care? Partner, we're a team. If you score with the ladies, it's like a victory for both of us."

I found that hard to believe. Mickey was always so competitive when it came to matters concerning the opposite sex. We were best friends, but in my heart, I always thought Mickey was happiest when I struck out with the ladies. Then I wouldn't be getting one over on him. I supposed we'd both be content if each one of us had a girlfriend. But if one did, and one didn't, that would never do.

He looked forward. "We're almost there. Now listen, don't worry about me. I'll just blend in. You won't even know I'm there."

It was time to set him straight. "Mick, I won't

know you're there because you *won't* be there. Once you see what you came for, then do me a favor and scram. I'll be nervous enough. I don't need a coach looking over my shoulder."

Mickey turned away. "Don't hold back. Say what's on your mind. Geez. If that's what you want, I'll just get off at the next stop and go home."

"Don't play hurt. You wouldn't want me hanging around you if the tables were turned, would you?"

He sighed. "Well…I guess not."

I reached over and pulled the cable that alerted the driver we wanted off at the next stop. We got up and moved to the center of the bus where the exit was. What happened in the next few seconds is still a blur. Just as the Mick and I were ready to hop off, there was a huge CRASH and the bus came to a sudden, unplanned stop. The old ladies started screaming. Mickey and I were thrown several feet. I landed on my stomach with my knees taking the worst of it. Mickey ended up on top of me.

"What the hell?" he said.

We got to our feet and looked out the large front windshield. What we saw was a white panel truck that had been cut nearly in half. Our bus had hit it broadside. I reached down to rub my knee. When I looked at my hand, I could see blood.

"Oh, great," I said. I soon realized that I had torn my jeans and cut my knee. "Well, this'll really impress a date."

Mickey glanced at my knee and gave me one of those looks—you know what I'm talking about—like it wasn't as bad as it looked, but in reality he didn't want to say how messed up it was.

"She probably won't even notice," he said unconvincingly.

The driver, who had exited the bus following the collision, hopped back on. "There's nothing to worry about, folks. A little fender bender is all it is. There'll be another bus by in a few minutes to pick you up."

"Like hell," Mickey whispered. "We're getting out of here." He reached over and pulled the cord. "Can you open the door back here, please," he yelled.

"Relax, kid," the driver said. "Just sit down and wait for the next bus."

"But this is our stop," Mickey said.

The driver shook his head disgustedly, leaned over, and pulled a lever on the dashboard. A moment later, the back door swung open. He motioned for us to exit.

We jumped off and walked to the intersection, where we joined a crowd of people who had gathered in the street following the accident. There were no emergency vehicles on the scene yet, but a few good Samaritans had sprung into action. They were trying to get the driver out of the panel van. He appeared to be trapped, but he was conscious and nodding.

"That guy's got one heck of a lawsuit," Mickey said.

"Unless he ran a red light or something." I looked down at my pant leg. "How am I going to explain this to Andie? I look like a real dope."

Mickey was smiling.

"What's so funny?" I asked.

"I'm not laughing at your ripped jeans. I was just thinking you've got the worst luck on buses."

What Mickey was referring to was an incident that had taken place last spring. He stopped by the house that morning to pick me up and we walked to the bus stop at Belmont. When we arrived, there had to have been six or seven other people waiting. The bus got there a few minutes later and people started boarding. I was at the end of the line. Usually that was no big deal, but this day it proved to be nothing short of tragic. I waited as the others in front of me hopped in. Then just as I stepped up into the doorway, the bus doors closed on my hands. I was hanging onto a pole in the entryway, and then these accordion doors closed from each side. That wasn't the worst part. The driver then pulled away from the curb with my body dangling from the bus. At this point I couldn't let go, so I just hung on for dear life. I might have been hanging outside the bus for a mile or two had not one of the old ladies on board yelled out, "There's a boy hanging out of the bus!" The driver then casually pulled over and opened the doors as I climbed in. Do you believe he didn't say boo to me? He didn't apologize or say he was sorry. He just waited for me to get in and he was back on his route.

"Yeah. Well, at least, I'll have another interesting story to tell people." We crossed the street and continued on our way. We saluted good old Anton J. Cermak College Prep as we passed by. We walked through the parking lot with the tennis courts in sight. I could feel my heart racing. What if Andie forgot about our little meeting? I'd look like a real jerk just standing there. We climbed up onto the bleachers and sat down.

"There she is," Mickey said.

The team was huddled around the coach, Mrs. Anderson. We couldn't hear what she was saying, but she was very animated. Moments later, the girls all put their hands in the middle of the circle and then raised them with an enthusiastic, "Team!" I watched Andie as she talked with some of the other girls. Then she grabbed her duffel bag and walked to the gate. She looked up into the bleachers where Mickey and I were sitting. I wanted to wave but was too nervous to. I didn't want to seem overly anxious. I managed a half smile. Then she looked away. It appeared she was looking for someone. Didn't she recognize me? I was only thirty feet away from her.

Then she smiled and my heart sank. Colton Brand, a linebacker on the football team, suddenly appeared. He walked up to the gate and grinned. Andie ran over, threw her arms around him, and kissed him. Colton took her duffel bag, and the two of them walked arm in arm to the parking lot.

"Colton Brand and Andie Walker." Mickey shook his head. "I never saw that coming." He turned to me. "Looks like she's off the market, pal. And did you see the way she kissed him? That didn't happen in the last twenty-four hours."

"How did I misread those signals so badly? I feel like a jerk."

"Paulie, let's face it. Girls are hard to figure out." He punched me lightly on the shoulder. "C'mon, let's get out of here."

We climbed down the bleachers and walked to the parking lot. We could see Andie getting into Colton's car. Right then I wanted to cry. We walked to the bus stop in total silence. I had no desire to converse, and Mickey seemed to pick up on that cue. We rode the bus home and made small talk along the way. At no time did the word *Andie* come up in our conversation. We talked about everything but girls.

When I got home, I went straight to my room to sulk. I lay on my bed and tried to imagine what life might have been like if Andie *had* remembered our date. Date, yeah, right. Who was I kidding? I couldn't get a date if I paid a girl to go out with me. And to be perfectly honest, I had no interest. If Andie wasn't available, then I'd just drift along with all the other losers. And there were a ton of them—guys who tried to be cool around girls but who didn't have a chance in hell of ever going out with any of them. I didn't want to be in that group. I hated that group. I thought my time with Guennie had prepared me for all of this. I thought it would make me more comfortable, more suave around girls. But apparently I was wrong. All I had managed to accomplish while in Pennsylvania was a special moment with one girl—that ended with a thud. She was gone, along with any hopes of ever having a meaningful relationship with another girl.

Chapter 3

I jumped up and went into the bathroom. I looked at myself in the mirror and shook my head. You're pathetic, I thought. I had to get out of this funk. Self-loathing was not attractive. I splashed some cold water on my face and groaned. All right, if Andie Walker was no longer available, then there had to be another girl at school who might be able to tolerate me. But I couldn't think of any. I had been so head over heels about Andie for so long I had stopped looking at other girls. I had stopped talking to them—as if I ever did in the first place. I wasn't sure who or what was out there. What choices did I have at this point? I needed to move on. But I couldn't. I wanted Andie Walker in my life—period. I wanted to see her break up with Colton and come running to me. But what was the likelihood of something like that ever happening?

I knew it could never take place if all I did was sit around and feel sorry for myself. If I wanted to accomplish the impossible, then I would have to make it happen myself. I closed the toilet seat and sat down. In the past, I had done some of my best thinking in this room. All right, so logic told me Andie was no longer attainable. She was dating a football player. A starter, even. One of the more popular guys on the team. She had to have been attracted to him because, like her, he was an athlete. So how does a guy like me, one who was only talented enough to play on intramural teams, compete with a real athlete? No matter how hard I tried, I would never find myself on one of Cermak's sports teams. I just didn't have those kinds of skills. So where did that leave me? My first response was—dead in the water. But I couldn't accept that. I just couldn't.

I began to think about my options. I could try to break up Andie and Colton. But how? Spread vicious rumors about him? Convince her he'd been cheating on her? Confront him and fight for the girl of my dreams? Um, forget the last idea—he'd kill me. The more I thought about it, the worse I felt. Was I the kind of person who would stoop so low as to sabotage a relationship? Part of me thought *yes*. But the more noble side of me decided I just couldn't do that. It wasn't me. I wasn't that big a jerk. At least, I didn't think so. Then what was I supposed to do? I guessed I could wait for them to break up. From my observations, most high school romances lasted a few months at best. It was more than likely this one would follow the same path. And if it did, then I had to be waiting in the wings.

That was it. I would do everything in my power to seem like her knight in shining armor. I would be cool. I'd talk to her in class and at lunch. I'd make sure she knew I was in the bleachers at her matches. And if she suddenly remembered she had forgotten about meeting up with me, I wouldn't make her feel bad. I would tell her it was no big deal. That I hadn't given it a second thought. That it hadn't fazed me in the least. That was my plan. I only hoped I could pull it off.

On Monday morning Mickey and I met up at the bus stop. We didn't talk much. I had to give him credit.

He didn't say anything about the mix-up on Saturday. I appreciated that. And I thought it would stay like that, but I was wrong. At about the halfway point on our morning trek, he caved. I should have known it.

"I hope you've put any notion of hooking up with Andie Walker out of your head, pal."

I turned and glared at him. I refused to answer. I wasn't ready to discuss my shortcomings.

"Well?"

I stared forward. I knew my unwillingness to discuss the matter was killing him.

"You can ignore me all you want," he said. "But I guarantee you'll feel better if you talk about it. It's only natural." He waited for a response. When none came, he began pushing more buttons. He put his finger to his lips. "Hmmm, so who can I get you a date with? Let me see."

I had heard enough. "Damn it, Mick, will you just drop it! Geez."

"See, I knew you wanted to talk about it."

"I don't want to talk about it. Andie Walker is ancient history. Okay?"

He sat back. "Fine by me." But he couldn't let it go. "There's a bunch of eligible girls out there. Now's the time to get back on your horse and ride."

I let out a long sigh. "If there are so many eligible girls out there, why haven't you made your move? Huh? It's not so easy, is it?"

Mickey smiled. "So that's it. Finally, you've come clean. It's hard for you to ask out a girl, isn't it? I should have known. Well, you've come to the right person. I'd be more than happy to work my magic and play Cupid for you."

That was it. I got up and moved to an empty seat. I didn't have to listen to this. I was perfectly capable of making my own breaks happen. I didn't need a matchmaker.

Mickey hopped up and sat back down next to me. "It's nothing to be ashamed of. So you struck out with one chick. Big deal. You were never going to make it with Andie anyway. She's in the majors. You're Double-A. No offense."

But I was offended. I really just wanted this conversation to end. I couldn't wait till we got to school. Then I'd be able to put a little distance between me and the Mick, who at this point was no more than a constant reminder of my failures.

"What do you think of Claudia Landry? She's kind of cute."

I turned and made a face. "Claudia Landry? Right. She's way too smart. I'd never be able to carry on an intelligent discussion with her. She'd see right through me."

"Who said anything about an intelligent discussion?" he said. "She's a kid just like us. She wants to be popular just like us. I'm sure she'd lower her standards to have a conversation with you."

I knew Mickey was trying to help, but did he have to insult me while he was doing it?

"I'm not a complete idiot, you know," I said. "If I wanted to, I could come up with something to talk about with her. But who says I want to? She looks so studious all the time—with those glasses and with her hair always up in a bun."

"Hey, if she lost the glasses and let her hair down, don't you think she'd be a real looker?"

"Maybe. But I've never talked to her. Hell, I have no interest in talking to her. Just drop it, will you?"

"Just trying to help is all."

I looked up and saw our stop just ahead. We had almost missed it. I jumped up and pulled the cord.

"Looks like we'll just have to continue this discussion after school," he said with a smile.

I shook my head and exited the bus. I waited momentarily before crossing the street. I walked in and headed straight for my locker. When I got there, I couldn't believe what I was seeing. Leaning against it was Andie Walker.

"I am so, so sorry, Paulie. When I got to school today, I suddenly remembered I was supposed to meet up with you on Saturday. I completely forgot. I hope you didn't come all the way to school to meet me."

I was tongue-tied. Why did this always happen? I couldn't blow this. Sure, she had a boyfriend, but this was an opportunity to make a few points with the girl of my dreams. I had to be cool.

"Don't worry about it," I said. "It's fine."

"So you did come Saturday, then?"

"It was no big deal. I didn't have anything else going on anyway. It's okay."

"I feel terrible," she said. "But I intend to make it up to you." She dug into her purse for her datebook. "Let me see. We don't have a Saturday practice for a couple of weeks. But how about if we meet up then. Does noon work again?"

"Sure," I said. "That's fine. But if it's inconvenient, you really don't have to."

"I insist. It's the least I can do."

The warning bell rang. Five minutes to first period.

"Listen, I'd better go," she said. "Sorry about Saturday."

"Don't think anything of it," I said with a grin.

"You're sweet. See you later." And she was off.

You're sweet? Did she actually say that? Did she actually mean it? Maybe I had been premature in thinking this little love affair was over. Maybe I still did have a chance. Well, I had a couple of weeks to showcase my talents. I would be so cool around her. I wouldn't let her know I had any romantic interest in her. Just friends. That was what I would make her think. Then when she and Colton broke up, I'd be ready to pounce.

I scooted to Mr. Drennan's English class and took my seat. I knew I had to concentrate on my studies if I had any intentions of turning around my academic career and getting into a real college, but I couldn't get Andie off my mind. *You're sweet.* She had actually said, "You're sweet."

"All right, folks," Mr. Drennan said. "Open up your literature books to page forty-seven. We're going to read *The Rime of the Ancient Mariner* by Samuel Taylor Coleridge." His request was met with a plethora of painful groans. "I don't know what's wrong with you people," he said. "This poem is a classic."

"How about if we don't read it but say we did," John Tucker shouted out from the back of the room. He was unable to control his own laughter. Snickers followed.

"Okay, Mr. Tucker, would you like to read the first stanza?"

"Not particularly."

"Well, do it anyway. And stand."

John extricated his large frame from his undersized desk and stood. "What page was it?"

Mr. Drennan sighed. "Page forty-seven."

John began paging through his lit book. "What is this thing about anyway?"

"It's about a ship. A ship that has to negotiate stormy seas as it makes its way to the South Pole. And then it continues on to the great Pacific Ocean. It's about the adventures an ancient mariner experiences on this journey." He paused. "Does that help?"

John shrugged. "Okay, here goes." He squinted. "It is an ancient mariner, and he stoppeth one of three. By thy long gray beard and glittering eye, now wherefore stopp'st thou me." He raised his eyes. "Stopp'st? What is that about?"

"It was simply a style of writing in merry old England back in 1834. Okay, the next stanza. Miss Michaels."

And on and on it went from one reader to the next—each reciting a single stanza from a brutal poem that seemed to never end. I tried to stay with it, but I kept thinking about Andie. She looked great today, by the way. She had her hair up in a high ponytail. I loved it when she wore it like that. Actually, I loved it any way she wore it. I thought about seeing her at lunch. That was only a couple of hours away. I had sat across from Andie Walker for the past two years in the cafeteria but had never managed to speak word one to her. I would just keep my head down and shovel in the three sandwiches my mom had made for me. I wasn't sure how Andie found the time to eat. She and her friends spent the entire lunch hour gabbing endlessly. I wasn't sure I'd be able to get a word in even if I wanted to. I would somehow need to work something into the conversation naturally. I didn't want to seem like I was eavesdropping. I needed to think of something to say, but how could I plan for that if I didn't know what they'd be talking about...

"Mr. Passero."

I was in a daze.

"Mr. Passero?"

Angela Fitzgerald, who sat in front of me, turned around and made a face. "Read the next stanza, Paulie."

I panicked. I looked up, and then down at my book. I would have been more than happy to read if I had any idea where we were.

"Angela, where are we?" I whispered.

She turned around disgustedly, turned a couple of pages in my book, and pointed at the correct stanza.

I cleared my throat. "God save thee, ancient Mariner."

"Stand, please," Mr. Drennan said. He sounded somewhat exasperated.

I stood and continued. "God save thee, ancient Mariner. From the fiends, that plague thee thus! Why look'st thou so? With my new cross-bow I shot the ALBATROSS." I looked up sheepishly. "Sorry," I said and sat back down.

Angela leaned back and rolled her eyes.

I sat up in my chair and tried to follow what was going on, but alas, before long I had lost my place yet again. I had other things—more important things—on my mind. I couldn't be bothered with this drivel. It must be stopp'st. You'll be happy to know I did manage to survive English class—barely. Then it was on to Spanish. I knew I'd have a hard time concentrating in there, but I didn't have a choice. I had to. Señora Mendez wasn't as lax as Mr. Drennan. Lose your place in her class and you'd be saddled with additional homework assignments. I had to work after school. More homework was the last thing I needed.

I found myself just staring at the clock. Only forty-five minutes until lunch—and Andie. I tried to concentrate, but nothing was working. I was worried Señora Mendez could sense I was antsy. She kept staring at me.

"Paulie, are you all right?"

"I'm fine."

"Why don't you clear the dust from your brain. Please count to fifty in Spanish aloud. That should bring you back to Earth."

I just sat there. I couldn't think. I knew how to count in Spanish. So why did I mess it up so badly?

"Uno, due, tre, quattro, cinque…"

"Whoa, whoa, whoa!" she said.

"What's wrong?"

"What's *wrong*? This is Spanish class, not Italian."

Whoops. Grandpa had been teaching me a few new Italian words each day. We had gone over numbers yesterday. I guess my brain cramped up.

"While I'm happy to see you're now *tri*-lingual, why don't we just speak Spanish while we're here. Can you do that?"

"Sure." I took a deep breath. I eventually managed to crank out the correct numbers, once I purged Andie from my mind. This girl was going to mess me up academically. I had made a pledge to turn things around in my junior year. I couldn't be bringing home more C's. That would never get me into a decent college. I had to control my thinking. Class was not the appropriate time to pine for the girl of your dreams. There'd be plenty of opportunities for that later. Back to business.

Chapter 4

Following Spanish, it was on to math class. Numbers had always come naturally to me. I could have—and should have—aced freshman and sophomore math. I always did well on the exams. It was my anemic homework record that cost me dearly. Now, as an upperclassman, I intended to change all that. I did my best to concentrate, but I still had Andie on the brain. Despite that, I was able to hold my own in class.

When the bell sounded, I sprinted to the cafeteria and positioned myself in the spot that would hopefully be directly across from Andie. The room began to fill up in the next few minutes. The decibel level also increased dramatically. From a distance I could see some of Andie's lunch crew. They were making their way to my table. A moment later, I saw her. She had stopped to talk to a group of boys on the football team. Oh, if only I had the skills and body type to play football. But that was never to be. I guess I'd just have to woo girls with my sparkling personality—not.

Soon Andie was seated across from me. I stared straight down at my three salami sandwiches. I was too nervous to make eye contact. I would just have to wait for the opportune moment to make my presence felt, which, if things were true to form, might or might not ever happen. As I delved into lunch, I sensed someone staring at me. I raised my eyes just enough to spot Andie trying to get my attention.

"Hi, Paulie," she said.

"Oh, hi."

She tried to see what I was eating. "What's for lunch?"

I lifted a piece of bread, unveiling four slices of salami dripping in mustard.

"Salami?" she said.

I nodded. "Salami's very popular in my house. As are most other Italian lunchmeats."

"I wish my mom would get more creative." She held up a bologna sandwich and frowned.

"Don't knock it," I said. "I'm a big fan of bologna."

She giggled.

This was going great. Who knew I could get this much material out of lunchmeat.

"Hey, I have an idea," I said. "Want to trade?" I picked up one of my sandwiches still wrapped in wax paper.

She seemed to be thinking to herself. And then a moment later, "Okay."

We exchanged sandwiches. My hand briefly brushed up against hers. It was soft and warm. I watched as she unwrapped my sandwich and sampled it. The expression on her face was priceless.

"Wow, that's got a bite to it," she said.

"Ooh, that stinks," Charlotte O'Keefe, one of her friends, said. Charlotte was kind of cute but in a hard way. Even though I really dug her freckles.

"It's not bad," Andie replied. "Although I think it's cleaning out my sinuses."

Her friends laughed. And soon the girl talk took over. I had become a mere spectator. But that was okay. I was fine with baby steps. My mini-conversation with Andie was the most I had ever spoken to a girl at lunch—or to a girl, period. Not, of course, counting Guennie this past summer. I concentrated on my lunch as the girls gabbed. I would occasionally glance at Andie and smile, but she was too busy with her friends to notice.

Charlotte tapped Andie on the shoulder. "Take a gander, girl." She pointed at Colton, Andie's boyfriend, who was leaning over one of the freshman girls a few tables over. "A little competition, huh?"

"Oh, don't be silly," Andie said. But she did look a little miffed. "That's Carolyn Mancuso. She just joined the tennis team. Colton's just being neighborly."

I couldn't help but watch. Colton was smiling, and Carolyn was laughing. It sure looked more than neighborly to me. And then I got to thinking. Wait a minute. This was just what I needed. If Colton got caught messing around with another girl, Andie would have to dump him. Sure. It was perfect. I was hoping he'd stay over there the entire lunch hour. He'd be getting himself in so deep he'd never be able to dig out. I watched Andie's face. She didn't look pleased.

"You'd better straighten him out," Charlotte said. "If I ever caught Jeremy slobbering over another girl like that, I'd kick him you know where."

"He's not slobbering over her," Andie said.

"Well, it sure looks that way to me," Charlotte said.

Andie was now stewing. This was fantastic. A minute later, Colton was making his way over to our table. Andie spotted him and turned away. Nice move. That'd show him.

"Hey, babe," Colton said. "What's hanging?"

"Who's your new girlfriend, Colt?" Charlotte said with a smirk.

Colton was caught off guard. "What are you talking about?"

"*Carolyn?*" Charlotte said.

Colton threw his head back. "Oh, her. She doesn't mean anything to me. She's new here. I was just giving her the official Anton J. Cermak welcome." He laughed nervously.

Andie turned toward him, breaking her silence. "Well, it sure looked to me like you were interested."

Colton threw up his arms. "What is this? The Inquisition? Can't a guy talk to a girl just friendly-like? Hell, Andie, you talk to the other guys on the team all the time, and I don't get all bent out of shape."

"That's different."

"What's different about it?"

"Because I don't fawn all over them and make goo-goo eyes at 'em," she said.

"I wasn't doing that." He shook his head. "Geez, you girls are all alike. You overreact to everything."

Charlotte jumped back into the fray. "Oh, it's because we're girls, is that it?"

"Well, yeah. You see things differently."

"And guys don't?" Andie said.

"Nope."

Andie looked determined. "Okay, let's just find out." She looked right at me. "Paulie, didn't it look to you like Colton was acting a little more than friendly with that girl?"

Oh, my God. Why would she drag me into this? The last thing I wanted to do was piss off Colton. He was a lot bigger than me.

"Yeah, *Paulie*," Colton said. "What did it look like to you? And be very careful."

Oh, great. Now he was threatening me.

"What do you expect him to say when you put it like that?" Charlotte said.

"I'd really rather stay out of this," I said. "I wasn't watching what was going on. Sorry."

Andie tilted her head and made a face. "He's not going to hurt you if I tell him not to."

As much as I wanted to be near Andie, I was suddenly sorry I sat down here today.

"You couldn't hear anything," I said. "How could you tell what was going on?"

Colton smiled. "See, nothing happened."

Andie turned and stared at him. "That's not what he said."

"Paulie, I'm talking about their body language. What did that tell you?"

If I told Andie what she wanted to hear, Colton would kick my ass. And she would never be able to protect me from that. But if it caused them to get into an even bigger fight, and if she were to dump him on account of it, then a few bruises might not be so bad.

I sighed. "To be perfectly honest, it just looked like a very friendly conversation. Colton must have said something funny, and she laughed. That's about all I saw."

"But did it look like he was hitting on her?" Charlotte said.

Charlotte was definitely asking the wrong person.

This wasn't my area of expertise. If I had known the proper technique for hitting on girls, I wouldn't have been so ill-prepared all these years. I glanced at Colton. He was now staring daggers at me. I wasn't sure how to get out of this fix. I had to say something. I looked into Andie's eyes. So blue. So welcoming. I couldn't let her down. I just couldn't.

"Well, yes, I suppose you could have interpreted it that way."

"See," Charlotte said.

Colton leaned over the table and got right in my face. "You little shit. You'll pay for that."

"Don't you touch him," Andie said. "Paulie, you let me know if he does anything, okay?"

Oh, great. Like that's going to stop this big SOB. I knew exactly what was going to happen. Colton was going to mess me up and then tell me if I said anything, I'd get it even worse.

I glanced at my watch. "Geez, it's late," I said. "I'd better be going." I cleaned up what was left from lunch and jammed it into the brown paper bag I had carried into the cafeteria. I stepped out into the aisle and made a beeline for the exit. I would now have to do my best to avoid Colton if I wanted to live to see seventeen. But when I got to the door, I felt a large hand on my shoulder.

"Hold on, pal," a voice said. It was Colton.

Oh, great. "Yeah?" I said. I was fairly certain I was safe since there were so many witnesses still in the room. He wouldn't try anything here.

"Why'd you have to go and say that?" he said.

I didn't respond at first.

"Huh?"

"I was just telling her how it looked," I said.

"Well, what the hell do you know anyway?"

I shrugged.

"That's all you have to say?"

"I don't know what else you want me to say." And then for some unknown reason, something came out of my mouth I would have liked to have taken back. "Maybe you should be more careful around other girls if you don't want Andie to see."

He placed his hand in my chest and shoved me. He was pissed. "I think *I am* gonna kick your ass. And I think I'm gonna do it right here. Just who the hell do you think you are, talking to me like that? I don't have to listen to a pipsqueak like you. You're nothin'."

I didn't have a good comeback. I really wished I had. But in order to come up with a snappy remark, you had to be fearless. You had to be prepared for the consequences of your actions. And that was something I wasn't prepared for.

The bell rang. Thank God.

He began poking his finger in my chest. "Just watch your step next time, *Paulie*. You got it?"

I nodded.

He turned around disgustedly as I made my escape. What had I gotten myself into? Was a girl, even a really great girl, worth a physical beating? I was starting to rethink things. I decided to lay low for the next couple of weeks. I avoided Andie's lunch table and sat with Mickey. He always sat with some friends from his neighborhood. They were a bunch of brainiac clods who were in their own little world, but the last thing I needed right now was another encounter with Colton. Steering clear of him also meant keeping my distance from Andie, and that killed me. I wondered if our rendezvous at the tennis courts was still on for this weekend. I was wondering what Colton would think if he saw the two of us together. I thought about canceling it, but I didn't know if I'd ever get another one-on-one chance with Andie again. I just had to hope he wouldn't show up on Saturday.

Mickey and I rode the bus home together that day. The topic of conversation was a familiar one.

"So have you thought about who you're going to ask to homecoming?" he said.

"When is that anyway?"

"Three weeks from Saturday."

To be honest, I hadn't given it a second thought. In order to ask a girl to homecoming, you had to have, at some point in your life, spoken to a girl, and presently there was no one but Andie on my radar. And she was currently unavailable.

"I'm thinking about going stag," Mickey said. "I don't like the idea of tying myself down to one girl. I'd rather spread it around."

"Spread what around?" I asked. "The bullshit?"

Mickey made a face. "Now is that the kind of thing you say to your best friend? That was harsh, guy."

"I'm sorry, Mick. I'm just in a pissy mood."

He winked. "Don't worry about it," he said. "Hey, are you still bent out of shape about that Andie thing at the tennis courts? I'm tellin' you, Paulie, you gotta forget about that girl. It's like she's married to Colton. You haven't got a chance with her."

Maybe. Maybe not. But what the Mick didn't know was Colton was stepping out on her. At least, that was how it looked. So maybe I'd get a chance at her after all.

"I know," I said. The remainder of the bus ride was more of the same—Mickey telling me I had better ask someone to homecoming, and me clamming up. I tried to change the subject repeatedly, but we kept coming back to the same topic—girls. For my own sake, I really needed to think about other things. I had a chemistry test coming up in a couple of days, as well as an article due for the paper. Our English teacher, Mr. Drennan, recently had a short story published in a national anthology, and I needed a thousand words on it by five p.m. on Friday. The only time I could talk to Mr. Drennan was during my gym period tomorrow. And because of that I would have to make up gym during my last period of the day, which was usually study hall.

The next day I made a pledge not to think about Andie until the weekend. This girl was taking a toll on my grades. When school started a few weeks back, I had decided to make a serious effort to raise my G.P.A. this year, and things had been moving in the right direction until the little dust-up with Colton in the cafeteria. I had to get back on course.

My meeting the next day with Mr. Drennan went well. He talked about how he had always dreamed of becoming a published author; about the struggles of selling a literary work; and about his favorite teacher in high school—his English teacher, of course. I was fairly certain I would have enough quotable material to crank out a thousand words. It was really kind of neat to sit down with a teacher in a non-class setting. He seemed more relaxed, and he joked around more than he did in class each day. It was almost as if he wasn't my teacher at all; it was like we were a couple of pals just sitting around chewing the fat.

The remainder of the day was relatively uneventful until eighth period—gym. Because I had to move classes around to fit in the interview, I found myself with a completely different group of guys in the locker room. There were a lot of jocks yelling and joking around. I recognized most of them from the football team. And then as I changed into my gym clothes, my life flashed before my eyes. Across the room I spotted Colton. This wasn't good. This wasn't good at all. He'd never be able to resist the temptation of knocking me around on the gym floor, and because of the sheer numbers of kids in class, it'd be easier for him to do so and get away with it. Our PE teacher, Mr. Renn, was the assistant basketball coach, and the biggest slacker on the faculty. He would usually just have us play basketball the entire period while he read the latest edition of the *Chicago Sun-Times*. And woe to the student who tried bothering him while he was engrossed in the day's news.

I hid behind a wall of lockers to avoid being detected by Colton. But a moment later he was standing right next to me.

"Well, if it ain't Paulie Passero—the kid who sees things that aren't really there. Are you in this class now? I sure hope so. It'll give us a better chance to get to know one another."

"No," I said. "It's just for today."

"Oh, that's a shame. It really is. I guess we'll have to make the most of the time we have together. Don't ya think?"

I was trying my best to think of a way to get out of gym for the day. I wondered about pretending I was sick. You couldn't very well force a sick kid to participate in gym, now could you? But I knew Mr. Renn would see right through it. The only way to convince him you weren't feeling well was to puke right in front of him—but be careful not to get any of it on his shoes. I saw that happen one time. It wasn't a pretty scene for the hurler.

"Well, I'll see you on the court," Colton said with a smirk.

I was about to be thrown to the lions, and there was nothing I could do.

Chapter 5

"All right," Mr. Renn said, "count off by fours."

We were about to be broken up into four groups. That way we'd be playing two half-court games of basketball. When it came time for me to shout out my number, I was so nervous that I forgot what the kid next to me had said. I paused momentarily.

Mr. Renn threw his head back and groaned. "What's the problem, Mr. Passero? You can't count to four?"

"I'm uh…uh," I stammered.

"You're three, dummy," a voice called out. It was Colton. He started counting the number of kids between us. Then he moved down a few spaces and squeezed back into the line.

I knew exactly what he was up to. He wanted to be in the *four* group. That way we would be mortal combatants on the floor. But when it came time for him to say his number, he suddenly realized he had screwed up. He had mistakenly positioned himself in the *one* group. He grabbed the kid to his right and yanked him into the number one position.

"I'm four and you're one, you got it?" he said. But it really wasn't a question. It was more like an order. And since this kid was even shorter than me, he accepted his fate without an argument. Mr. Renn saw what was taking place but did nothing to stop it. That, of course, would require him to do his job, and since he had failed to do so the entire time he had worked at Cermak Prep, there was no reason to start now. Why ruin his perfect record?

Colton bent forward, looked down the line, and winked at me. I was clearly in his crosshairs. And he wasn't about to misfire.

"Okay, groups one and two on this court, and three and four on the far one." Mr. Renn said. He grabbed a pair of basketballs from a barrel of balls and tossed them in the direction of the teams. "All right. Call your own fouls and get along. I don't want to have to break up any disputes, or you'll be sorry."

"Let's play man-to-man," Colton told his teammates. "And I'm guarding this kid," he said pointing to me.

"Colton," a member of his team said, "you should be guarding a taller kid, not him."

"Oh, so you're the coach now?" Colton fired back.

"Well, I was just—"

Colton walked over to his teammate. His sheer size made him a very imposing figure.

"Maybe you didn't hear what I said. I said I got *him*," he said gesturing again in my direction.

"All right, all right."

"We'll take the ball out first," Colton said. "Anybody got a problem with that?" No one did. He tossed the ball to a teammate and the game began.

I did my best to stay as far away from him as possible. Wherever he went, I managed to be on the opposite side of the court. That seemed to do the trick for the first couple of minutes, but before long, Colton was all over me—even when I didn't have the ball. When I miraculously pulled down a rebound—usually unheard of for someone of my size—I began dribbling out to the free-throw line. The entire time Colton was slapping my arms—a typical foul on every court but ours, apparently. It was up to the ball handler to call the foul, and since I didn't want to seem like a wuss, I said nothing. I passed the ball as soon as I spotted an open man. I thought that would get me a little breathing room, but no such luck. Colton was all over me like flies on shit. That was how it went for the bulk of the period. He repeatedly jabbed and shoved and elbowed and slapped at me. And his aggressive behavior became pretty obvious to everyone else on the court.

"Hey, Passero, don't be a martyr. You can call a foul if you want," Tim O'Brien, a kid on my team said.

"What are you talking about," Colton said. "I didn't foul him."

Tim looked at me and shrugged.

"It's all right," I said. "The period's almost over."

"C'mon, guys, let's go," Colton snapped.

I glanced at the clock overhead. Less than five minutes before Mr. Renn would halt play and send us to the showers. I was going to survive this.

A minute later, Tim got trapped in the corner with the ball and was looking for help. I needed to come to his aid and return the favor. I made a beeline for an open spot. Colton sensed the opportunity he had been waiting for the entire period. He shifted his feet, slid into my lane, and set a pick. I never saw him. It was like colliding with a brick wall. All I remembered was smashing into something really hard and hitting the floor. I couldn't remember much else. A minute later, I opened my eyes and Mr. Renn was kneeling over me.

"You okay, Passero?"

I grabbed the back of my head. I must have hit it on the gym floor and blacked out momentarily.

"Go get the nurse," Mr. Renn told one of the kids. "Don't get up," he told me.

When I tried to anyway, he pushed me back down. Nurse Wilson came running over a few minutes later. She sat me up and asked me my name, the name of our school, and who the president was. Although I don't recall answering, I must have aced the test, because within a few seconds, she was helping me to my feet. I reached back and felt a bump on the back of my noggin and a pounding in my head. The next thing I remembered was sitting in her office holding an ice pack to the back of my head.

"I'm not going to release you until I'm sure you're all right."

"I feel fine," I said. "But the room is spinning."

She walked over and shined a light into my eyes. "Unless you make a miraculous recovery, I'm going to run you over to the emergency room."

"Oh, I don't think that'll be necessary. I'll be fine."

Nurse Wilson placed her hands on her hips. "I'll be the judge of that, mister."

Twenty minutes later I was starting to feel better. The pounding and the spinning had stopped, but the back of my head was still sore.

"I feel a lot better. Can I go?"

"Are you telling me the truth?" the nurse said.

"I am. I really do feel better."

"Okay, you can go. But I want you to stop in here to see me when you get in tomorrow morning. You got it?"

I nodded.

"Concussions are dangerous. I want to make sure you're okay."

"Thanks." I got up and walked into the locker room to change. It was empty. I got dressed and headed down the hallway to my locker. The entire school seemed deserted. When I exited the front door, I looked around for Mickey. He was long gone. He must have wondered what had happened to me, but then he probably took off. I was headed for the bus stop when a figure emerged from behind a row of bushes on the front lawn. It was Colton. Had he stuck around to finish the job?

"Hey, Passero, you all right?"

"I'm okay."

"Well, I just wanted to tell you I set a legal pick. You should have seen me. It was your own fault. I didn't do anything wrong."

I should have known Colton hadn't waited around to see how I was doing. He wanted to make sure he wasn't in trouble.

"I'm fine," I said. "Forget about it."

"I just don't want you blabbin' to Feingold about this."

Mr. Feingold was the school disciplinarian. If you were a candidate for detention or worse, you needed to cross paths with the man. I had no intention of turning this into an international incident.

"Don't worry, I'm not going to Feingold," I said.

"Well, you'd better not."

I turned and began walking in the direction of the bus stop. Once I had reassured Colton this matter was behind us, he had lost interest in torturing me. When I looked back, he was gone.

When I got home, my mom informed me Mickey had called a couple of times and wanted me to call him back. I went into the basement for a little privacy and picked up the extension. A moment later, Mickey picked up.

"Hey, it's me," I said.

"Dude, what happened to you? I waited for like fifteen minutes."

"Sorry. I couldn't tell you what was going on."

"Well, what did happen?" he asked.

"I got hurt at gym."

"What?"

I wasn't sure how much detail to go into. Should I tell him Colton laid a trap for me? Or should I accept responsibility and admit it was partially my own fault?

"We were playing basketball at gym, and I fell and hit my head on the floor."

"Are you okay?"

"Yeah, I went to the nurse's office. She made me stay there for a little while. But I'm okay."

"That's good to hear. I thought you went home sick or something."

I chuckled. "I wish I had." We chatted for a few more minutes. Then I went up to my room and lay down on my bed. I still had a headache. I went back downstairs into the kitchen and popped a couple of aspirin. My mom was at the stove.

"I'll have your dinner ready in about fifteen minutes," she said.

I looked at the clock. It wasn't even four o'clock yet. "Why so early?"

"You have to work tonight. Did you forget?"

Oh, brother. I had forgotten. "Okay, thanks." Stocking shelves was the last thing I wanted to be doing tonight. I just wanted to crash. Instead, I'd have to work five-plus hours and then come home and do homework until God knows when. I decided to go upstairs and lie down for a few minutes to try and get rid of this headache. I fell onto my bed and closed my eyes. The next thing I remembered was my mom standing next to my bed shaking me.

"Paulie, wake up," she said. "You're going to be late. Now come on down and eat something before you have to leave."

I changed, grabbed a quick bite, and headed out. The headache was still there. As was the bump. When I got to the store, I headed up to the lunchroom, hung up my coat, grabbed an apron, and got to work. The next five hours dragged on unmercifully. It was as if things were moving in slow motion. More than once, one of my coworkers asked me if anything was wrong. I just said I was a little tired. At nine-thirty, I hung up my apron and headed home. It was about a half-hour walk. Sometimes, usually on a Saturday, I'd be able to take the car to work. But on weeknights, because I had to leave before my dad got home from work, I would have to walk.

When I opened the front door, I found my parents watching the ten o'clock news. There was a story on about how Richard Nixon still had a six percent lead in the polls over Hubert Humphrey. The general election was a month away. A few months ago, I would have had little to no interest in politics. But since I was now a bona fide reporter for the Anton J. Cermak *Gazette*, I needed to become better informed when it came to the goings-on in the world of politics. I stopped momentarily to watch the story, then retreated to my room, where I opened up my folder to figure out how much homework I had and how late I'd be up. When I realized nothing was due tomorrow, it was an easy decision to go straight to bed. Since I wasn't working tomorrow night, I knew I'd have time to get the work done. I set my alarm, lay down, and fell asleep with my clothes on.

The next morning, I woke up feeling kind of scummy. I jumped in the shower, got dressed, had breakfast, and headed to the bus stop to meet Mickey. It was the first time in about eighteen hours I didn't have a headache. That was an improvement. Then I began thinking about tomorrow—Saturday. It was the day I was supposed to meet up with Andie on the tennis courts after practice. When we had originally set that date, I was excited. But between then and now, a lot had changed. Colton had now entered the picture. He was determined to make my life miserable—and he was doing a great job of it. I was praying he wouldn't show up tomorrow morning. I hoped Andie had another ride home. I wasn't sure how he'd react seeing the two of us on the court together. A part of me wanted to cancel the meeting. But the chance to be one-on-one with Andie was too great an opportunity to pass up. I had to be there. If I wanted to end up with Andie someday, I needed some quality face-time with her. I needed to make myself the natural option to become her next boyfriend if and/or when she and Colton broke up.

Mickey and I talked about the usual nonsense on the bus ride to school. And then the same old topic arose—girls.

"Hey, have you decided who you're taking to homecoming?"

Who was I going to take? That was a good one. Give me a break, Mick. He knew as well as I did I didn't know any girls well enough to just walk up to one of them and ask them to go to homecoming. It wasn't going to happen.

"I don't think I'll be going this year." Or any year.

"What you need is a little help from your friendly matchmaker."

I laughed. "If you can't get your own date, what makes you so sure you can get one for me?"

"Who said I can't get a date?"

"You were the one who told me you'd be going stag to homecoming."

He made a face. "Well, it's not because I can't get a date. Who do you think you're talking to? You're talking to the Mick. To Mr. Suave. Mr. Debonair."

"Who's only gone on two dates in his life. One with your cousin, which didn't count, and one where you puked on your date. Sorry to say, but you don't have much of a track record when it comes to the opposite sex."

He seemed offended. "You really know how to hurt a guy, don't you?"

"Listen, Mick, I'm not trying to be a jerk. But let's face it—you're as inexperienced as I am when it comes to girls. We both talk a good game, but in reality, we suck at dating."

He let out a long sigh and stared forward. He apparently didn't want to hear the truth. It was painful for both of us. Following an awkward pause, we decided to change the subject. Complaining about teachers and classes was a much safer topic. That went on for a few minutes...and then, all at once, I got this sinking feeling in the pit of my stomach. Oh, my God. What had I done? When I got home from work last night, I had decided to go to bed. Since I didn't have any assignments due today, I figured it was safe. But what I was forgetting was the fact that I had a chemistry test today...and an article due for the *Gazette*. I had whiffed on both. What was I going to do? I was thinking through my options while Mickey continued to gab. I never heard a word of what he said for the last half of the bus ride.

By the time we got to school, I still wasn't sure how to handle things. I supposed I could tell my teacher I got knocked out at gym class and spent time in the nurse's office, and hadn't felt well enough last night to study. But I didn't want to sound like a wimp. I hated it when kids pulled that kind of cream-puff crap. There had to be another way. Let's see. I had no study periods between now and chemistry class. Without a killer excuse, I would be taking the exam completely unprepared. That was nothing new for the old Paulie. I rarely studied for exams the first two years of my high school career, but junior and senior years were going to be different—at least, I had thought they were. So much for the new me.

When I looked back on this day, I could honestly say it was one of my darkest academic days at Cermak. How did things ultimately fare, you ask? Not well. I managed to record a C- on my chemistry test, and Mrs. Geraty, the newspaper advisor, let me have it for missing a deadline. She didn't say she was angry with me. I wish she had. Instead, she told me she was *disappointed* in me. It was ten times worse when teachers said they were disappointed in you. I would have much preferred getting bawled out instead of hearing that. It always left such an unpleasant taste in my mouth. After that, all I could do was lick my wounds and hope for an amazing day with Andie tomorrow—one that would pick up my spirits and help me to forget this very forgettable day.

Chapter 6

I had a hard time sleeping that night. I kept thinking about what I would do if Colton showed up at the tennis courts. Would I forge ahead, or would I bail? I really didn't know. One thing was certain—I didn't want to end up in the nurse's office again. The bump on the back of my head was still a little sensitive to the touch, but at least it had gone down somewhat. I only really felt it when I combed my hair or when I lay down on my pillow at bedtime. At least, it was improving.

For this rendezvous with Andie, I decided to go solo. No Mickey. Not that he would cramp my style or anything—it was more like not wanting him to see me pull a giant fail if Colton was there. I got to the bus stop about eleven fifteen. It was now October and starting to get cool outside. It didn't help that the wind was howling. I faced away from it and waited another ten minutes for the bus to show up. When it did, I couldn't believe how crowded it was. Where was everyone going on a Saturday anyway? I noticed some of the people on board were holding signs. One read, "Stop the War!" Another said, "No More Innocent Blood Shed on Foreign Soil." A third read, "Withdraw from Vietnam Now!" And then I remembered seeing something in the *Trib* the other day about some anti-war demonstration taking place downtown this weekend. So that explained the crowd.

I eventually found a seat about three-quarters of the way back. There was an empty seat next to me—the only seat not taken. I always hated sitting next to strangers. I was hoping no one got on between here and my stop. I stared out the window and thought about Andie. Lately I had found myself daydreaming about the same thing. I would imagine Andie and Colton had broken up, or his dad had gotten transferred to another state and he'd have to move, or that he would somehow or some way just disappear one day and never be heard from again. I didn't know how something like that would happen, but it felt good thinking about it.

The bus driver pulled over at a stop a few blocks away. Oh, no. I prayed it wasn't some large, smelly person. Maybe it was someone who preferred the front of the bus and who would stand the rest of the way. I leaned over into the aisle to get a peek at the new passenger. When I did, my heart suddenly began racing. My mouth got dry. I felt a hollowness in my chest. I got lightheaded. Walking down the aisle in my direction was Violet, the untouchable girl who had ridden our bus for the last two years but we hadn't seen yet this school year. As she got closer, I got a better look at her. She was chewing gum. Her hair was ratted as usual. Her eye makeup was thick. And, praise the Lord, she was in an unusually short skirt. I wanted her to take the seat next to me so badly. But I was also fearful she would.

She stopped when she saw the empty seat. She stared at it and at me. Then she moved a couple of rows farther down. She clearly was looking for another option. She apparently didn't want to join me. I definitely wasn't her type. She knew it and I knew it. A moment later she was standing next to me again.

"Is that seat taken?" she asked.

I opened my mouth, but nothing came out, so I just shook my head. She dropped into the seat and crossed her legs. Her perfume was dizzying. It was so strong. But that was okay with me. I glanced over and noticed she was carrying a paperback book and a notebook. The book immediately got my attention—*Lost Horizon* by James Hilton. That was the book I had read in one sitting at Uncle Buddy's a couple of months back. I loved that story. It was a perfect opportunity to start up a conversation. I could easily talk about it. I remembered every page of the book.

I had a decision to make. Did I have the guts to talk to her? I sighed. Did I even have to ask? The answer was an unequivocal *no*. I couldn't talk to a normal girl, let alone a goddess. I guessed some things would never change. Then I thought about traveling to Pennsylvania in August with my dad for my grandmother's funeral. I had met the most amazing girl and actually talked to her—a lot. I could do this, I thought. I didn't know how far Violet was going. I might not have much time. I would never again have an opportunity like this. It was the stuff of daydreams—Violet just happens to sit down next to me? What were the chances of that ever happening again? I could feel my heart beating right through my chest. If I opened my mouth, would anything come out? And if I did, would I make any sense? What if she didn't say anything back? What if she got up to get away from me? Was it worth total humiliation?

Then I thought about something my dad once told me. It happened to him a few years ago. He was in a restaurant in Chicago and he spotted Joe DiMaggio sitting at the bar. He had been a huge Yankee Clipper fan for most of his life. He wanted desperately to go and say hello, but he just couldn't work up the nerve. During his entire dinner, he kept thinking about Joe. Then about a half hour later, when he finally found enough courage to act, he got up and walked to the bar—only to find Joe had left. He said he had learned a valuable lesson that night—he would never again pass up an opportunity like that. Was this my Joe DiMaggio moment? If I waited much longer, would I end up like my dad? Had I learned nothing from his story? He told it to me for a reason. I needed to act—and I needed to act now.

I took a long breath, licked my lips, and opened my mouth.

"I see you're reading *Lost Horizon*. Let me tell you—that is a great book. I loved it." I waited for a response.

She glanced at the book, and then at me. "I'm having a hard time getting into it," she said. "The first couple of chapters are really dry."

Her voice didn't sound anything like I had expected. It was higher-pitched than I had imagined. But she had actually answered me. Violet had spoken to me. Mickey would never believe this.

"You know, I felt the same way. But you have to stick with it. Just wait until the plane goes down and they end up in Shangri-La. It's the absolute best."

She smiled. "I'm headed to a study group right now to discuss the book. We were all supposed to have read it. But I didn't. I guess I'm not a very good student."

Initially I wasn't sure how to respond. So Violet wasn't a scholar. So what? It actually sounded like something the old Paulie would have done. I completely understood where she was coming from. Then I suddenly realized an amazing opportunity had just fallen into my lap. I needed to seize it. I had to. I just had to.

"If you want, I can tell you as much about it as I remember. Where do you get off?"

"Mobile Avenue. The Ridgeway stop."

"Okay, then, we only have a few minutes."

Violet smiled and opened her notebook. She found a pencil in her purse. "Okay. Go," she said.

For the next ten minutes, I told her the amazing story of *Lost Horizon* and a utopian society in the Himalayas known as Shangri-La. I told her about Hugh Conway, a member of the British diplomatic service, who finds inner peace and love in a strange land, only to lose it all. But the story doesn't end there. Now normally I don't make a habit of giving away a book's ending, but this time I did. And Violet seemed to appreciate it. She was smiling the entire time. I glanced at her notebook. Her scribble was impossible to read. Hopefully she could decipher it. I looked outside and saw her stop coming up.

"I guess that's about as much as I can tell you. You get off pretty soon."

"That was fantastic. You're a lifesaver." She held out her hand to shake. "I'm Violet."

I reached out and took her hand. It was warm and soft. Her fingernails were painted black, and they were really long.

"I'm Paulie...Paulie Passero."

"Where do you go to school?" she asked.

"Cermak."

She got up and turned to leave.

I couldn't let things end like this. I needed a clever comment to leave her with.

"Maybe I'll see you again on the bus sometime," I said. It wasn't much, but at least it was something.

"I'm afraid you will. I broke up with my boyfriend last night. So no more rides to school. It's back to the bus for me." She reached over and pulled the cord, alerting the driver she wanted to get off. She moved toward the front door.

I leaned into the aisle to watch her go. I couldn't take my eyes off her.

Right before she reached the front, she turned around and looked back. She smiled and waved.

I waved back and watched her exit. Then I scooted across the seat, looked out the window, and watched her walk in the direction of Ridgeway. I couldn't believe what had just happened. I had actually talked to Violet. And she wasn't scary or anything. She was really nice. She shook my hand. She smiled at me. She waved to me. Was this the beginning of something amazing? Was she destined to be my soul mate? I didn't want to get ahead of myself, but you never know. Stranger things had happened. We were from two different worlds, but that didn't mean we couldn't end up together someday. It wasn't only possible, it was probable. Yeah. Me and Violet. I can see it now.

And then my thoughts turned to Andie. It was hard to believe. For a guy who was a complete clod around girls a few weeks ago, here I was with *two* irons in the fire. I was starting to feel pretty good about myself.

And it got me to thinking. Maybe Andie and Colton would never break up, and the chance of me sneaking in somehow and whisking her away was not only unlikely, it was downright impossible. Maybe this was the way things were supposed to be. I guess I'd have to scratch Andie off the list and add Violet. But what if the Violet thing was no more than two ships passing in the night? Maybe she'd never talk to me again, or smile at me, or wave to me. Maybe I was making more of this moment than it actually was. Then I would need Andie back in my life.

I needed to take things one step at a time. This was no time for a rush to judgment. I decided to play both hands and see which one came up aces. If one didn't pan out, maybe the other would. I glanced out the window and noticed the bus approaching my stop. I jumped up, pulled the cord, and hopped off.

I walked around to the back of school where the sports complex was located. Since we were playing Lincoln under the lights tonight, the football practice field was empty. When I got to the tennis courts, I climbed up onto the bleachers. I could see the girls were scattered. Some were scrimmaging. Others were running sprints. Still others were just milling around and talking. Mrs. Anderson, the tennis coach, began waving her arms.

"Okay, girls, finish up what you're doing and meet in the center court for a team meeting."

I spotted Andie retrieving balls with some of the other girls. She had her hair in the high ponytail again. I always loved that. And I sure didn't mind those short tennis skirts. I looked around for Colton. He didn't appear to be anywhere. Things were getting better all the time. I could only hope Andie hadn't forgotten about our little date. But realistically, who was I fooling? This wasn't a real date or anything. It was a tennis lesson of sorts—and probably nothing more.

Then I heard a sound that seemed to be coming from directly beneath me. It was a like a shriek of some sort. I couldn't tell if it had come from a person or an animal. When I heard it again a few seconds later, I was now sure it was a person. And it sounded like a girl. Then I heard the same voice say, "Stop it! I said, stop it!" To this day, I have no idea what made me get up and walk to the opening that led under the bleachers. What I saw, I will never forget. It was Colton and that girl Carolyn, the girl from the tennis team, the one he had been flirting with at lunch. She was holding down her shirt, and Colton kept trying to get his hands under it.

"If you don't stop, I'm going to scream," she said.

I didn't know what to do. Should I say something? Should I do something? Should I get the hell out of there? I was frozen. My feet wouldn't move. I couldn't take my eyes off them.

"Since when are you this big tease?" Colton said.

"I don't want you to do that," she said.

"Oh, come on, you know you want it." He slid his hand under her shirt. "Don't play so hard to get."

Carolyn's face was red. She tried to fight him off, but he was too strong for her.

"Somebody, help m—" she managed to blurt out before Colton put his hand over her mouth. He picked up one of her legs and she fell backward to the ground. He positioned himself on top of her.

She reached up and scratched his face.

He wiped his cheek. There was blood on his hand. "Why, you little bitch, you're gonna get it now."

I knew I should be doing something. But how was I supposed to stop Colton? He'd kill me. I watched as he tried to pull down her skirt. I tried to look away, but I couldn't. I crouched down and moved a few feet farther away from them. I had always wondered how I might handle an emergency situation if I was ever faced with one. I had imagined myself doing the right thing. I saw myself risking life and limb for a noble cause. And so here I was in my own personal moment of truth. Would I step up and do something, or would I stay put and not get involved? As much as I hated to say it, my fears were beginning to overwhelm me. I began thinking about saving my own neck and not this girl's reputation. I felt so bad for her, but not bad enough to speak up.

Then, from the tennis courts, I heard someone yell, "Carolyn, where are you? Are you here?"

Colton stopped and turned toward the voice. "Don't say a word," he told his victim.

But when the single voice turned into a sea of voices calling out her name, a frightened Colton slid off her. Carolyn immediately jumped to her feet and ran toward the opening in the bleachers. She was whimpering.

I immediately scooted over and hid my face. Since she seemed completely focused on the exit, I was fairly certain she hadn't seen me.

A moment later, Colton got up, ran to the opening in the bleachers, and stopped. He turned and spotted me cowering in the corner. Our eyes met momentarily before I turned away.

"You didn't see shit, Passero. You got it?"

I said nothing. How had I gotten myself into this jam? Right now, I just wanted to be home, in bed, under the covers, and away from all this.

"You rat me out and you're dead," he said as he ran out and headed in the direction of the parking lot.

I was still frozen in place. I couldn't move. All I could think about was what might have happened. I would never have forgiven myself if something really bad had taken place. Thankfully, Colton hadn't succeeded. I let out a long sigh. I was so relieved I hadn't been forced to intervene, as if I actually would have. To save face, I could probably tell myself I would have eventually done something, but I knew in my heart I would never have managed to work up enough courage to do so.

I stood up and made my way out from under the bleachers when one of the girls from the tennis team spotted me.

"There's a boy over here, Mrs. Anderson. He might be the one."

The one? Wait a minute. Wait just a minute. Was this girl suggesting *I* had something to do with what had happened to Carolyn? That was crazy.

Mrs. Anderson jogged up to the opening and glared at me. "What were you doing under there?" she asked.

"I was just waiting for Andie Walker. She was going to give me a few tennis tips."

"What's your name?" she said.

"Paulie Passero."

"Bring Carolyn over here," the coach told the other girls.

A moment later Carolyn Mancuso approached.

Two of her teammates were supporting her.

"Is this the boy?" Mrs. Anderson asked her.

She fought back tears. "No, he's not the one. It was…" Carolyn stopped and glanced in Andie's direction. "It was Colton Brand. He tried to rape me."

"That's a lie," Andie said. "He wouldn't do that."

Oh, yes, he would, I thought. Andie didn't know him as well as she thought she did.

"Colton? From the football team?" Mrs. Anderson asked.

Carolyn nodded. Then she turned toward me. "You must have seen something. Tell them what you saw. Tell them I'm not making this up."

A million thoughts crossed my mind at that very moment. And not one of them found me being a stand-up guy and confirming her story. I could only think of what Colton would do to me if I spoke up. Then the true coward in me emerged.

"I didn't see anything," I said. "When I went under the bleachers, no one was there. I'm sorry."

Carolyn began sobbing. "You have to believe me, Mrs. Anderson. It was Colton."

"She's lying," Andie said.

"Why would I lie about something like that?"

"Because you can't have him for yourself," Andie said. "I saw you waving your tail in his face in the cafeteria the other day." A few of the other girls were nodding.

"What are you talking about?" Carolyn said.

"All right, all right," Mrs. Anderson said. "This is a very serious allegation, Carolyn."

"But he did it. He really did," she said.

"I'm going to have to speak to the principal," Mrs.

Anderson said. She put her arm around Carolyn and walked her back to the tennis courts.

I just stood there. I wasn't sure what to do. After all the excitement, I wondered if Andie and I were still on for today. That question was answered a moment later when Andie walked up to me.

"Paulie, would you mind giving me a rain check? I'm just not in the mood to teach anybody anything today. Okay?"

"Sure, no problem," I said. "We can do this another time." But I wondered if it would ever happen. "Well, I'll see you then." I turned to leave.

"Paulie?" she said.

"Yeah?"

"So you really didn't see anything?"

I shook my head. "No, nothing."

"I'm glad. Thanks." She smiled weakly and retrieved her tennis bag.

I couldn't believe what a schmuck I was. I wanted so badly to tell her what I saw. I wanted her to know her boyfriend was a real creep. Why was this so difficult for me? Why was I such a chicken? Right at that moment, I didn't like myself very much. I didn't like what I had become. Was this who I would turn out to be? Was it my destiny to be a coward? I walked back to the bus stop. Another red-letter day for the Passeros.

Chapter 7

Word of the Colton-Carolyn incident spread quickly. When I got home, my mom told me Mickey was trying to reach me. Since I didn't want my parents to overhear our conversation, I decided to walk over to his house to discuss the matter. He was shooting hoops in his alley when I got there.

"Paulie, did you hear what happened?"

I decided to play dumb. I didn't want Mickey to know I had wussed out.

"No. What?"

"Colton Brand tried to molest a freshman girl under the bleachers by the tennis courts a little while ago."

"Whoa. How did you find out?"

"Karen Phillips is on the team. She was there. She told her brother, Todd, who told Henry who told Marcus who told me."

"So did it really happen?"

"That's what everybody thinks, but no one actually saw it going down. It's her word against his. It's possible the coach'll hold him out of the game tonight until they figure out what really happened, or he'll skate, which is what Colton usually manages to do."

"And there were no witnesses?"

"Karen said no one saw anything. She did say there

was a kid they found under the bleachers. But he apparently didn't see anything."

This story was now taking on a life of its own. Since I didn't want Mickey finding out about my involvement from someone else, I decided it was time to come clean.

"Mick...um...I...um...was the kid they found under the bleachers."

"What? What are you talking about? What were you doing there?"

"Don't you remember—Andie Walker offered to give me a few tennis tips. Well, today was the day."

Mickey set the ball on the ground and walked over. "So what were you doing *under* there?"

"Well, I was sitting there when I thought I heard something coming from under the bleachers, so I went to check."

"And what'd you see?"

"I didn't see anything."

"Colton wasn't there, huh?"

I wasn't sure how to answer. I wanted to tell him so badly. I wanted to unburden myself. It would have felt so much better to share this story with someone. But since I didn't come to Carolyn's rescue, I didn't want people thinking the worst of me. On the other hand, Mickey was my best friend. Surely, he would understand. My mind kept playing games with me. Should I tell him or not? Should I tell him how I saw everything but did nothing to prevent it? Should I advertise the fact I was a loser—that I didn't have the guts to do anything? If I did, what would Mickey think of me? Would he be able to put himself in my shoes and see why I acted the way I did? Or would he be disappointed in me? Would he even want to be my friend anymore? All these things ran through my head. I tried to imagine his reaction to a lie…and to the truth. I decided to hide behind the lie.

"I didn't see anyone."

"This is a pretty big deal. Marcus said it was a girl on the tennis team—a new girl."

"Her name is Carolyn Mancuso. You'd probably recognize her if you saw her. She's pretty cute."

Mickey shook his head. "You know, I wouldn't put anything like that past Colton. He's such a jerk."

"That he is. Hey, can we change the subject?" I didn't want to talk about this anymore. I didn't want to be reminded of my cowardice. The more I thought about it, the more depressed I got. There had to be some other topic we could discuss. And then I remembered my encounter with Violet on the bus this morning. It was doubtful Mickey would believe I had actually spoken to her, but it might be fun to get him a little worked up.

"Well, tell me one thing," he said. "Did you have your little rendezvous with Andie Walker at the tennis courts?"

"No, after all the Colton stuff went down, she wasn't in the mood to give me a lesson."

"Trust me, my friend, she's never gonna be in the mood to give you a lesson."

Okay, Mick, you might be right. Maybe nothing will ever happen with Andie. But just wait until you hear the Violet story. This would either make his day or ruin it.

"Something funny happened on the bus ride to school this morning."

"Yes!" Mickey had just nailed a fifteen-foot jumper. "What was that?"

"I talked to Violet."

He stopped and stared. "You talked to Violet? Our Violet?"

I nodded.

"Yeah, right."

"I did. I swear."

"Have you forgotten? She doesn't ride the bus anymore."

"She did this morning. And she's gonna from now on."

Mickey shook his head and laughed. "And how do you know that?"

"She told me."

"She told you?"

"Yeah, she said she broke up with her boyfriend, so she'll be riding the bus for a while."

He smiled. "Is that so? What else did you talk about?"

"*Lost Horizon*."

"Huh?"

"*Lost Horizon*, the book by James Hilton."

"Never heard of it."

"Well, it's a great book. You should read it sometime."

"So why would you be talking about some book with Violet?"

I sat down on a garbage can. "Okay, here's what happened. I was sitting next to her when I noticed she was carrying a copy of *Lost Horizon*."

"Wait a minute," he said. "Back up. Just how did you manage to be sitting next to Violet?"

"Well, when she got on the bus, the only empty seat was next to me."

"The bus was filled? On a Saturday? Gimme a break."

"There were a bunch of people on board headed to some anti-war rally downtown today."

Mickey appeared skeptical. "I never heard anything about it."

"You should read the paper."

"And you're such a news hound, is that it?"

"For the last month, I've made it a point to read the *Chicago Tribune* every day."

"All right, forget about that," he said. "How did you manage to talk to Violet?"

"Like I said, after she sat down, I noticed she was carrying a copy of *Lost Horizon*. And since I had read it this summer, I decided to strike up a conversation with her. I just leaned over and told her it was a great book."

"Just like that?"

"Just like that. And then she said she was headed to a study group at Ridgeway, but she hadn't finished the book. So I offered to tell her about it, and she took me up on it."

Mickey's eyes narrowed. "That's a pretty good story, Paulie. How long have you been practicing it?"

"I'm telling you, Mick, it's the truth. How could I make up something like that?"

"There's one way to find out for sure if you made it up or not. We'll just see what happens when she gets on the bus Monday morning—*if* she actually gets on the bus Monday morning."

"I told you. She broke up with her boyfriend. She'll be there."

"Okay, Mr. Passero, let's bet on it. I bet you five dollars she never gets on the bus, and if she does, she'll ignore you the way she always does."

Five dollars was a lot of money. I wasn't sure if I wanted to risk it. Violet *had* told me she'd be taking the bus again. I was fairly sure of that. But would she remember me? I wanted to believe she would. Heck, I had saved her neck. We were kind of friends now. Well, maybe not friends—more like acquaintances. She couldn't possibly forget me forty-eight hours later. Could she?

"Well, what do you say? Is it a bet?" he said.

I knew he was expecting me to take a pass on the bet. That would confirm his theory the whole thing was made up. On the other hand, if I agreed to the bet, it would definitely mess him up. I decided it was worth five dollars to have a little fun with the Mick.

"Okay, five bucks," I said. I held out my hand to shake on it.

Mickey seemed hesitant to make the bet official. "She has to be on the bus, and she has to say *hi* or wave or do something. Got it?"

"Got it."

He reluctantly shook my hand. Then he smiled and seemed to be thinking about something.

"What is it?"

"I was just trying to figure out how to spend the five dollars."

"Okay, you do that," I said.

He picked up the basketball and passed it to me. "Let's play some horse."

And so, for the next hour we engaged in a series of roundball contests—horse, pig, cow, 21, and around the world. The Colton-Carolyn story came up a few more times before I asked Mickey to just drop it. Every time he brought it up, I'd get this knot in my stomach. I wasn't sure how long it would be before that incident wouldn't bother me anymore. Right now, it was too painful to think about.

Then he'd bring up Violet. And that was one topic I was perfectly fine with. I could talk about Violet all day. It made me feel better about myself when I thought about meeting up with her. For the remainder of the weekend, whenever I would find myself thinking about what I had seen under the bleachers, I would immediately try to visualize sitting next to Violet on the bus. I'd think about what I had said to her, what she had said to me, and how we had shaken hands. Her hand was so soft. I tried to imagine what it would be like to be on a date with her—to hold hands with her—to kiss her. But I knew I was starting to get ahead of myself. I didn't have a snowball's chance in hell of ever going out with her. For one thing, I didn't have a car. And that seemed kind of important to her. Let's face it, this girl was completely out of my league. I soon came to the realization our little encounter on the bus was a once-in-a-million chance meeting that would never happen again.

When Monday morning rolled around, I began thinking about what I would say if I were to bump into Colton, Carolyn, or Andie at school. The Colton conversation would be quick and dirty. It would consist of him threatening to kill me if I ever told anyone what I had seen. Running into Carolyn would be really awkward. I would probably just look away. There was nothing I had to say to her. Although, if I had any guts, there was a lot I could tell her. Here she was, trying to defend her honor, and the only person who could corroborate her story was a weakling who didn't have the courage to speak up. I was such a loser. And what would happen if I were to bump into Andie? I'd smile. I'd try to find something clever to say. I'd try to stay in her good graces. As long as Colton was around, that was the best I could do.

And then, all of a sudden, I thought of something. *As long as Colton was around*...that was it. If I told the principal what I had seen under the bleachers, Colton might get expelled. That could be the answer to my problems. But wait a minute. Just because he'd no longer go to Cermak, it didn't mean he was out of my life. It wasn't like he'd be moving away or anything. He'd still be in the area. He'd just go to another school. And I knew exactly what he'd do. He'd wait around for me after school. He'd wait until the streets were deserted, and then he'd pulverize me. No, that wasn't going to work. And Andie would probably hate me if she ever learned I had ratted him out. The more I thought about it, the more I realized speaking up was one bad idea. It appeared laying low was the best strategy. It wasn't the most noble of gestures, but it was the best thing for my physical well-being.

When Mickey and I hopped on the bus that morning, all he could talk about was winning the five dollars. He was convinced Violet would never be on our bus, and if for some strange reason she was, he was sure she'd never look my way. When the bus pulled over to her corner, I held my breath. Two or three kids and one older lady got on. No Violet. Mickey punched me in the shoulder.

"Pay up, partner."

The bus started back up, then stopped abruptly. The doors opened, and—wouldn't you know it—Violet had arrived. I glanced at the Mick and smiled.

"Just wait," he said. "Let's see what she does."

I leaned into the aisle so she could see me.

She was looking around, probably for a friend.

Our eyes met momentarily. I was hoping she would acknowledge me, but nothing happened. She recognized a girl about halfway back and sat down next to her.

Mickey grinned. "No offense, Paulie, but I knew you were full of shit."

I sat there and stewed. This could have been a legendary moment in my life. Why had I even said word one to Mickey about meeting up with her? Why had I told him anything about it? I should have known nothing would happen.

Mickey held his hand out, palm up, and grinned.

Having to come up with five bucks wasn't the worst part of it. It was being sold out by Violet. I had done her a huge favor. All I was asking for in return was a gesture. Would it have killed her to have smiled at me or waved to me? She probably had used a lot of the information I had supplied when she met up with her group. Apparently, it was all for nothing. I reached into my back pocket for my wallet. I had a whopping three dollars. I slid them out and dropped them into Mickey's hand.

"I'll have to owe you the rest."

He closed his hand. "I'm sure you're good for it."

And then out of the corner of my eye, I saw someone walking in my direction. When I looked up,

Violet was standing next to me.

"Hi, Paulie," she said.

"H-…Hi."

"Well, I just wanted to thank you again for bailing me out on Saturday."

"Oh, you're welcome," I mumbled.

"It really helped. It made me sound like I had actually read the book. So thanks." She smiled.

"I'm glad I was able to help." And then deep from within, I found the courage to continue the conversation. "Let me know the next book you're supposed to read. If I've read it, I'd be happy to help you out."

She laughed. "That's an idea." She stood there a few more seconds. "Well, thanks again."

I nodded as she made her way back to her seat. I glanced in Mickey's direction. He was, in a word, dumbfounded. I held out my hand, palm up, and cleared my throat.

"You were saying."

"I don't believe it. I cannot believe it."

I sat back and just enjoyed the moment—one of the best ever.

Chapter 8

The moment we walked into school, things were buzzing. There were various groups of kids huddled together in conversation. Something was up, and it didn't take long to pick up on the details. The Colton-Carolyn incident was high on the list of discussion topics. Since I hadn't spoken to anyone but Mickey all weekend, I hadn't realized that Mrs. Anderson, the girls' tennis coach, had talked to the football coach and the principal about what had taken place under the bleachers on Saturday. Apparently, the principal had pressured the coach to hold Colton out of the game until the matter was resolved. And wouldn't you know it, we lost. We lost to a team we should have creamed. Everyone was saying the benching of Colton lost us the game. And now, everyone was pissed at Carolyn. Without knowing anything about what had happened, the majority of the student body was siding with Colton.

I was the one person who could have come to Carolyn's aid. I had had plenty of opportunities to speak up, but each time, I had choked. I kept trying to rationalize: since nothing really had happened, it would be okay for me to stay mum. Of course, that was from the perspective of a male. I had no idea what it was like to have been violated the way Carolyn was. The more I tried to think about it from her perspective, the worse I felt. Even though Colton hadn't hit a home run, he *had* made it to second base, and that was an awful thing for Carolyn. I knew that now. I tried to tell myself what had taken place could have been much worse, but since it hadn't actually happened, then it wasn't so bad. But it was. It really was. If you thought someone was about to rape you, even though they weren't successful, that fear would stay with you for a long time—maybe even a lifetime. I suddenly was right back where I had started. Should I say something, or should I keep my mouth shut?

It didn't take long for kids to figure out *I* was the mystery man—the material witness—the one who walked out from under the bleachers shortly after Carolyn was seen leaving—the one who said he had seen nothing. As I walked through the hallways on my way to class, I could tell people were staring at me, but no one said a word. When I ran into some of the guys on the football team, they all nodded, smiled, and gave me a thumbs-up. It felt kind of good, but when I thought more about how I had earned that response, I was ashamed of myself. Were those feelings of shame enough to make me do the right thing? If I did, not only would Colton be on my case, the entire football team would be. My head felt like it was going to explode. Why was I protecting a thug like Colton? It just wasn't like me. We ran in different circles. He wasn't the kind of person I'd be friends with—and for good reason.

It was hard to concentrate in class. I kept feeling as though there were dozens of eyes on me the entire period. It was difficult to take notes. The only way I could get this out of my head was to think about Violet.

I thought about our little exchange on the bus this morning. And Mickey's reaction. It was awesome. I wondered what I'd do if I were ever given the choice of being Violet's boyfriend or Andie's boyfriend. If I chose Violet, I'd need a whole new wardrobe—a greaser wardrobe—leather jacket, baggy gray pants, and pointed black shoes with two-inch heels. I didn't have any of those things. If I chose Andie, I wouldn't have to change a thing. I could just be me. The decision suddenly had gotten much easier. The Violet thing was fun to think about, but in reality, I knew it could and would never happen. What was I thinking? I had to reprioritize things. If Andie was destined to be the future Mrs. Paulie Passero, I had to concentrate on her—and her alone.

When I entered the cafeteria, I could see things had heated up. The group of friends who usually sat with Carolyn at lunch had abandoned her. She was now sitting alone. I felt really bad for her. Two tables over, Colton and his band of merry men were taunting her. They were throwing things at her—grapes, peanuts, pretzels, and other food items. Carolyn kept her head down. Her eyes were closed most of the time. There was something wrong here. She was the victim. How could this be happening? This just wasn't right.

I glanced over at Andie's table. The usual crew was in place. Some of them were pointing at Carolyn and yelling things. Andie wasn't participating. I tried not to listen. I knew I couldn't return to Andie's table, not after the dust-ups with Colton. I looked where Mickey was sitting—a bunch of dorky kids from his neighborhood. If I decided to break down and join them for lunch, my social status would go right down the tubes. With the conditions I had set for myself, there was literally no place to sit. But one. I don't know what made me do it—maybe guilt—but I strolled over to where Carolyn was sitting. I just stood there for a few seconds waiting for her to look up. But she never did.

"Excuse me," I said. "Is there anyone sitting here?"

Carolyn lifted her head slightly and wiped her eyes. She had been crying. "No," she said. It seemed as if she was trying to avoid eye contact with me. When she did finally look up, I could tell she recognized me, but she said nothing.

"Do you mind if I sit here?"

She didn't respond right away. That wasn't a good sign. When a few more seconds passed, I got the hint. I took her silence as a *no* and turned to leave.

"Wait a minute," she said.

I looked back.

"You can sit here if you like."

"Are you sure?"

She nodded.

I hesitated but eventually made my move. I sat down across from her. For the first couple of minutes, neither of us spoke. It was kind of awkward. Then a grape came flying from two tables over and hit me in the side of the head.

"What the—"

Carolyn looked up. "I'm afraid that was meant for me," she said. "I'm sorry. If you want to move, go ahead."

I could hear the guys at the football table laughing. When I looked over, I noticed they were all having a good time but Colton. He was staring daggers at me. He had to be wondering why I was sitting with Carolyn.

Heck, I was wondering why I was sitting with her. But something made me do it. Guilt maybe. Or was there some higher power taking over, forcing me to do the right thing? I wasn't sure.

"As long as they're just throwing grapes, I think I'll be fine," I said.

She forced a weak smile. Right at that moment, she seemed so vulnerable. I was starting to feel bad. I needed to do something to make things better.

"I don't think we've formally met. I'm Paulie Passero." I moved my hand in her direction. When she didn't reciprocate right away, I pulled it back.

"Oh, sorry," she said. She reached out to shake. "I'm Carolyn. Carolyn Mancuso."

I was really starting to enjoy shaking hands with girls lately. Their skin was always so soft. I noticed Carolyn's hand was unusually warm. I wasn't sure why that was.

She looked down and continued eating her sandwich. She took really small bites. Not like me. I could down an entire sandwich in four bites or less. Neither of us spoke for the next couple of minutes. Then, right on cue, another grape came flying over. This one hit me right in the eye.

"Damn it," I said.

"Are you okay?" she asked.

I rubbed my eye. "Yeah, I'm fine." But I wasn't. That thing had nailed me in the open eye. Things were a little blurry.

"It isn't safe to sit here," she said. "We should leave."

But there wasn't anywhere else to go. We weren't allowed to leave the cafeteria until the bell rang. I looked around for room at another table, but there didn't appear to be any. I glanced at the clock on the far wall. We would somehow need to kill five more minutes.

I looked over at the football table. "Those guys are a bunch of jerks."

She smiled. "Yeah, I know." She was looking anywhere but right at me.

With the time remaining, I knew exactly what I should do. I should tell her I was sorry for what happened to her on Saturday, and that I had seen everything that had taken place under the bleachers. I should have offered to go with her to the principal's office to tell him what I had seen. I wanted to do those things, but I was afraid of what would happen if I did. Why was I such a coward anyway? I ate quietly for the next few minutes and said nothing. There was no hero in me today. When the bell finally rang, Carolyn cleaned up her place, smiled, and left. I knew I had wasted the perfect opportunity to come clean. The guilt was eating me up.

And that was how it went for the remainder of the week. The day would start out on an upbeat note because Violet would smile at me on the bus. When I'd get to school, the eyes of my classmates were still on me. Then at lunch I'd sit at Carolyn's table and little to nothing would come out of my mouth. Each day the harassment from the football team and some of Andie's friends got worse. The jeers were louder and more vulgar. The food items flying in our direction in the cafeteria got worse. On Wednesday, they started throwing crumpled up lunch bags. On Thursday, Carolyn got hit in the shoulder with an orange. This was getting out of hand. After lunch that day, I walked with her to class. When we entered the hallway, it was a scene right out of the Ten Commandments: The seas parted. Or in this case, kids moved out of our way and avoided us as if we were lepers.

I didn't think things could get much worse, but by the time Friday rolled around, there was a new low. I sat down at Carolyn's table and decided it was time for a real conversation. It wouldn't be easy. She would barely make eye contact the entire lunch period. Since she didn't appear to have any friends left, it was up to me to get her talking. Maybe she would feel better if she did.

I cleared my throat. "So how you holdin' up?"

She lifted her head. She had a look on her face that said everything. She wiped her eyes. Her mascara was running.

"I've been better."

"People have pretty short memories around here, you know," I said. "I think things will get back to normal pretty soon."

"You do? Well, I don't."

I leaned closer to her. "You just gotta hang in there. You gotta be tough."

She sat up and sighed. "Nothing I do will change anything. But at least I won't have to put up with it much longer."

"What do you mean?"

She smiled weakly. "I'm transferring at the end of the semester."

What?! I couldn't believe what I was hearing. So Colton and his crew had won. These creeps were running her off. It wasn't right. A person shouldn't have to leave school in order to be treated in a civil manner. But that's exactly what was happening here.

"What school would you go to? Not Ridgeway, I hope?"

"My parents are helping me figure that out. Ridgeway's an option."

"You don't belong at Ridgeway," I said. "You wouldn't fit in with that crowd."

"I don't seem to be fitting in here too well these days, or haven't you noticed?"

How could I argue with that? It all made perfect sense. Carolyn was destined to be the ugly duckling at Cermak for as long as people believed she had made up the story about Colton. Take the jocks, for instance—I didn't think any of them cared if he had done it or not. They just didn't like seeing one of their own getting ratted out—by a freshman, no less. Most of the kids who attended Cermak were decent human beings—at least I had always thought they were. If they knew the truth, they wouldn't be treating Carolyn the way they had been. But one thing was clear—unless I spoke up, she would continue to get persecuted. I felt so bad for her.

"It looks like you'll be needing a new lunch partner soon," she said.

That was the least of my concerns. Right now, I had to think of a way to help this girl. But the only possible way was just too painful. Could I find the courage within to do the right thing? The lunch bell rang.

"See ya Monday," she said.

"Carolyn?"

She paused.

Ready or not, it was time—time for me to be a man. "Can I talk to you after school? It's important."

"I have tennis practice until four-thirty."

I had to get this off my chest. "That's fine. I'll go to the library and work there until then. I'll meet you by the courts after that."

"Okay, I guess." She had a slightly hopeful look on her face when she left.

I sat there momentarily and thought about the decision I was making. Would I actually have the guts to go through with it? Would I finally share the details of what I had seen last Saturday? The thought of it was making me nervous. I knew there would be ramifications. If I spoke up and bailed out Carolyn, I'd be digging a deep hole for myself—one I might never be able to climb out of. Once I told her what I had seen, I would then have to admit I had lied to the tennis coach. I would undoubtedly have to tell my story to the principal. And I wouldn't just be ratting out any old kid—I'd be targeting one of the most popular kids at school. I'd be making enemies left and right. And, you know, it just might end up being me who would have to consider transferring to another school.

Chapter 9

I stared at the clock that hung behind the circulation desk in the library. It read three thirty. In an hour, I would either confront my demons or shirk my responsibilities. With each minute that passed, my heart seemed to beat faster. I was making myself a nervous wreck. I had managed to read only two pages in my chemistry book for the last half hour. I just couldn't concentrate. I knew in my heart I was about to do the right thing—the noble thing. Why was it so hard? I wished now I hadn't kept it all bottled up. Why hadn't I told Mickey? He was my best friend, for Pete's sake. You're supposed to be able to tell your best friend anything. I guess I was afraid he'd disapprove of me for staying mum. And then he'd bug me day and night until I finally spilled my guts.

What about my parents? Why hadn't I told them? Wait a minute. Forget that last thought. There was no way I could have told my folks. If my dad found out I hadn't come to some girl's rescue, he'd be really pissed at me, and he'd never let me forget it. He'd tell me some story of when he was young and how he had to stick his neck out—and how he was a better man today because of it. And my mom? Well, she'd be disappointed in me, although she'd never actually say it. Her body language would say it all. There didn't appear to be anyone I could share this with. Then I thought about my teachers, but I didn't have the kind of relationship with any of them to be able to discuss a subject of this nature.

I squeezed my temples. Wasn't there anyone I could talk to about all of this? And then, all at once, a name popped into my head—of course, Mr. Drennan. We had gotten to be pals recently when I did that news article on the short story he had written. By the end of the interview, I remembered, I felt so relaxed and comfortable with him. I looked up at the clock. What were the chances he was still at school? I packed up my stuff and made a beeline for his classroom. As I walked down the hallway, I told myself if I found him in his classroom, it would be a sign I was supposed to unburden myself and share what I knew with the authorities. Or, if he wasn't there, then I would keep it to myself and not show up to meet Carolyn after practice. I reached his classroom and stood outside for a minute. Now I wasn't sure if I wanted him to be there or not. I took a deep breath and poked my head in. He was sitting at his desk grading papers. When the door closed behind me, he looked up. I wasn't sure if I should proceed, but it was too late to turn back.

"Paulie? What can I do for you?"

"I was just passing by and…" I hesitated. C'mon, kid, man up, I told myself. Do the right thing for once in your life. "…I wondered if you had a minute to talk."

He slid the pile of papers on his desk to the side. "Sure, come on in and sit down. What is it?"

I walked in and plopped down at the desk closest to his. I set my books on the floor.

He was staring at me but smiling.

"Um, I don't know where to begin."

He sat back in his chair. "Just start wherever you want."

I had a hard time looking him in the eye. I cleared my throat. "You know all this talk going around school about Colton Brand and Carolyn Mancuso and what happened under the tennis bleachers on Saturday?"

"I've heard about it, yes."

"So what do you think about it?" I thought it best to get his take on the whole thing first before lowering the boom.

"Well, I only know what I hear. And since I wasn't there, I don't really know who to believe."

"Are you leaning one way or the other?"

He sat up. "Paulie, I'm not really sure we should be having this conversation. This is an administrative matter now. It's out of our hands."

"But what if the administration doesn't have all the facts?"

"What facts are we talking about?" he asked.

I stared at the floor and didn't speak.

"Paulie? Do you know something about what happened? I understand you were there."

"Yeah, I was there."

"Coach Anderson says you didn't see anything. Is that right?"

I looked at him with what had to have been the guiltiest face ever.

"You did see what happened, didn't you?"

I looked away and nodded.

"Would you like to talk about it?"

"I thought I did, but now I'm having second thoughts."

He got up from his desk and walked around to where I was sitting. He slipped into the desk next to mine and sat sideways. He reached over and put his hand on my shoulder.

All of a sudden, I felt my eyes watering up. Oh, no, I couldn't cry. Not here. Not now.

"It's really hard to talk about," I said. I glanced at the clock. I was supposed to meet Carolyn in fifteen minutes. What would I say to her? For that matter, what would I say to Mr. Drennan?

"You might feel better getting this off your chest," he said.

"I'm just worried about what will happen if I do."

"Why do you say that?"

"Colton's twice as big as me. He'd kill me."

"That won't happen. We can make sure of that."

"You can't watch over me twenty-four hours a day."

He leaned over and placed his head close to mine. "Why don't you tell me what you saw. Just me. And if you don't want me to tell the principal, I won't. It'll just be between you and me. How's that?"

I considered his proposition for a moment. The more I thought about it, the more I realized it was a win-win offer. If I chickened out after telling him, I wouldn't be under any pressure to share this information with anyone else. I wondered if I should take him up on it. For some reason, I enjoyed talking to this man. I felt safe.

"What do you say?" he said.

I looked up and nodded reluctantly.

"Okay, good. Just take your time. Don't worry about anything."

I let out a long sigh. "Okay, here goes." I paused. "I was at the tennis courts on Saturday. I had arranged to meet Andie Walker there. She had offered to give me a few tennis pointers after practice."

"Okay."

"Then while I was sitting there, I heard noises coming from under the bleachers. I decided to see what they were." I looked at Mr. Drennan. "I wish now I had never gone to look."

He put his hand on my shoulder again. "Maybe you were supposed to. Things happen for a reason, you know."

"When I got there, I couldn't believe what I was seeing. Colton Brand and Carolyn Mancuso were under there. He was trying to have his way with her."

"What do you mean?"

"He kept trying to put his hand under her shirt. She kept saying *no*, but he wouldn't listen. Then he pushed her down on her back and got on top of her. She reached up and scratched his face. That really pissed him off. He put one hand over her mouth, and the other under her shirt. Then he…" I started to lose my breath.

"Take your time. You're doing great."

"Then he tried to pull down her skirt, and I think he might have succeeded but someone called out her name, and he stopped. Someone from the team was looking for her. Colton told her to keep her mouth shut. Then more girls started calling out her name. That's when he must have gotten nervous. He got up off her, and she jumped up and ran past me, but I don't think she saw me. Then he started to run, but he stopped when he saw me. He made it very clear that if I told anyone what I had seen, he'd make life very unpleasant for me."

"Don't worry about him." Mr. Drennan said.

"I wasn't sure what to do. Should I say anything? Should I forget what I saw? I decided to get the heck out of there, but when I did, one of the girls on the tennis team saw me. She made it sound like I was the one who had attacked Carolyn. Mrs. Anderson came running over. She asked me who I was and what I had seen." I dropped my head. I was ashamed to admit what I had done—or rather, what I hadn't done.

"Paulie, I understand perfectly why you didn't say anything. What's more important is that you're talking about it now. This takes a ton of courage to do."

"I told Mrs. Anderson I hadn't seen a thing. I said that with Carolyn standing right there. I felt awful." I made a fist. "And now everyone believes she was lying about Colton. Nobody'll talk to her. They throw stuff at her in the cafeteria. It's awful. And at lunch today she told me she plans to transfer out of Cermak at the end of the semester. They're driving her out...all because of me."

"It's not because of you."

"If I had had any bal—any guts—none of this would have happened."

"Do you know how much guts it takes to tell me this?" he asked. "You should be very proud of yourself."

"Then why do I feel so miserable?"

"You're going to feel better soon, very soon. Trust me."

I looked at Mr. Drennan. "Are you going to tell people what I told you?"

"Am *I* going to? No, but I hope you will. And I

plan on being right at your side when you do. If you do."

I rubbed my forehead. "I don't know what to do."

He put his arm around me. "I think you know what you need to do."

"Before I came in here, I was waiting around till tennis practice was over. I was so mad at the way people were treating Carolyn, I was going to tell her what I had seen." I glanced at the clock over Mr. Drennan's desk. "Now I'm not sure if I have the courage to go through with it."

"I sure as hell think you do," he said. "If you had the courage to tell me, you have what it takes to tell her."

"But she'll hate me. I could have saved her a lot of grief if only I had spoken up earlier."

"Hate you? No chance. She'll be relieved you're speaking up. I'll tell you what. Why don't both of us go over to the tennis courts and tell her together."

It was an interesting offer. With Mr. Drennan there, Carolyn would be less likely to get pissed at me. I nodded.

"Give me a minute to clean things up here," he said. He scooped up a pile of papers from his desk and dumped them into his briefcase. He grabbed his sport coat off the back of his chair and threw it over his arm. "Ready?"

I smiled. I let Mr. Drennan do all the talking as we walked out the back door of school and headed for the athletic complex. When we got there, the girls were all huddled around Mrs. Anderson for a team meeting. A minute or so later, it broke up and the girls scattered. I couldn't help but notice most of the girls were in groups of two or three, but Carolyn was walking alone.

Mr. Drennan walked up to Mrs. Anderson and said something to her. She leaned over and glanced at me. Then she nodded.

"Carolyn," she said, "can you come over here for a minute."

Mr. Drennan waved me over. This wasn't exactly what I had in mind. It was just supposed to be me and Carolyn. Now the adults were involved. I guess they just wanted to make it official.

"Carolyn," Mrs. Anderson said, "I think Paulie has something he wants to tell you."

I looked at Mr. Drennan, who smiled. I blew out some air. And then I dove in.

"I did see what happened under the bleachers on Saturday." I glanced at Mrs. Anderson. "I'm sorry for not telling you what I saw. It was just as Carolyn described it. Colton was trying to—well, you know— and Carolyn was trying to fight him off. She managed to scratch his face before she got away." I stared at Carolyn. "I'm sorry. I'm really sorry for not sticking up for you. I know now I should have. When I saw how rotten the other kids were treating you, I knew I had to do something." Carolyn started crying.

"Why didn't you speak up right away?" Mrs. Anderson asked.

"Colton knows I saw everything. He…"

"He threatened Paulie if he spoke up," Mr. Drennan said.

Mrs. Anderson nodded. She put her arm around Carolyn. "Honey, I'm so sorry this happened to you. And I'm even sorrier we doubted you."

"Am I going to have to tell the principal this

story?" I asked.

"He may have a few questions for you," Mrs. Anderson said, "but Mr. Drennan and I will speak to him first. We'll do the heavy lifting for you. Okay?"

"Okay."

She put her hand on my shoulder. "Paulie, it took a lot of courage for you to speak up. I'm so glad you did."

"Me too," Carolyn said as she wiped her eyes. "Thank you."

"It's over, Paulie," Mr. Drennan said with a smile.

"Is it?" I replied.

Chapter 10

I turned to leave. I felt like a huge weight had been lifted off my shoulders. But I also felt like there was now a huge target on my back. I had no idea what would happen on Monday when word leaked out. I would probably have to start looking over my shoulder everywhere I went. Mr. Drennan had said nothing bad would happen to me, that he'd see to that. But I knew better. He might be able to convince Colton to leave me alone, but there was no way he could stop the entire football team. Why couldn't those guys see I had done them a favor? I had done the entire school a favor. Colton was a cancer. He had to be exposed. Who knew how many other girls he would have assaulted? Why couldn't people see Carolyn could have been someone's sister or girlfriend? They would naturally want to get the guy who had molested her.

I thought hard about what I had done and the consequences of my actions. Maybe I was being too hard on myself. Maybe people *would* approve of my decision to come clean. Maybe they'd view me as a hero. Yeah. Maybe this would all work out okay.

"Paulie?"

I turned around to find Carolyn standing there.

"I just wanted to thank you for what you did. I'm sure it wasn't easy."

I smiled weakly. "It was something I should have done days ago. I'm sorry for that. I'm sorry for what you had to go through."

"It's all right," she said.

"If you want me to move to another lunch table, I would understand. It's fine."

"What are you talking about?" she said. "You're more than welcome to sit with me. Nobody else will."

"I bet that's all going to change now. You'll see. Once people know the truth about Colton, they'll understand. And I bet you won't have to transfer to another school."

"I don't know about that," she said. "I think I'm going to need a fresh start."

"I honestly hope that doesn't happen."

"We'll see." She looked away momentarily. "Well, thank you again. I'll see you on Monday?"

"Yeah, sure. I'll see you then." I watched her jog back in the direction of the tennis courts. I couldn't help but notice she had passed someone on her way back. The person seemed to be heading in my direction. A few seconds later, I could see it was Andie Walker. She was running toward me. Andie was the last person I wanted to see right now. When she found out what I'd said about Colton, she was going to hate me. I knew it. And that would put an official end to the romance I had dreamed about. But wait. Maybe I was jumping to conclusions. Maybe she wouldn't be upset. Maybe she would be happy to find out the kind of creep Colton really was. Maybe she'd thank me for getting her out of what might have been a really bad situation. I had to think positively. I could only hope and pray it would turn out that way.

"Paulie," she called out. "Wait up."

I stopped and turned around.

She was out of breath when she finally stopped. "Hey, can I talk to you for a minute?"

I nodded.

"What was all that about back there with the coach and Mr. Drennan?"

Oh, God. What should I tell her? Should I make up a story? Should I tell her it was all nothing? Or should I just tell her the truth? She was going to find out anyway, no matter what I did. And I guessed I'd rather have her hear the bad news from me than from some stranger.

"Um, it's kind of complicated," I said.

"Like how?"

I was having a hard time blurting it out. I knew she didn't want to hear it.

"Does it have something to do with Colton and what happened on Saturday?"

"Yeah."

"So what is it?"

"Well…do you remember when someone found me under the bleachers that day?"

"Yeah," she said. "What about it?"

"I told Mrs. Anderson I hadn't seen anything…but I lied. I saw the whole thing. Carolyn was telling the truth. Colton was…you know."

"No, I don't know," she said angrily.

Oh, boy. I was afraid of that reaction. But what could I do? I couldn't change my story now. She needed to know the truth.

"He was molesting her, Andie. And she was trying to fight him off."

"Is that what you told Coach Anderson and Mr. Drennan?"

"Uh-huh."

She threw her racket down. "Paulie, how could you do that? How could you? Colton's not like that. I don't know what you think you saw, but you have it all wrong."

"I'm sorry, but it's the truth."

She ran her fingers through her hair. "Do you know what's going to happen now? He's probably going to be suspended. And maybe get kicked off the football team." She stopped and seemed to be thinking to herself. "He better not get expelled, that's all I have to say."

"I don't know what's going to happen. I'm sorry."

"You're sorry? That's all you have to say? This is serious stuff. I hope you know that."

"I do."

"Paulie Passero, I don't want to talk to you ever again. I don't want to see you. I don't want to have anything to do with you. Understand?"

I didn't think she was looking for an actual answer to the question.

She started to cry. "How could you?" She picked up her racket and began running toward the tennis courts.

Well, I guess the worst had finally happened. She was going to tell Colton, and all her friends, and all his friends, and the entire football team. I was dead meat. There was no way I was going to survive this. I should just kill myself right now. It'd save me a lot of agony in the future. I swallowed hard. I was having a hard time catching my breath. There was no way Mr. Drennan could stop all this. The entire school was going to hate me. Why couldn't Andie see the big picture? Why couldn't she see things from my perspective or from Carolyn's? Why was she so sure about her cheating boyfriend? Apparently, she didn't know the real Colton. Didn't she realize the same kind of thing would have eventually happened to her? I had saved her from the pain and misery of an attack of some kind. Why couldn't she see that?

I sat alone on the bus ride home. Believe me, that was a blessing. I was in no mood to make idle conversation with some stranger. I just wanted to be left alone. For the remainder of the ride, I sat there and felt sorry for myself. When I got home, I found my mom in the kitchen whipping up a batch of pizzelle with the hot iron. When I saw them, I smiled. I loved pizzelle, especially when they were still warm. It was the first good thing that had happened to me today.

"You look like you could use a few of these," she said. She sprinkled confectioner's sugar on some of the pizzelle, placed them on a napkin, and slid them in front of me.

"Thanks," I said.

"You're late today. A newspaper meeting or something?"

"Huh? Oh, yeah, a newspaper meeting."

"I can't wait to read your next story," she said. "Do you know what it's going to be about yet?"

"Um…no, not yet. We'll get our assignments next week." I knew the longer I sat there, the more I'd be lying about things. I didn't like lying to my mom. She had always been a straight shooter with me. She had bailed me out countless times when I had gotten into a squabble with my dad.

"I think I'm gonna take these upstairs and get a start on my homework," I said.

"Okay," she said. "Dinner's at the usual time."

I trudged up the stairs and passed my grandfather's room. The door was open. He was sitting in a rocking chair listening to a Dick Contino record. Before Grandpa had come to live with us, I'd had no idea who Dick Contino was. I soon learned he was this amazing Italian musician who played the accordion—really well, I might add.

"Hey, Paulo," Grandpa said. "Come in. Sit with me."

I loved the old guy, but I just wasn't in the mood to chat.

He patted his hand on the end of his bed. "Come see me."

I wanted to tell him the truth—that I wasn't in the mood—but I couldn't. He was a really nice old man who had lost his wife a couple of months ago. The last thing he needed was some bratty, selfish teenager ignoring his invitation. I set my books on his bed and joined him.

"There's nobody like Dick Contino. He can really play the squeeze-a-box. Do you think your mom and dad might buy you an accordion someday? It's a great instrument for a boy, you know."

"I don't know, Gramps. We've never talked about it."

"You want me to ask them for you?"

In a word...*no*. With school, the newspaper, work, and my social life—make that my non-existent social life—I had little to no time to learn a musical instrument.

"Let me think about it. Okay?"

"Sure, sure. You do that." He smiled. "What are you eating?" His eyes lit up. "Did your momma make pizzelle?"

"Yep. She's making them right now. You want me to get you some?"

"No, I'll go downstairs myself. I like to talk to your momma." He rubbed the top of my head, turned off the phonograph, and left.

I went into my room, threw my books on the desk, and lay down on my bed. I wanted to go to sleep and wake up ten years later. I was sure my future had to end up better than my past had. How could it get any worse? I closed my eyes, and that was the last thing I remembered before my mom woke me up for dinner.

When I went downstairs, I found my dad watching a prizefight on TV. I stood there for a minute and stared at the fighters. Nothing much was happening. They were just dancing around.

"They don't seem to be doing anything," I said.

"Be patient. They will be," my dad said.

"Why are they holding their gloves in front of their faces like that?"

"That's how you box, son. When you're not throwing a punch, you have to protect your face at all times…or you won't be on your feet for long."

My mom walked into the living room. "Peter, please turn that off. It's time to eat?

Dinner conversation was relatively dull. I didn't really participate. Afterward, I went up to my room where I proceeded to feel sorry for myself—a practice I had gotten pretty good at lately. I tried to do homework, but I kept thinking about what had happened today, and what was likely to happen on Monday. I turned in early and just lay there unable to sleep.

I wasn't sure how things had gotten so messed up. When I made the decision to tell people what I had really seen, I thought it would be a breakthrough moment for me. I thought once I had unburdened myself and told the truth, I would hear angels playing harps and hordes of fans cheering uncontrollably. People would hoist me up on their shoulders and parade me around town. It would be my greatest hour.

But that didn't happen. It wasn't even close. I would have been better off keeping my mouth shut and taking the secret to my grave. The members of the football team would still be my allies since I hadn't ratted out Colton. And Andie would be appreciative her boyfriend had not been singled out. The only collateral damage would have been Carolyn. I felt really bad about how she had been treated, and that was why I had finally spoken up. But what if I hadn't? What if I had said nothing? What would it have hurt? Carolyn was planning on transferring at the end of the semester anyway. She was cute. She would find a whole flock of friends at her new school. She would have been fine.

I was now having serious misgivings about what I had done. Mr. Drennan thought it was a brave thing, but he wasn't the one who would have to survive the onslaught of Colton supporters. He wasn't the one who'd have to walk the halls and be treated like an outcast. I closed my eyes tightly and willed myself to sleep. The longer I stayed awake, the more depressed I became. Within a few minutes, I was out.

The next morning I got up and went downstairs for

breakfast. My mom was washing the dishes. I looked around for my dad but didn't see him.

"Where's dad?" I asked.

"Oh, he had to go in to work today," she said. "Every once in a while, he has to go in on a Saturday."

I tried to hide my joy. Now don't get me wrong, I loved my dad. But every weekend when he was around, he had these projects for me that would kill the better part of the day—scrape the old paint off the fence in the back yard, clean the awnings, weed the garden, mow the lawn and rake it up, et cetera, et cetera. The raking was the part that made me crazy. And it was all because my dad was the cheapest man on earth. Last spring, our mower died. I couldn't have been happier. The old mower didn't have a grass catcher that picked up all the grass. I prayed for the longest time for the old one to die so we'd have to get a new mower—one with a grass catcher.

So we go over to Goldblatt's to get a new one. My dad complained about the prices the entire time. When he found a relatively cheap mower, he shrugged and wheeled it to the counter. When I saw it had a grass catcher, I was in my glory. No more raking up the grass. A salesman approached us.

"That's a real beauty," he said. "You're gonna love it. A lot of horsepower. It'll cut even tall, wet grass in a breeze."

"That's all fine," my dad said. "But it's still too expensive. Is this all you've got?"

"Well, I do have one in the back that's ten dollars cheaper."

"What's wrong with it?"

"Nothing," the man said. "Give me just a second

and I'll get it." He disappeared momentarily. A minute later he reappeared with another mower. "Here we go. It's actually the same model as the one you have there. It just doesn't have a grass catcher."

What? Say it ain't so! I looked at my dad. Please, please, don't do it.

"Ten dollars cheaper, you say?"

"Yep."

"Dad, it doesn't have a grass catcher. That means we'll still have to rake the yard."

"No, it means *you'll* still have to rake the yard." He turned to the salesman. "I'll take it."

So you can see why I had no problem with my dad having to work today. Every time I mowed the lawn, I thought about how much easier my job would have been with a grass catcher. It still makes me crazy.

"What are your plans today?" my mom asked.

"I have a ton of homework. But first I thought I'd run over to Mickey's."

"Will you be here for lunch?"

"I don't know. But don't worry about it. I'll find something in the fridge."

After breakfast, I walked over to the Mick's house. I was trying to decide if I should tell him everything that had happened the day before. If I didn't and he found out about it from someone else, I knew he'd be sore. It probably was best to tell him everything. I was still worried about how he might react to my unwillingness to speak up for Carolyn when I had a chance. I figured it really didn't matter anymore. I would have to live with my own poor decisions.

When I got to his house, he was in the back mowing the lawn. Of course, his mower had a grass catcher. He didn't see me at first when I walked into the back yard. The mower was pretty loud. I plopped down on a white wooden swing that sat on a concrete patio directly behind the house. I waited a few seconds until he caught sight of me. He turned off the mower.

"Paulie, what are you doing here?"

I shrugged. "Just thought I'd stop over to shoot the shit."

"Perfect. I need a breather now anyway." He sat down next to me.

"So what's up?"

I let out a long sigh. "A lot's happened in the past twenty-four hours."

"Like what?"

"Okay, here goes—the whole painful saga."

His eyes narrowed. "I'm all ears."

"Remember the Colton-Carolyn drama that happened a week ago?"

"Yeah."

"And do you recall I was under the bleachers when it happened, and I told people I hadn't seen anything?"

He nodded.

"Well, I lied. I saw everything."

"What?"

I then proceeded to tell him the entire story—about what Colton had done to Carolyn—about how she fought to free herself—about how Colton threatened me on his way out—about how I had lied to Coach Anderson—about my conversations with Carolyn this past week in the cafeteria—about my conversation with Mr. Drennan—about my ultimate confession—about Carolyn's reaction to it—and about Andie flipping out.

"Holy shit," he said. "Paulie, are you okay?"

"Not really. I don't know what's gonna happen now. I don't know if everyone will hate me or support me. I just don't know what to expect."

"Well, in my book, it took balls to do what you did."

"Thanks. That makes me feel a little better."

"I don't see how people can get on your case. You were an eyewitness to an assault. You told people what you saw—even with the threat of violence hanging over you."

"Don't remind me."

"You told them what Colton said to you, right?"

I nodded.

"Then he wouldn't dare lay a hand on you. If anything bad happened, he'd be the first person they'd suspect. He's not that stupid. Well, he is stupid, just not that stupid."

"I hope you're right. But I'm worried about how the football team will react. Those guys are like a cult. They stick together no matter what."

"We don't really hang around with any of them. But I would sure keep my distance if I were you."

"No kidding."

"I suppose this kind of dashes your dreams of ever going out with Andie Walker."

I managed a half smile. "Big time. That's never gonna happen now—as if it was ever gonna happen anyway."

Mickey patted me on the back. "I'm proud to call you my friend. You've got stones, Paulie. I don't know how I would have handled this mess." He grinned. "You know, I think this whole thing is gonna blow over. And you'll come out of it a hero. That's what I think."

"Really?" I was suddenly feeling much better about things. Maybe Mickey was right. Maybe everyone would admire me for speaking up in the face of intimidation. Yeah. Maybe people would look at me differently now. Maybe this was the best thing that could have happened to me. Maybe, just maybe, everything would work out just fine.

Chapter 11

When my alarm went off on Monday morning, I just lay there for a few minutes. Today could end up being one of the best days of my life. On the other hand, it also had the potential of being one of my darkest days. I tried to think positively. I had spent the better part of Sunday afternoon knocking out a series of homework assignments. I had to read *Romeo and Juliet* for Mr. Drennan's class. As I read, I kept imagining myself as the ill-fated Romeo and Andie as the elusive Juliet. Maybe that was a solution to my problem, I thought. Since, like Romeo, I couldn't have the girl of my dreams, maybe ending it all was an option. But I didn't think Andie would react the way Juliet had. Andie was not about to cash in her chips for someone like me. Let's face it—she hated me. And there didn't appear to be anything I could do to change that. But I wasn't so sure Romeo's solution was the answer. Would I actually consider killing myself over a girl? I just couldn't see it.

I sat up in bed and thought about what was waiting for me at good old Anton J. Cermak College Prep today. I wondered how I would feel a few hours from now when I got home from school. Would I be rejoicing, or would I be licking my wounds? As much as I was hoping for a positive outcome, I kept obsessing on the worst-case scenario. It was making me crazy.

When I got to the bus stop that morning, Mickey was already there. He glanced at his watch.

"I was worried about you," he said. "I didn't think you were coming."

"I sure didn't want to."

"Like I said, I don't think you have anything to worry about. You might get a little heat from the football guys, but that'll die down eventually. And the rest of the kids will be really supportive. You wait and see."

I sighed. "I hope you're right." I could see the bus coming. I dug into my pocket for change.

Mickey patted me on the back. "It's all gonna be okay, pal."

When we boarded the bus, we took refuge in our private sanctuary—the seats in the back. I watched as other kids from school hopped on. I was waiting for sneers and jeers, but most of them didn't even make eye contact. That was encouraging. Two stops later, a familiar face appeared. It was Violet. She looked good—really good—despite the ratted hair. When she spotted me, she smiled and waved. I returned the smile and glanced at Mickey. I was waiting for his reaction.

"I still can't believe you talked to her."

"Me neither. It's all kind of surreal."

Mickey poked me in the ribs. "Hey, I got an idea."

"What?"

"Since you still don't have a date for the homecoming dance this weekend, why don't you ask Violet?" He grinned.

"Yeah, right. As if she'd ever say yes."

"That seemed like a pretty friendly wave a minute

ago. Just go for it, tiger."

I shook my head. "You're crazy."

"Am I? Since the girl of your dreams is no longer in the picture, what have you got to lose? And if Violet says no, then tough shit. You're no worse off than you were a few minutes ago. So do it."

I knew Mickey would never expect me to walk up to Violet and ask her to a dance. He knew I'd never do it. He was just giving me crap. But wouldn't he be shocked if I did go over there and ask her? I tried to imagine what I'd say, and then what she'd say in response. But I didn't have the guts to do it, and Mickey was counting on that.

"You don't have a date," I said. "Why don't you ask her?"

He chuckled. "She doesn't know me from Adam. On the other hand, you two seem to be best buds."

I stared at the floor.

"It looks like I'm going to have to think of some other way to motivate you." He sat up in his seat. "Paulie Passero, if you don't ask out Violet right here and now, then you don't have a hair on your ass." He smiled. He seemed proud of himself for issuing an ultimatum.

"And wouldn't you be surprised if I went over there and started talking to her."

"You and I both know that's never going to happen." He was still grinning.

Boy, would I love to have shaken him up at that very moment. I had a notion to jump up, go over to where Violet and her friends were sitting, and ask her out. Just like that.

Mickey folded his arms. "I knew it. Your ass is as

smooth and clean as a newborn baby's butt. Chalk up another whiff for lover boy."

Mickey was really pissing me off. I glanced at Violet. She was gabbing with her friends. Did I have the guts to ask her? Would the words actually come out of my mouth? Would I strike out in the clutch? I thought to myself. I wanted to ask her. I really did. Andie was now ancient history. I glanced at Mickey. I was trying to imagine the look on his face if I decided to accept his challenge. He'd shit his pants if I walked over there right now. I took a couple of deep breaths. Could I do this? Could I actually do it?

"She gets off pretty soon, you know. This is your last chance."

I just sat there.

"I knew it." He was looking really smug about now.

I bit down on my lip. It was do or die. Time for action. I leaned into the aisle, let out a long sigh, and stood up. I winked at Mickey. I moved one foot forward, then the other. I was inching closer to Violet. At this rate, I'd make it up to where she was sitting in about an hour. With each step forward, I could feel my heart pounding faster. When I finally reached her group, I could hear her friends gabbing about how someone named Michelle was a real slut. I cleared my throat, and the conversation stopped.

Violet looked up at me and smiled. "Hi, Paulie." She turned to her friends. "This guy saved my life on Saturday. He told me everything about a book I was supposed to have read." She turned to me. "Did you need something?"

"Well...um...I was just wondering..." I started to

stammer. "This Saturday is our homecoming. And there's a dance, you know, in the Cermak gym that night. I'm sure you probably have other plans, but I was just wondering if you'd like to go with me?"

Violet's girlfriends started giggling. Why did girls always have to do that anyway?

"This Saturday night?" she said.

"Yeah. If it's not enough notice, I understand."

One of her friends turned to her. "You've always wanted to see what a dance at Cermak was like." She raised her eyebrows.

Violet thought about it for a moment and then smiled. 'You know what, it might be fun. And since I'm single again, why not?" She patted her lap with both hands. "I'd love to," she said.

"Really?" I said.

"Sure. So what time does it start?"

"Eight o'clock."

"Why don't you pick me up at about seven forty-five?"

"Great. Great."

I turned and floated back to my seat.

I smiled at Mickey. "I'm picking her up at seven forty-five." I plopped down and started humming. It was a victory song.

"It's impossible. I don't believe it."

"Eat your heart out, Mick." I leaned back and gloated.

"So if she actually said yes, then tell me this— where does she live? I assume she gave you her address."

I sat up. Oh, shit. I had no idea where she lived. Hell, I didn't even know her last name. I got up and set my books on the seat. I worked my way up to where her group was sitting. Their backs were to me. Just as I got there, I could hear them talking—about me.

"I can't believe you said yes," one of her friends said.

"I felt like I had to," Violet said. "He helped me out of a jam. So I'm just returning the favor."

"Who knows, maybe it'll turn into a passionate romance," another friend said with a smile.

"Are you kidding?" Violet said. "This is a one-time-only *pity* date."

My heart sank. A *pity* date? Those were the worst. I suddenly felt a queasiness in my stomach. I felt like I was gonna puke right there. I took several deep breaths. I had to pull myself together. I wanted to tell them I had heard the entire conversation. I wanted to tell them how cruel and shallow they were. Instead I pretended I hadn't heard a thing. I shuffled my feet to get their attention.

"Excuse me…Violet?"

"Oh, hi again." She had a guilty look on her face. "Did you need something else?"

I forced a laugh. "I'm afraid I don't know your address."

"Oh," she said as she opened up her notebook and tore off a small piece of paper. She dug into her purse and pulled out a pen. Then she began jotting something on the paper. "Here you go," she said.

I looked at it—3113 N. Neva Avenue. I knew exactly where that was.

"Anything else?" she said.

"Well, I'm a little embarrassed to admit I don't know your last name."

She laughed. "It's Kulick. Violet Cassandra Kulick. Do you need to know anything more about me? Height? Weight?"

Her friends giggled. "How about her bra size?" one of them said.

"No, that's good. Thanks." I turned to leave.

"Paulie, what kind of car do you have?"

Do *I* have? I didn't want to tell her my means of transportation was the same as that of my parents.

"It's a brown 1966 Chevy Bel Air."

The expression on her face suggested she didn't approve. "Oh, that's nice." She rolled her eyes.

"See you at seven forty-five this Saturday then," I said.

"Can't wait," she said with a smile, but I knew she said it sarcastically.

I headed in Mickey's direction. I could see he was all eyes. He was dying to know what had just transpired.

"Well?" he said. "What was that all about?"

I handed him the piece of paper.

"So this is where old Violet lives, huh?"

"Violet Cassandra Kulick lives there."

"And this is legit? She's going to the dance with you?"

"Come and see for yourself," I said matter-of-factly. I sat down and proceeded to sulk. This was not how I expected to be feeling after having scored the winning touchdown. It felt more like a fumble.

"For a guy who just pulled off the impossible, you're acting pretty glum," he said.

If Mickey only knew what I had overheard, he wouldn't have been surprised by my reaction. But I had no intention of telling him this was a pity date. It would take all the fun out of it. Maybe *fun* wasn't the right word. On one hand, I felt like I had just accomplished something that had been haunting me for years. I had actually asked a girl out on a date. But instead, I was feeling hollow inside. I knew it wasn't a real date. I knew it would never go anywhere. Once her obligation was met, I wasn't sure Violet would even acknowledge me on the bus anymore. I had always thought she was so special. She was this unattainable goddess who walked into our lives for a few minutes each morning. It was fun just looking at her. But now that had been tainted. I finally had met the real Violet, and I didn't especially like what I had found out. She was a tease, a skank, a tramp. Part of me wanted to march right up to her and call this whole thing off. But another part of me wanted to walk into the Cermak gym with a real looker on my arm. Even though everything would come to a screeching halt when the dance ended, I still wanted to go through with it. This was the type of thing that would elevate me socially, and I dearly needed that.

I didn't remember what the Mick and I talked about for the remainder of our ride. I kept thinking about the *pity* date I was about to experience on Saturday night. How did a girl act when she was on a date she didn't really care about? Would she talk to me? Would she dance with me? Would she be embarrassed to be seen with me? I was suddenly wondering if this date would actually make me a social climber, or if it would drop me to new depths of nerd-dom. Violet would at least be polite, right? I wanted to ask Mickey's opinion of the whole thing, but I didn't dare. I was having too much fun watching him squirm. This would be the first time in our long friendship that I had a date and he didn't. Most of the time, we were both attending these things stag.

And then something popped into my head. Oh, no. I had no idea if the car would be free Saturday night. My parents rarely went out on the weekends. When we did, it was usually a Sunday afternoon dinner at my grandparents' home—the ones on my mom's side. But sometimes they'd have dinner at one of their cousins' homes. My parents were one of four couples who got together every month or so, and it was always on a Saturday. I hoped—I prayed this wasn't one of those days. What would I do if I had no wheels? I couldn't take Violet to the dance on the bus. No self-respecting male teen would be caught dead taking his date on the bus. And where would I borrow a car? I didn't have any close friends who had their own rides. I should have thought to ask my parents first. But how could I have? I didn't know I'd be going out until a few minutes ago. The minute I got home tonight, I'd need to find out.

Moments later, the bus pulled up in front of Cermak.

"Well, you'll know soon enough," Mickey said.

"Know what?"

"The *Colton-Carolyn-Andie* saga? Have you forgotten?"

Shit. I had forgotten—for a few minutes at least. The Violet thing had preoccupied me for the better part of the bus ride. I thought to myself for a minute. You know, life really sucked. I was using one problem to forget about another problem. It didn't seem fair. I hopped off the bus, waited for traffic to lighten, and crossed the street. As I approached the front door of school, I suddenly could feel a knot in the pit of my stomach. Standing in front of the building were members of the football team. They had their arms crossed and they were staring right at me.

"This doesn't look good," Mickey said.

"They're not waiting for me, I hope."

But as we moved closer, it soon became apparent they were. Where was Mr. Drennan when I needed him? He was going to protect me. Yeah, right. The players were standing in a line blocking the entrance. When Mickey approached, one of them moved away, creating an opening. He looked back at me, then turned and slipped through. As I moved closer, team members quickly closed ranks. What the hell was going to happen here? Were they going to kick the shit out of me right in front of school? They couldn't. They wouldn't. There'd be like fifty witnesses. I was starting to breathe heavily. I was worried about hyperventilating. I stared at the pavement as I moved forward. Then I heard this low rumble of voices. They were all chanting the same word under their breaths over and over. "Rat, rat, rat, rat…"

Chapter 12

The closer I got, the more erect they stood. When I was no more than six feet away from the line of players, I could see they were not going to move aside the way they had done for Mickey. I looked around. They seemed to be letting everyone else through—but not me. The *rat* chant continued. I moved a little closer with my head still down.

"Excuse me," I said. "Can I get through?" But no dice. No one moved. I waited a few more seconds and then tried again with the same result. I glanced at my watch. The first period bell would ring in five minutes. How long were these guys willing to stand out here? In a few minutes, they'd all be facing detention. Somehow, I had a feeling they weren't worried about being a few minutes late for class. They had a more important statement to make. And they were coming through loud and clear.

"Guys, can I get by? I don't want to be late."

All I heard was, "Rat, rat, rat…"

I looked down at the end of the line. Maybe I could get around them. I decided to try. I walked past the group without making eye contact. When I got to the end, Tom Webster, a two-hundred-and-seventy-pound offensive lineman, stared me down.

"You ain't gettin' past me, twerp."

This was now getting ridiculous, and to tell you the truth, I was getting a little scared. I walked down to the other end of the line. Standing there was Brian Lambert, the team's fullback. Brian was a junior like me. I had had a few classes with him the last couple of years. He always seemed like a decent guy. And he was actually pretty smart, not like the better part of the jocks at school. When I looked up at him, I noticed he wasn't chanting. He was just standing there with his arms at his sides. I smiled sheepishly and tried to move around him. Surprisingly he was about to let me pass when someone down the line caught a glimpse of what was going on.

"Don't let his ass through, Lambert!" a voice called out.

"Sorry," Brian said. "Can't do it."

Oh, great. Now what? How was I ever going to get in the front door? I walked back to the center of the line. Over my shoulder, I saw Andie and her friends approaching. When our eyes met, I quickly looked away. She walked right up to me.

"I think you should know what you did, Paulie," she said. "Colton got suspended, and he might get expelled. Are you happy now?"

"I'm not happy about any of this," I said.

"Then why did you do it?"

"Yeah," some of the players yelled out.

I looked around. Every eye was on me. Did they all hate me? Or just the majority of them? I had to defend myself. I couldn't just stand there and take it. These people had to know the truth.

"Why did I do it?" I said. "Because Colton did a terrible thing, and somebody had to speak up."

"Liar!" one of Andie's friends yelled out.

"Can't you see?" I said to her. "This could have happened to you, or any one of your friends."

"Well, it didn't," Andie said. "It didn't because he's innocent. He would never do that."

"Do you want us to kick his ass right here, Andie?" one of the players said. "Just say the word."

She looked right at me. "No, I think you made your point. You might as well just let him through."

"What can I say to make you believe me?" I said to her.

"Nothing!" she said.

She nodded to her friends, who followed her past the players and into school. And with that, the showdown was over. The players turned and walked in the front door.

I waited a few seconds to make sure the same reception wasn't waiting for me when I entered the building. Sensing the commotion was over, I walked in and headed to my locker. When I got there, I found a gift from Colton and the boys. A stuffed rat had been taped to the front of the locker. On it was written, "Passero the Rat." I wasn't sure how much more of this I would be subjected to for the remainder of the day— or for the rest of my life, for that matter. I yanked off the rat, opened the locker, and tossed it in. I threw my lunch inside and grabbed books for morning classes. I looked over my shoulder, and for some reason, I had the sensation there were hundreds of classmates watching me. I didn't actually see anyone, but I just felt it. Or was I just becoming paranoid?

I turned and merged into the throng of kids in the hallway. I was headed for Mr. Drennan's class when I looked up and noticed Carolyn passing by. She stopped momentarily, shook her head, and continued on her way. She didn't say a thing. It was clear from her expression she knew everything that had just happened outside school. I felt bad for her. None of this was her fault. It wasn't fair. She had become a virtual pariah at school, and now I had joined her. I thought back to the summer preceding my freshman year. I'd had such huge plans. I was going to be a standout academically as well as socially. It would be my coming-out party. Well, it looked as though I had gotten my wish. I had managed to become a standout—but for all the wrong reasons. Right at that moment, I wanted to be home—in bed—with the covers pulled over me. I wanted to stay there for the rest of my life.

I walked into Mr. Drennan's classroom and found a seat. I kept my head down. I didn't want to face anyone. I was wondering if everyone, not just the football team, hated my guts. Colton was a fairly popular guy, but he was also a jerk. And I couldn't be the only kid at school who had noticed that, even before this thing with Carolyn. You would tend to think that if someone had the guts to bring down one of the bullies at school, there would be people who would be on your side—people who would rally around you. But the problem with high school kids was no one ever said much about someone, even someone you didn't care for, if that person just happened to tower over you. I wanted to believe I wasn't alone, but there were no indications anyone was willing to come to my aid. Most of them just blended in and kept to themselves. No one wanted to get involved. I did, and now I was paying for it.

I sat there feeling sorry for myself, until I began to

wonder what I would do if this had happened to someone else. What if another person had come forward about an incident at school? I liked to think I would step up and show my support for that person. But the more I thought about it, the more I felt like I would just do what everyone else was doing—nothing. So, I didn't really blame these other kids for not defending me. It was what most of us would do. And that didn't mean they were bad people, it just meant these kids weren't willing to stick their necks out for someone else. It might have been the right thing to do, but it wasn't the popular position most people would take. They would think one thing and do another.

When I managed to emerge from my personal pity party, I realized class had begun. We were in the midst of a discussion of *Romeo and Juliet*. I had read it the day before, so I was somewhat prepared for the discussion. I tried my best to follow what was going on, but I kept getting distracted. Would the football team be waiting for me in front of school every morning? Would they continue to hassle me? What other surprises did they have for me today? I tried to pay attention to the conversation, but I kept obsessing on my uncertain future. I was fearful it wouldn't be long before my physical well-being would be at stake. And if that did happen, what would I do? Would I tell someone in a position of authority? Would I be a rat again? Oh, great, now I was referring to myself by that name.

But that was just it—I wasn't a rat. If someone decided to make my life miserable, I was fairly certain I would probably just put up with it and not tell anyone. Speaking up in that case would make you a tattler. But the Colton/Carolyn situation was completely different. It had nothing to do with something that had happened to me. I was able to justify my actions because I was trying to help a third party who had been wronged. I was an eyewitness, not a rat or a snitch or an informer or a squealer. Why couldn't anyone else see that?

I kept trying to clear my head and join the classroom discussion, but I just couldn't. I kept imagining the worst possible scenarios. And each one ended with me getting my head handed to me. I wasn't a physical person. I didn't look for trouble. I didn't have the size to throw my weight around. I couldn't remember the last time I had been in a scrape. If any of the football players, all guys bigger than me, were planning on roughing me up, I would be at their mercy. I'd have to take it and keep my mouth shut. It wasn't a very pleasant outlook, and I couldn't stop thinking about it. When the bell rang ending the period, I headed for the door, but something made me stop and stare at Mr. Drennan. He was erasing the blackboard. This was the man who had promised me if I spoke up, nothing would happen to me. He would see to that. I decided to let him know he was wrong.

"Mr. Drennan?"

"Yeah, Paulie, what is it?"

"I suppose you heard about what happened to me this morning out in front of school."

He stopped and set the eraser down. "Why, no, I didn't hear anything. What happened?"

I sighed. "It was no big deal...if you don't count having to cross a line of football players blocking the front door and chanting, 'Rat, rat, rat,' endlessly."

He frowned and sat down behind his desk. "I'm

very sorry that happened. I'll speak to Mr. Feingold and Coach Walters about it. I'll make sure they address it with the players at practice today. I can promise you won't be subjected to anything like that again."

"Please don't say anything," I said. "These guys already think I'm a rat."

"But they can't get away with this," he said. "We can't allow students to intimidate one another. It's just not right."

"Don't you see?" I said. "I can't have you fighting my battles for me. As much as I would welcome your help, it would only make matters worse. I know you said you'd look out for me if I came forward, but it's just not possible. You're just one person. You can't take on the whole world. The entire student body thinks I ratted out a star football player. There's nothing anyone can do."

"I wish I did have an answer for you, I really do." He stood up and walked around to the front of his desk and leaned on it. "If you don't want me to talk to the players or the coaches, I don't know how I can help."

I stood there for a minute. I didn't know what else to say. Mr. Drennan was a nice guy and everything, but I couldn't help but think he had given me bum advice. If I had kept my mouth shut, none of this would have happened. The only loser would have been Carolyn. I didn't really owe her anything. I barely knew her, for Christ sake. I felt bad for her, yeah, but why did I have to suffer with her? If I had said nothing, she would have transferred to a new school at the end of the semester, started a new life, and everything would have been fine. I would have gone on living the same old ho-hum life, but to tell you the truth, *ho-hum* sounded pretty good right about now.

"Paulie, if you're determined to handle this thing yourself, do you mind if I give you a little advice?"

Oh, great. I hoped it wouldn't turn out to be as lame as his last heart-to-heart.

"Sure," I said.

"What you're facing, I wouldn't wish on anyone."

I thought this was supposed to be a pep talk. Now I was feeling even worse.

"I had honestly thought the reaction of your classmates would be different. I was hopeful they would recognize the gravity of what had taken place. I thought they would admire the courage it took for you to come forward. To call out a bully. To come to the aid of a fellow student." He sighed. "But instead they seem to have taken the easy way out. *Don't get involved. Don't be a snitch. Stick your head in the sand."* He shook his head. "I guess I'm not surprised by the reaction of the football team. They tend to stick together. They rally around one of their own—even if that one did an unspeakable thing." He leaned over and picked up his briefcase from the floor and opened it. He pulled out a stack of papers and held them up. "Maybe these will help."

"What are those?"

"There's an emergency school board meeting tonight to address the Colton Brand situation. The board has to decide what sort of discipline to dole out. And one of their options is expulsion." He waved the papers. "I've written everything down right here. I've been asked to speak to the board regarding the matter. And I'm going to push hard to have Colton expelled from Cermak."

"Expelled? Really?"

"Yes. We can't have thugs roaming the halls at this school. You wait and see, Paulie. Once Colton is gone, the football team will forget all about him and get on with their lives. He'll be yesterday's news. Then your problems will vanish. Once we purge the cancer, the body will heal. Trust me on this one."

I wanted to. I really wanted to. "Do you really think so?"

"I do," he said. "Hey, what are you doing tonight?"

"Just homework and stuff."

"I want you at this meeting. It starts at seven in the principal's conference room. Once the board hears from an eyewitness, they won't be able to do anything but give Colton his walking papers."

I wasn't sure what I'd be expected to do. "Would I have to talk?"

"It's possible. But I'll be right there. All you'd have to do is tell them what you saw under the bleachers that day. You were able to tell me and Coach Anderson and Mr. Feingold. How much more difficult could it be? What do you say?"

If Mr. Drennan was right…if expelling Colton could make all my problems go away, then I needed to do everything in my power to make it happen. Of course, one of the casualties of this strategy would be losing Andie for good. If Colton got tossed, she would hate me for the rest of my life. But I think I could live with that if it meant everyone would get off my case and let me live a normal life. It would be a huge price to pay, but right at this moment, self preservation seemed a better option than worrying about a failed romance.

I let out a long sigh. "Okay, I'll do it."

"I'm so glad to hear that," Mr. Drennan said. "I'd better contact the principal about having you there to field questions. I'm sure he'll be fine with it." He glanced at the clock in the back of the room. "Hey, you'd better get going. You're going to be late for second period."

I grabbed my books and headed to Spanish class. The hallways were busy, but fortunately there was no one blocking my path this time. That was definitely an improvement. I slipped into class and found a seat just as the bell sounded. Señora Mendez took attendance and then picked up a record jacket from her desk and slipped out an LP. She walked it over to the phonograph and set it on the turntable. A moment later, groans filled the classroom. We were about to listen to a conversation in Spanish. Today's lesson was *El Pícnic*. That's *The Picnic* for nitwits who can't figure it out. Whenever Señora Mendez would play recorded conversations in Spanish, she just expected us to follow along as if we were native Spaniards. But it wasn't that simple. In fact, it was next to impossible.

Have you ever listened to a foreign language conversation? The speakers talk a million miles an hour. No one, unless of course you were a Spanish teacher, could translate word one. And so, for the next fifty minutes, we managed to muddle through. Like my other classes this morning, I did my best to concentrate but found myself thinking about the school board meeting tonight. I was having second thoughts about showing up. Why had I agreed to come anyway? What was expected of me? Would someone be asking me questions? Would these people believe me? Or would they try to intimidate me? I suddenly wanted out, but I had given Mr. Drennan my word. Oh, what had I gotten myself into?

Chapter 13

At lunch that day, I decided to sit with Mickey and his nerdy friends. These guys were all physics geeks. You couldn't have a normal conversation with them. All they ever talked about was antimatter and entropy and neutrinos and Planck time and time dilation. It was like sitting through another foreign language class. There was nothing I could add to the conversation that any of these guys would appreciate. Cars and girls and parties would never be found in their vocabulary.

I leaned over and whispered to Mickey. "Big news. I'll tell you on the bus."

"Hey, you can't leave me hanging like that," he said. "Spill it right now."

I motioned to his dorky friends and mouthed, "Not here."

He threw his head back and whined.

"Relax. We'll be headed home in no time."

But I had misspoken. By the time I had survived the remainder of the lunch hour, chemistry, PE, and study hall, it felt as if eons had passed. After the final bell rang, and I managed to snag stuff from my locker, I poked my head out the front door of school to see if there was another reception committee in my path. When I was fairly certain there was no one waiting to dismember me, I met up with Mickey at the bus stop.

When I arrived, he was barely able to contain himself.

"Okay, now, so what's going on? I couldn't think straight the entire afternoon."

"I gotta come back here tonight," I said.

"For what?"

"There apparently is an emergency meeting of the school board."

"Why would you have to be here for that?" he asked.

"They're meeting to decide what to do with Colton."

Mickey's eyes widened. "Do you think they're going to expel him?"

"That's one option," I said. "And that's what I'm hoping for. Mr. Drennan thinks my problems will be over if the school boots him. He thinks Colton will be yesterday's news, and everyone will get on with their lives."

"Now don't get me wrong, Paulie, but that's asking for an awful lot."

"Well, it makes sense, doesn't it?" I said. "If Colton disappears, so do my problems."

"You might be right, but what are the chances those Bozos will give him the old heave-ho? Don't you remember what happened last year when there was another emergency school board meeting?"

"I'm not sure."

"Does the name Tom Reynolds ring a bell?"

"Oh, yeah."

"All Tom got was a slap on the wrist for exposing himself in the girls' locker room during gym class. Of course, who wanted to be the one who suspended a star basketball player before the playoffs? The guys on the school board are all members of the booster club. They were jocks themselves. They saved his ass."

"But what Colton did was a lot worse than that. He wasn't just showing. He was touching."

"You saw what happened last weekend when he didn't play," Mickey said. "Do you actually believe they're gonna let that happen again?"

"Mick, come on. The least they would do is throw him off the team. They gotta do that."

"Winning means an awful lot to those old farts. I wouldn't put anything past them."

When the bus finally arrived, we headed to the back and resumed our conversation. By the time we reached our stop, I was convinced Mickey was right. They weren't going to do anything. I wasn't sure I needed to show up. If I hadn't told Mr. Drennan I'd be there, I was tempted not to go.

My mom was cleaning the blinds in the living room when I got home. I needed to tell her I had to go back to school tonight. I wasn't sure why I was hesitant to tell her about the whole Colton/Carolyn incident, but I was. It was a little embarrassing to talk to your mom about things like that. I decided to take another path.

"There's a fresh batch of chocolate chip cookies on the kitchen table if you're interested."

"Okay, thanks," I said. "Hey, Mom, I need to go back to school tonight for something."

"For what?"

"There's a school board meeting I need to be there for."

"Why is that?" she said.

"I was asked to cover it for the school newspaper." I wasn't proud of myself for lying, but I needed something that sounded legit.

"Oh, okay. Do you need to eat dinner earlier? What time do you have to be there?"

"Well, if the car's available, I'd need to leave about six-thirty."

"I don't think your dad or I are doing anything tonight. That should be fine."

And then it hit me. I had forgotten all about Violet. I needed the car on Saturday night for the homecoming dance. If it wasn't available, I didn't know what I was going to do.

"Mom, do you know if the car will be available on Saturday night? I've got a thing I have to be at."

"This Saturday?"

I nodded.

"Honey, we're having dinner with our cousins that night. I'm afraid we need the car."

I just stood there. Why in God's name did I ask Violet out before checking on the car first? What the hell was I gonna do?

"Why did you need it?" my mom asked.

"Well..." I hesitated. I wasn't in the habit of telling my mom anything that had to do with girls. It just wasn't the type of conversation you had with your parents. I had placed them on a strict need-to-know basis years ago.

My mom was waiting for an answer.

And then I reconsidered my options. Maybe I should tell her the truth. Maybe I could guilt her into letting *me*, the boy who never asks out girls, use the car. It was worth a shot.

"Um, I have a date."

She raised her eyebrows, and then she smiled. "Oh,

really. Who with?"

I had never really planned on telling my parents anything about Violet. She wasn't the kind of girl your mom would pick for you if she had the chance. Moms were not big fans of floozies. I would need to leave out that part.

"It's just this girl named Violet."

"Violet what? Do we know her...or maybe her family?"

Um, no way, Mom. I guarantee she would have definitely remembered meeting her.

"No, I don't think so," I said.

"Does she go to your school?"

I knew that if I told her Violet went to Ridgeway, it wouldn't go over particularly well. But I was trying to be truthful here. I decided to share all the sordid details. Well, not all of them.

"No, she goes to Ridgeway."

The expression on my mom's face was priceless. Without uttering a word, she was showing her displeasure with the fact some hussy was about to corrupt her little boy.

"How would you know a girl from Ridgeway?" my mom asked.

"Well, I met her on the bus."

My mom frowned.

I knew this wasn't going well. Maybe I had made a mistake telling her the truth. Maybe she couldn't take it. I had a feeling my dad would actually have reacted better to me having a date with a Ridgeway girl than my mom. Dads tended to live vicariously through their sons. And they hoped to see them walk on the wild side occasionally. It was a guy thing.

"Well, I don't know what to tell you," she said.

"Mom, this is our homecoming dance. I can't very well take a date on the bus. Is there any way you could get a ride from someone?"

It had now become painfully clear to me honesty had not been the best strategy. My mom was not embracing my choice of young lady. I should have blurted out the name of a girl from Cermak, and better yet, one from a family she already knew. Whoever said honesty was the best policy?

"What do you say, Mom?"

"Let me think about it. I suppose we could ask Bob and Nancy to swing by our house on Saturday. It wouldn't be too much out of the way for them. But even if they said yes, your father is the real problem here."

For as long as I could remember, my dad hated asking favors from other people. He never wanted to admit he needed anyone else's help. He was funny that way. He especially disliked asking for assistance because once you were the recipient of a charitable deed, you were on the hook for returning the favor. He didn't like owing anybody anything.

"You know how he is about that sort of thing," she said.

"Could you ask him anyway?"

She made a face. "Is this Violet your girlfriend or something?"

I chuckled. "Ah, no. This is a one-time-only date. I won't be asking her out again. This is really a friend-friend thing, not a boyfriend-girlfriend thing."

She looked pleased to hear she wouldn't be having a Jezebel for a daughter-in-law.

"I'll see what I can do," she said with a smile. "Leave it to me."

Phew. That was a close one. It wasn't a slam dunk by any means, but my mom knew all the best ways of guilting my dad into doing something. I headed into the kitchen, grabbed a couple of cookies off the table, and went up to my room. Since I had no idea how long I'd be at school tonight, I decided to crank out some homework so I wasn't up till midnight.

A couple of hours later, I was seated at the dinner table opposite my dad. He didn't look happy. It was apparent my mom had already spoken to him about Saturday night. I could tell he wanted to say something but he was holding back. A minute later, he let loose.

"Why didn't you check with us first to see if the car was available before asking out this girl? We would have told you to ask her out some other day."

"Dad, I'm sorry. It all happened kind of fast. I didn't really know ahead of time. And plus, this Saturday night is our homecoming dance. It wouldn't have helped to have asked her out for another day."

He shook his head angrily and turned to my mom. "I hate owing that damn Bob anything. I know he's going to ask to use my new pruning shears. I just know it."

I stared at my plate and said nothing.

He glanced in my direction. "A girl from Ridgeway? Really? You couldn't find someone from your own school? Those Ridgeway kids are all gonna be jailbirds someday, you know."

"Oh, Peter, be serious," my mom said.

"I am. The police are over at that school every day for something."

"It's just one date," she said. "He won't be asking her out again." She looked at me. "Right, Paulie?"

"Right," I said. "One and done."

My dad sighed. That ended the dinner conversation, which was fine with me. I wolfed down healthy portions of mashed potatoes, green beans, roast beef, and salad. Then I exited the kitchen. Since my dad had never actually said I couldn't use the car on Saturday, I assumed my mom's pleading had been successful. Thank God. I couldn't imagine having to tell Violet we'd be taking the bus to the dance.

I quickly brushed my teeth and headed out. As I drove to school, I thought about what was awaiting me. I had no idea what to expect. I wasn't sure if it would be like being a witness in a courtroom. Would I have to place one hand on a Bible and swear to tell the truth? Would it be that crazy, or would it be more laid back? I wondered if Carolyn would be there. She would be a great witness. Who in his right mind is going to challenge a girl who was actually molested? The more I thought about what I had witnessed, the more I was convinced Mickey was wrong. No matter how badly these folks wanted to see Colton back on the football field, they just couldn't ignore the facts. He not only broke school rules, he broke the law. He should have been arrested. He'd be lucky if he was only expelled.

I pulled into the school parking lot about six-fifty. There were a half dozen cars already there—probably the school board. I wasn't sure if Mr. Drennan was here yet. I didn't know what kind of car he drove. When I got to the front entrance, I spotted a security guard sitting behind a desk just inside the door. I waved to get his attention. He made a face, grabbed a clipboard off the desk, and moved in my direction. The door opened just a crack.

"Can I help you?" he said.

"I'm here for the school board meeting."

"Name?"

"Paul Passero."

He moved a finger down the list on his clipboard and stopped. He looked at me suspiciously. He had to be wondering why a kid would show up for a school board meeting. He motioned for me to come in.

"The meeting takes place in the principal's conference room. Do you know where that is?"

I nodded. Not every kid in school knew where that was. If you were on Mr. Feingold's list of troublemakers, you knew exactly where it was. Or if you just happened to be on the staff of the school newspaper, you also knew all about it. A couple of weeks ago, a pipe burst in the basement and flooded the newspaper office. We held our staff meeting that week in the principal's conference room.

I turned at the end of a long hallway and made my way past a series of administrative offices. When I got to the conference room, I spotted Mr. Drennan sitting on a chair outside the entrance.

"Paulie, I'm glad you made it. I was starting to worry you had changed your mind about coming."

"Well, to be perfectly honest, I did think about skipping. But since I had given you my word, I thought I'd better show up."

He smiled. "It's nice to know you're a man of your word. I wish I could say that about some of your classmates."

I shrugged and smiled. I wasn't sure how I was

supposed to respond to a statement like that.

Mr. Drennan patted the chair next to him. I sat down and stared at the floor.

"There's nothing to worry about," he said. "Everything will be fine."

"I hope so. I'm just worried they won't believe me."

"Trust me. That won't happen. We have the statement from Carolyn, and your story corroborates that. This meeting isn't to determine if Colton's actions actually took place, it's to determine what type of punishment he should receive."

I crossed my fingers. "I hate to say it, but I'm hoping he gets expelled. He deserves it."

"I couldn't agree with you more."

The door to the conference room opened and a man in a dark green windbreaker appeared. On it were the words *Anton J. Cermak Class of 1950*.

"Mr. Drennan, we're ready for you."

Mr. Drennan stood, winked at me, flashed a thumbs-up, and disappeared behind the door.

Now what? I wondered. Now I just had to wait, I guessed. I put my head back against the wall and actually managed to doze off for a few minutes. When I woke up, I glanced at my watch. It was seven-fifteen. I assumed if someone had come out to get me, they would have awakened me. I apparently hadn't missed a thing. I stood up to stretch my legs and walked a few feet before turning around and walking back. I sat back down and tried to recall the entire ugly scene under the bleachers. It was hard to forget. I wanted to get the details straight. They'd be comparing my account of what happened with Carolyn's story of the events. A moment later, the door opened, and the same gentleman in the alumni jacket appeared.

"We're ready for you, son."

I nodded and followed him in. Ready or not, this was it. Wish me luck. But what was about to take place couldn't have turned out any worse.

Chapter 14

"I'm not finished," Mr. Drennan snapped.

"Thank you for your input," a balding man with graying temples said. He moved a few papers in front of him, studied one briefly, and looked up. The nameplate in front of him read *Wyatt Kimbrell*.

"So you must be Mr. Passero, I assume?" he said.

"Excuse me, Mr. Chairman!" Mr. Drennan said. He was livid.

I had never seen him so angry before. I didn't like where this was going.

"Mr. Drennan, would you please sit down," Mr. Kimbrell said. "You had your opportunity to address this forum. And we've taken your comments into consideration. Now it's time to move on."

Mr. Drennan stood up and pointed at the board members. "All I can say, gentlemen, is your attitude, in my opinion, is very cavalier. It's clear to me your decision tonight will very likely come back to bite you in the ass. The ladies, on the other hand, seem to appreciate the seriousness of the matter."

Mr. Kimbrell glared at Mr. Drennan momentarily and then turned to me. "Young man, I hope you have more substantive things to share with this body than your English teacher does."

I smiled weakly. I stood up and faced the front. I

took a good look at the five adults behind the table. Beside Mr. Kimbrell was the alum with the Cermak jacket. He appeared to be Gary Lisowski. Then there was Mr. Payne, who was the principal, and two women, Sheila Munson and Linda Murphy. I recognized only the principal.

"Can you please tell us exactly what you saw under the bleachers that day?"

"I'll try," I said. I glanced over at Mr. Drennan. He was staring at the board members with his arms folded and his jaw locked. It didn't look like I'd be getting any support from him. He was fighting his own battle at the moment. "Well, I was at the tennis courts that day to meet up with one of the players after practice."

"And who would that be?" Mrs. Munson asked.

"Andie Walker? She's on the tennis team."

"Continue, please," she said.

"Then I thought I heard voices coming from under where I was sitting. So I got up and went down there. I found two people under the bleachers—Carolyn Mancuso and Colton Brand."

"What did you do or say when you found them?" the principal asked.

I stared at the floor sheepishly. "Well, I'm not proud to say that once I saw who was down there, I hid. I didn't want to be seen."

"And why was that?" Mrs. Murphy said.

"You see, Colton isn't particularly fond of me right now. I didn't want him to think I was spying on him."

"That seems like exactly what you were doing," Mr. Lisowski said.

"Gary, let the boy finish," Mrs. Murphy said. She turned to me. "Go ahead, son."

"It seemed pretty clear to me Colton wanted to mess around with Carolyn but she wasn't interested."

"What do you mean by *messing around*?" Mr. Lisowski asked.

"You know, sex stuff."

"No, I don't know," he said.

"I think we know what was going on, Gary," Mrs. Munson said.

"We have a young man's academic and athletic career in our hands here. I just want to know exactly what happened," he said.

This was getting crazy. I guess I needed to be more specific.

"He was trying to molest her," I said.

"And how do you know that?" Mr. Kimbrell said.

"Because I saw him put his hand under her shirt," I said.

"Is that good enough for you?" Mrs. Munson said. "Please continue."

I took a deep breath. "Carolyn told him if he didn't stop, she was going to scream."

"How are we supposed to know if the girl wasn't leading him on?" Mr. Lisowski said.

"What's wrong with you?" Mrs. Murphy said. "If someone says, 'If you don't stop, I'm going to scream,' that person is hardly leading him on."

"We don't know what was said before this young man arrived," Mr. Kimbrell said. "I have to agree with Gary. This is simply a case of he-said, she-said."

Mrs. Murphy stood up. She appeared angry. "He-said, she-said can only occur if there are no witnesses. We have an eyewitness." She looked at me and nodded.

"Colton said something like, 'Don't play so hard to

get.' Then she tried to scream, but he put his hand over her mouth." I paused for a moment and tried to remember exactly what I saw. "Then Colton picked up one of her legs and she fell onto her back. He got on top of her. She was fighting him the entire time. At one point, she reached up and scratched his face. Then he wiped his cheek and saw there was blood. He got really upset, and called her...you know...the b-word."

Mr. Lisowski tapped his fingers on the table. "Young man, I'm afraid I'm not buying any of this."

"What is wrong with you people?" Mr. Drennan blurted out. He couldn't contain himself.

Mr. Payne held up his hand. "Okay, time out here." He turned to Mr. Drennan. "Bill, you had an opportunity to tell your story. Any more outbursts and we'll have to ask you to leave."

"Steve," he said, "why would this boy lie? He's been threatened by Colton Brand and many other members of the football team. Why would he put himself through that if it weren't true? He has no incentive to lie. If anything, he'd be better off if he had never spoken up in the first place. This is credible testimony, and the board must accept it as fact." He pounded his fist on the table.

"He looks like an honest young man," Mr. Kimbrell said. "But I have no idea if he's telling the truth or not. We just have to trust our guts to determine if these are facts or lies."

Mrs. Murphy sighed. "Why is it so difficult for the men on this board to believe anything unseemly about a Cermak athlete? You're protecting a young man who nearly raped one of our students. I just can't believe this."

Principal Payne held up his hands to restore order. When the participants had calmed down, he turned to me. "Anything else, Mr. Passero?"

"At one point, Colton tried to pull down Carolyn's skirt. Then he stopped when some of the other players called out her name. He got off her, and she ran out from under the bleachers. Then he left, but before he did, he spotted me. He told me if I ratted him out, I was dead. Then he ran off. And that's about it."

"Well, I think we've heard enough," Mr. Lisowski said. "I think I'm ready to vote."

"Yes," Mrs. Murphy said. "I think we have more than enough information here."

"Very well," the principal said. "Paul, thank you for coming tonight. We appreciate how difficult it was for you to share your account of the events that took place that day. You may leave now."

I glanced at the others. I guessed I had done all right. I stood and began to move toward the door. When I passed Mr. Drennan, he grabbed my arm.

"Wait for me out there," he whispered.

I left the room, closed the door behind me, and sat down on one of the chairs in the hallway. I wasn't sure what to expect. There definitely were people who appeared to be on Colton's side. And the ladies seemed to believe me and Carolyn. I just wasn't sure about the principal. I put my head back and rested it against the wall. I tried to relax. But it was no use. I was so wound up I couldn't concentrate on anything else. I knew whatever decision was made here tonight would greatly affect my future well-being. I couldn't tell how the vote would go. I kept my fingers crossed and hoped the board would do the right thing and expel Colton.

I could hear voices from inside the conference room. They were loud. Someone was shouting, but I couldn't tell what was being said. Then someone else piped in. At times, it seemed as though five or more people were speaking at the same time. And it got pretty heated. I waited in the hallway for a good twenty minutes before the arguing ended. A short time later, Mr. Drennan appeared. He didn't look happy. He looked at me, shook his head, and sighed.

"They didn't kick him out, I assume," I said.

"No," Mr. Drennan said. He chuckled, but it wasn't because something was funny. It seemed to be because he couldn't believe what had just taken place. "How are you getting home tonight?"

"I drove."

"C'mon," he said. "I'll walk you to the parking lot." When we got to where our cars were parked, Mr. Drennan exploded. "Morons! They're all morons!" He turned to me. "Do you want to know how they voted?"

I nodded.

"The two women on the board voted for expulsion. The two male idiots voted for a suspension. And not a lengthy suspension. They want him to get *time served*."

"I don't understand."

"They want him to be able to come back to school tomorrow. Can you believe that?"

"Well, if it was two to two, what happened?"

"Our wise and omniscient principal had to break the tie," he said sarcastically. "That man is such a wuss. He bends to pressure every time, and he always defers to the sports boosters."

"Colton's coming back to school tomorrow?"

"No, he'll have to serve out his suspension for the

remainder of the week. He'll be back in class on Monday."

"Oh, well," I said. "We tried."

"Oh, and one more thing," Mr. Drennan said. "Our star pupil will actually make his return sooner than Monday."

"Huh?"

"The principal and our favorite boosters didn't want to deny him the opportunity of playing in Saturday's game, *and* attending the homecoming dance that night."

Normally, that wouldn't have bothered me. I wasn't in the habit of attending many Cermak dances. If you didn't have a date, and I never did, then there wasn't much reason to go. And I didn't want to go stag. Those guys always looked so desperate. But this dance was different. I *did* have a date. I *would* be there. After everything I had told the school board about Colton's actions that day, I wasn't feeling too good about confronting him on the dance floor. He would be with Andie, naturally. It promised to be very unpleasant. I didn't want Violet to have to see any of the abuse that might get heaped on me. I sure hoped everyone acted like gentlemen.

"Do you have plans to be at the dance?"

"Yep."

"Well, good. I'll see you there. My wife and I will be helping chaperone the event. If you're worried about anything that night, don't. I'll keep my eyes on Colton and his crowd. You should be perfectly safe."

I remembered one other time Mr. Drennan told me he'd take care of everything. That hadn't worked out so well. But I appreciated the offer.

"Thanks," I said.

"It's getting late," he said. "Our alarms will be going off in a few hours. We'd better hit the road." He worked up a half-smile. "We tried, Paulie. But, you know, I think these board members had their minds made up long before tonight's meeting. I'm not sure anything we said made a difference. I'm sorry. I know you were hoping for a different result. All you can do now is face these bullies head on. Don't shy away or run away from them. They don't expect you to stick up for yourself. Show them you're not afraid. I know it may sound a little scary, but I believe in my heart you'll find you may have more allies out there than you think." He patted me on the head, and we got into our respective vehicles.

As I drove home, I thought about Saturday night and every day after that. Would I be facing a no-win situation on a daily basis? Maybe I could avoid my enemies or never make eye contact with them. But what would that accomplish? That would be like running away from my troubles. And right at that moment, I thought back to my first day of high school. I thought about something my dad told me. I wondered why I hadn't remembered it before.

That day at school I met up with some upperclassmen who'd decided to have a little fun with me. They hijacked my books and my lunch and the only three dollars I had to my name, and refused to give them back to me. I knew I couldn't report them. Once you're labeled as a snitch, your fun-loving high school days were over. I had to solve this problem on my own, or wait until these guys were done having their fun.

I walked into the cafeteria that day with no lunch

and no lunch money. Fortunately, Mickey was there. He shared half of a spiced ham sandwich with me. At dinner that night, my mom asked me how my first day went. I started tearing up and ran from the table to my room. She followed me. I refused to talk to her. I was embarrassed. Embarrassed to have cried at the dinner table. And embarrassed about allowing three senior thugs to have their way with me, and not having the courage to stand up to them. After my mom left the room, I could hear her talking to my dad out in the hallway. A minute later, he came in.

"Do you want to talk about it?" he said.

I shook my head. Now you have to understand my dad. He was never a touchy-feely kind of guy. We didn't really hug or kiss. And we never had heart-to-heart meetings. So this was completely out of character for him. I wasn't sure I could talk to him even if I wanted to. He sat down on my bed.

"I remember my first day at school," he said. "I couldn't speak a word of English. Your grandparents only spoke Italian to us. I guess they thought that would be good enough. But it wasn't. It was fine in our home, but whenever we left there, we were in a strange world where we didn't fit in. As you can imagine, every time I opened my mouth in class, the other kids would start laughing. I ran all the way home from school that day. I told my dad I never wanted to go back. But he made me go back. He told me not to pay attention to the other kids. Just to do my best. He told me everyone in this world is a little different, and I had as much right to be in that classroom as the others. He encouraged me to stick it out and stay the course. And never, never to let the other kids think they had gotten to me. I decided to take his advice. And it was some of the best advice anyone has ever given to me. From that day on, I never backed down. I stood up to all the kids who laughed at me. And with each passing day, I would learn a little more English. And pretty soon, the teasing stopped. Either they got tired of it, or they were afraid of what I'd do to them."

"Did you get into a lot of fights back then?" I asked.

"Hell, no. But I was Italian, and those were the days of Al Capone. So most of these kids figured if your name ended with a vowel, you were all in the mafia or knew somebody who was." He smiled. "Paulie, your first day at school, any school, is like a test. Somebody is always trying to find out what you're made of. And they have to learn, right away, you won't put up with their shit."

I smiled. I wanted to get this off my chest. "There were these seniors messing with me today," I said. "They took my books, my lunch, and my lunch money. I never got any of them back. I just felt so helpless." I groaned.

"Paulie, the world is full of tough guys, or better yet, guys who talk tough. But you know what I've learned? Most of it is just tough talk. They have no interest in an altercation. Now, I'm not telling you to take on a whole battalion of seniors yourself, but you have to let them know you won't put up with their crap. I'm not telling you to mix it up with these guys. I'm just telling you they tested you today—and you failed. Go back tomorrow and stand up to them. You have to face a problem head on, son. You have to battle through it. You have to fight the good fight. And you can never,

never let them see you cry. Try it. And trust me, I'm not giving you a bum steer." He smiled and patted me on the back. "C'mon, your dinner's getting cold."

All I could think of right at that moment was how I so dearly wished my dad and I had had more chats like that one over the years. This was a different side of him I rarely saw. It wasn't that he was unwilling to help me with a problem in the past, but you had to catch him at the right time, when he wasn't busy. You would never want to interrupt him when he was doing something. He placed a high premium on his own to-do list. For some reason, that night he didn't mind having his dinner get cold. He knew I was in a jam, and he knew how to help me through it. It was one of the first times he displayed a little compassion. And I loved the story he told. It couldn't have been easy growing up like that. But he survived, and maybe I could too.

So the next day, I found the trio of thugs who had picked on me the day before. They were standing in the hallway near their lockers. I approached them. I could feel my heart beating right through my chest. *Dad, I hope you're right.* I tapped the tallest one on the shoulder.

"Excuse me, don't you have something for me?" I said.

They all started to laugh. The tall one had dark, wavy hair and a pimple on his chin.

"We don't got nothing of yours, little man," he said.

Now it was time for me to talk tough. "I want my books and my money. The lunch has spoiled by now. You can keep it. And I want them right now."

"Whoa, the little man thinks he's a big man," he

said. He patted me on the back and grinned. "This kid's got balls—steel balls. I can't believe it. I like that." He turned to one of his cohorts. "Larry, give him his stuff."

Larry walked over to his locker and opened it. He reached in and came out with my books and five one-dollar bills. He handed them to me.

I stared down at the money in my palm. "You only owe me three dollars. This is too much."

The tall one grinned. "Consider it a tip. A tip that you earned. It took a lot of guts to do what you did." Then he waved his finger at me. "Now don't get too full of yourself. I don't ordinarily let people talk to me like that, but I like your style, freshie. What's your name?"

"Paulie Passero."

He put his arm around me. "Paulie Passero, you're okay. And by the way, tell your mom she makes one hell of a salami sandwich." He laughed.

I smiled and went on my way. I can honestly say I was a wiser man that day because of our little dust-up. I had applied my dad's advice, and it had worked. Why hadn't I thought about this story when the whole Colton problem first occurred? I wondered if I could use these same words of wisdom with today's set of problems. Granted, these issues were a little more complicated, but I couldn't see why the same advice wouldn't work. I needed to...*face the problem head on...learn to battle through it...fight the good fight...and never, never let them see me cry.*

It was now time to implement Plan B.

Chapter 15

The next morning when I reached the bus stop, I did so with a little more confidence than I had had the day before. Things just seemed brighter than they had been twenty-four hours earlier. I had no idea why I felt that way. There was no reason for it. If anything, I should have been all bummed about the school board backing down and letting Colton return. But I guess I never really believed he would be expelled. It would have been too easy. And my life lately had been anything but easy.

"Hey, Paulie," Mickey called out. He ran up to the bus stop. "What happened last night? What'd they decide to do?"

"They're letting him back in on Monday."

"I knew it. What did I tell you? He's a cash cow on the football field. I'm surprised they won't let him play on Saturday."

"Let me correct myself. Colton won't be back in *class* until Monday, but they're letting him play football on Saturday, *and* attend the dance that night."

"Those guys are such assholes."

I shrugged. "Outa my hands."

The bus pulled up. We hopped on and made our way to the rear.

"I'm wondering if your fan club will be waiting for

you again in front of school," Mickey said.

"Oh, God. I hope not. I don't want to go through that ever again."

"Yeah, that was bad news. I sure don't want those guys getting pissed off at me."

"They can be intimidating, that's for sure."

Two stops later, a familiar face hopped on board—Violet. When she saw me, she made a beeline for the back of the bus.

"Hey, I might be running a few minutes late on Saturday," she said.

"Oh, that's okay," I said.

"My aunt's doing my hair, and she has an appointment with her parole officer right before that."

I was speechless. I didn't know how to respond. "That's fine. Don't worry about it."

She smiled. "Okay, see you then." She turned and met up with her friends a few rows away.

"Her parole officer?" Mickey whispered. "Holy shit. Maybe Violet's an ex-con herself. Just what have you gotten yourself into, partner?"

All I could think about was my dad's comment the other day regarding the Ridgeway kids. Maybe he wasn't so far off base.

Mickey opened one of his books. "I got a vocab quiz in Spanish today. I'd better look this over."

It was relatively quiet for the remainder of the ride. I found myself juggling anxieties—the Violet date and Colton's return. One was good stress. The other, well, you know. I counted off the blocks until we arrived at school. As soon as we were close enough to get a peek at the front door, I closed my eyes and held my breath.

"I can't look," I said. "Are they out there?"

"Look for yourself," Mickey said.

I slowly opened my eyes. To my delight, there was no blockade by the front door. It looked like a relatively normal setting.

"Maybe yesterday was it," I said. "Maybe they won't be back."

We exited the bus, waited for the traffic to lessen, and crossed the street. I managed to walk in the front door of school without incident. I wondered if things were finally settling down. That would be so great. I headed to my locker to get stuff for morning classes. No stuffed rats or other vandalism. That was a good sign. I grabbed my books, slammed the door, locked it, and headed out. Just as I was about to turn into Mr. Drennan's classroom, I spotted Brian Lambert, the fullback on the football team, in the hallway. We looked at each other at the exact same time. I looked away at first, and then I thought about what my dad had told me about facing your problems a while back. It was worth a try. I looked right at Brian.

"Hi, Brian, how you doin'?"

I didn't know what to expect. A day earlier, he had almost let me get around him and into school until some idiot butted in. Maybe he didn't hate me like all the others. I glanced back in his direction. He looked at me with a half smile and nodded. He actually nodded. That was a good sign, right? Heck, yeah. That was a great sign. I was halfway through the doorway leading to Mr. Drennan's classroom when he called out.

"Hey, Passero, wait up."

I stopped in my tracks. What was this all about, I wondered. I was blocking the entrance to the classroom. I stepped aside and waited for him to come over. I sure hoped he wasn't going to remind me I was still a rat.

"Hey," Brian said. He looked away momentarily and seemed to be thinking of what to say. "Sorry about yesterday," he said. "I didn't want to do it, but I had to go along with the other guys."

"That's okay. It was no big deal."

"By the way, I don't think you're a rat. You did what you had to do. You actually did the right thing. Colton can be a real jerk sometimes." He looked around to make sure he hadn't been overheard. "Well, I just wanted to tell you that. See ya later." And he was off just like that.

"Thanks, Brian," I said but I wasn't sure he had heard me. Right at that moment, I felt as if I had just won the World Series. If one guy could see Colton was a creep, it had to mean others would eventually come forward. Maybe the tide was turning. Maybe each guy on the team would eventually see the light. Maybe they'd hoist me up on their shoulders and parade me around school. It was unlikely, of course, but it wasn't impossible. And just as I was beginning to feel better about myself, two beefy linemen from the football team sandwiched me from either side, knocking both me and my books to the floor. They turned back and laughed. It looked as if this wasn't over, by a long shot.

As the hours passed, most of my morning classes were fairly routine. No unexpected surprises. When we changed classes, there were no more signs of support, and no more hallway ambushes. Just the same old shit. When the lunch hour rolled around, I arrived in the cafeteria determined to find somewhere else to sit. Couldn't sit near Andie. That was playing with fire. She still hated me. And I was hesitant about rejoining

Carolyn. She was at the center of a major controversy, although it seemed to be dying down now that the school board had made its ruling. Who would ever have imagined Colton would actually be vindicated? I eventually surrendered and sat with Mickey and the nerds.

Right before the period ended, I saw Brian Lambert get up from the football table and walk over to where Carolyn was sitting. I couldn't hear what they were saying, but when the conversation ended, they were both smiling. How do you like that? First Brian apologizes to me, and then he's seen talking to Colton's victim, and smiling, no less. He apparently wasn't worried about what his teammates thought. Well, good for him. I had to give the guy credit. It was a ballsy move. If our roles had been reversed, I liked to think it was the type of thing I might have done, but knowing my penchant for avoiding confrontation, it was doubtful I would have acted as courageously.

The remainder of the week was relatively unremarkable. No one else on the team bothered to apologize for the blockade on Monday. And I was on the receiving end of a few glares and sneers from some of the jocks, but nothing physical. I was thankful for that. By the time Friday rolled around I was a nervous wreck, and it had nothing to do with Colton or Andie. It was all about Violet. This date business had finally sunk in. Had I actually asked her out on a dare? What was I thinking? I had no idea what I was doing. And here she was, one of the greatest-looking girls I had ever seen, going out with a wimp like me. My confidence had gotten a boost when she agreed to go to the dance with me, but when I overheard her telling her friends it was a one-time-only pity date, I felt like a real loser. It would have been easier if she had just turned me down. I wished now she had. I found myself actually hoping she would get sick or something and not be able to go.

My weeklong fling with Guennie a couple of months back seemed like a million years ago. Whatever confidence I had gained from that short relationship had now been dashed. It was like starting from scratch. What would I say to Violet? How could I keep a conversation going all night? This *was* a pity date—even I had to agree. We were completely and totally mismatched. If I hadn't overheard her, I think I still would have predicted Saturday night was a one and done.

On Friday afternoon's bus ride home, I wasn't feeling any better about things. In fact, I was getting even more nervous.

"So, you all ready for the big date?" Mickey said.

"No."

"What do you mean?" he said. "You've been fantasizing about going on a date with Violet for over two years. And you're not stoked about it? What's the deal?"

"Mickey, I don't have to tell you I'm no Romeo around girls. And Violet is no regular girl. She's a goddess."

"More like a skanky goddess. But still a goddess."

"I don't know what the hell I'm doing. How do I act around a girl like that anyway?"

"Just ask her if she's seen any good movies lately."

"Okay, that'll last about thirty seconds. Then what?"

"Ask her what her favorite subject in school is?"

I smiled. "Something tells me she doesn't have a favorite subject."

Mickey laughed. "You're probably right. Violet's no scholar. Hey, ask her which subject is her least favorite. And then which teacher she hates the most."

I smiled. "Those might just work," I said.

"I think I might avoid asking her if she's going to college," Mickey said. "I don't suppose too many kids from Ridgeway make the jump."

"You're probably right." I glanced out the window and noticed our stop was coming up. I reached up and pulled the cord. When the bus stopped, the Mick and I hopped off.

"You want to do something tonight?" he said.

"Can't, I gotta work." I had to be at the High-Low by five p.m. It was probably a good thing. I needed something to keep my mind off Violet. I was driving myself crazy with worry about screwing something up.

"So what color is Violet's dress?" he asked.

"How would I know that?"

"Didn't you ask her?"

"No."

"Then how do you know what color corsage to get her?"

Oh, my God! I had completely forgotten about that. Actually it had never even crossed my mind. Since this was my first official date, I didn't know the protocol about things like that. I didn't answer Mickey right away.

He stopped. "You didn't get her a corsage, did you?"

"This is gonna be a disaster." I held my head in my

hands. "I should just call her up and cancel the whole thing."

"Paulie, don't worry. You got time. The dance isn't till tomorrow night. You can run by a florist tomorrow and pick one up. But you're gonna have to find out the color of her dress."

I shook my head. "How do I find that out?"

"Earth to Paulie. Just call her up and ask."

And then it hit me. "I never bothered to get her phone number."

"Okay, here's what you do. You go into the florist and tell them you don't know the color of your date's dress. Just ask for something neutral. They'll probably give you something with whites or pastels."

I grabbed Mickey by the shoulders. "How do you know all this shit? I don't ever remember you buying a corsage for anybody."

He smiled. "I never did. But you forget I have a sister. I know all about it."

Of course. Mickey had an older sister who was a sophomore in nursing school. She was really nice...and cute. Her name was Judy. I never admitted it to anyone, but I'd had a crush on her for quite some time. Judy was always so easy to talk to. For some reason, I was comfortable around her. I guess the age difference helped with that. I used to joke with her all the time. She'd laugh at all my jokes. She was a great audience. Judy was the best part about going over to Mickey's house.

"I remember one time when Judy was going to her junior prom," Mickey said. "The boy she was going with had never asked her what color dress she was wearing. I remember her being concerned about that.

She was afraid he'd show up with some God-awful color that would clash with her dress. When the kid showed, he had a corsage with whites and pastels. She was relieved." He smiled. "So that's why I know all about it."

"Okay. Good. I'll run over to the florist tomorrow morning." I grinned. "Thanks, pal. You saved my life."

"Just remember that the next time you get pissed off at me for something."

"All right."

I peeled off and headed to the old homestead while Mickey continued on his way. When I opened the back door, no one was around. My mom had left a note on the counter. It read: *Running errands. Back soon. I'm picking up your suit from the cleaners. You'll need it for tomorrow night. Love, Mom.* I was sure glad she remembered my suit. Apparently you have to dress up for these things. I was so clueless about this stuff. It would be a miracle if I could pull this thing off.

I went upstairs to my room and rested for a while. I placed my hands behind my head and stared up at the ceiling. I was trying to imagine the looks on people's faces when I waltzed into the gym with Violet on my arm. No doubt she'd look great. She always did. I began to rehearse what I'd say to her. I had to get this stuff down. I had to be ready with an endless supply of topics. Any lull in the conversation could spell disaster. While I was making a mental note of what to say, I managed to doze off.

When my mom called from downstairs letting me know my dinner was ready, I jumped off the bed. I did my best quick-change-artist routine and headed down and into the kitchen. A plate of mashed potatoes, green beans, and my least favorite entrée, liver, was waiting for me. I dug my fork into the liver and held it up.

"Mom, why do we have to eat this stuff?"

My mom sighed. "We're not trying to kill you, Paulie. The medical community says it's good for you."

"Liver?"

"Yes, liver. Just eat it and don't complain."

So I did. Every morsel of it. But I made sure I drowned each piece in mashed potatoes. That helped kill some of the taste. And it wasn't just the taste, it was the texture. It was like eating rubber. Awful. When I finished, I said goodbye and headed out. It promised to be a typical Friday night at work. On Fridays we would get a large shipment of groceries for the Saturday onslaught of customers. We would have to break open each box and get everything on the shelves.

When I got to work, I punched my timecard in the lunchroom and headed out into the grocery area. Waiting for us, as usual, were pallets of boxes. I grabbed an apron and a box cutter from the back room and hit the ground running. I had been working for an hour or so when I heard someone trying to get my attention. I was on my knees loading up the large jars of applesauce, with my back to the aisle.

"Excuse me, can you tell me how to find the instant milk?"

When I got to my feet, my legs started to wobble. I was staring at Andie Walker.

"Oh, hi," I said.

"I didn't know you worked here," she said. She was all business. "The instant milk?"

"Aisle six, about halfway down on your left."

"Thank you, sir." She turned to leave.

I had to make her understand what I did wasn't personal. I had to do it for Carolyn's sake.

"Andie?"

She turned around with a disgusted look on her face.

"Yes, what is it? You know, I shouldn't even be talking to you, considering what you did."

"I wish you could try to understand why I had to do it."

"I'll never understand."

"Andie, if someone attacked you, and someone else had seen it, wouldn't you want that person to speak up?"

"Yes, of course."

"That's all I did."

"What you did was lie," she said.

"I'm not the kind of person who makes up stories like that."

She let out a long, loud sigh. "I don't know what kind of person you are." She put her hand on her hip. "Are we done here?"

"Yeah, I guess. But someday you'll find out I told the truth."

"I don't think so." She turned to leave.

"Well, I'll see you tomorrow night, I guess," I said.

She spun around with a surprised look on her face. "You're going to the dance? With who?" She said it like she was interrogating me.

"You wouldn't know her."

"I know most of the girls in our school."

"She's not from Cermak," I said.

"Where's she from?"

I knew this would get a reaction. "Ridgeway."

Her jaw dropped. "You're kidding?"

I shook my head.

"Well, it actually makes sense. You have a lot in common with those kids." She smirked. Then she turned and left.

Wow, that was kind of mean. I didn't think she was like that. But you know what, after all the nasty things she had said to me, I still wasn't mad at her. I couldn't be mad at her. Andie Walker, warts and all, was still the girl of my dreams. I thought to myself for a minute. Who would I rather be taking to the homecoming dance? Andie or Violet? I didn't even have to think about it. It was Andie in a landslide. Now don't get me wrong—Violet was gorgeous. And most guys would drool just thinking about her. But she and I were from two different planets. We would never, and could never, become an item. I definitely was not her type. And that was fine. Violet would be a lot to handle, and I was sure not the guy to handle her. After the dance, everything would just return to the way it was. The coach would turn back into a pumpkin, and we'd all live happily ever after. Not.

Chapter 16

When I got home from work on Friday night, I decided not to set an alarm. I didn't get to bed until eleven-thirty. Two of the stock boys had called in sick, and we couldn't leave until everything was on the shelves. When I joined the living the next morning, the clock radio next to my bed read ten-fifteen. Geez, what was I doing? I had to get to a florist. I dressed, ran downstairs, threw a couple of pieces of toast down the hatch, and headed out.

I knew there was a florist a few blocks away, on the corner of Belmont and Harlem, kitty-corner from the White Castle. When I walked in, the place was up for grabs. They apparently were filling an order for a wedding, and there was a missing bouquet. You would have thought the Russians had dropped the H-bomb on us. There were a lot of people scrambling and yelling. I waited in a corner out of the way. I didn't want to get involved. When two of the customers left the store, things began to settle down.

"Go make up that bouquet right now," one of the managers yelled out to a teenage girl. "And then you're going to have to drive it to St. Matthew's...by noon. Get to it."

The girl seemed flustered. She looked in my direction momentarily. I smiled. It didn't register. She disappeared into a back room.

I decided it was safe to walk up to the counter.

"Yes? Can I help you?" a skinny woman with gray hair said. She was wearing glasses that hung from a chain around her neck.

"Um, I need a corsage."

"When do you need it?" she said.

"Tonight," I said without making eye contact.

"Tonight! You're joking, right?" the woman said.

"Um…no, sorry."

She shook her head. "What's this for anyway?"

"A homecoming dance."

"And how long have you known about this dance?" she asked.

"A few days, I guess."

"So why couldn't you have ordered it a few days ago?"

This felt like the French Inquisition. I understood this was kind of late, but what good did it do to browbeat me? While she was standing there asking me all these questions, she could have been making up the corsage. This was nuts.

"I don't know. To tell you the truth, I didn't know I had to have one until somebody told me."

"You're going to a homecoming dance, and you didn't know you had to have a corsage for your date? Do you live in a vacuum?"

"I'm sorry."

She stared at a clock overhead. We close at six. I'll have it ready for you at five fifty-five. Don't be late."

"I won't. Don't worry."

"What color is your date's dress?" the woman said.

I just stood there and smiled sheepishly.

"You don't know what color her dress is, do you?"

I shook my head.

"I should have known." She sighed. "I'll put together something with some neutral colors."

"How much will this be?" I asked.

"I should hit you with an extra fee for a rush job."

I made a face.

"Eight dollars." She picked up a pad of order forms. "What's your last name?"

"Passero."

"Spell it."

"P-A-S-S-E-R-O."

"Phone number?"

"Five-five-five-three-two-eight-four."

She looked up. "Please tell me you don't need something else."

"No, that was it."

She dropped her pad on the counter. "I'll see you at five-fifty-five, not a minute sooner, not a minute later. Got it?"

I nodded. Then I made a beeline for the exit. I wouldn't be coming back here again, that was for damn sure. I headed home and practiced the small talk I would make with Violet tonight. I liked Mickey's idea about asking her about her least favorite subject and teacher. I was sure I'd be able to get some mileage out of that. Then I'd ask her if she has to read any more novels for English class. If I was lucky, it might just be something I had already read. I'd be able to tell her all about the plot and characters. And if that happened, she might feel like she owed me another favor. Another favor? God, no. This date was already too stressful. I couldn't handle another one. I thought dating was supposed to be fun. I didn't think you were supposed to be a nervous wreck.

I was just about home when I thought again about what it might be like to be taking Andie Walker to the dance instead of Violet. Then everything would be completely different. Sure, I'd be nervous. Who wouldn't be? But it wouldn't be nearly as stressful. And I'd really be looking forward to it. I wouldn't have to practice my small talk. Talking to her would be effortless. I just couldn't understand what she saw in Colton. He was such a complete asshole. And she was so nice, most of the time. Lately, she hadn't been the nicest to me, but I understood why she was acting the way she was. She was protecting her boyfriend—the same way she'd protect me if we were going out. She might be a little misguided, but she was loyal. I had to give her that.

When I walked in the back door, I found my mom in the kitchen baking bread.

"Where were you?" she asked.

"I had to order a corsage for tonight."

"You just put the order in now?"

Oh, please, not again. I didn't need to get beat up a second time.

"I know it's last minute, but I had completely forgotten about ordering one. To be honest, I didn't know I needed to."

She shook the flour from her hands and smiled. "That's my fault," she said. "A good mother would have thought about that and reminded you sooner."

"No, Mom, it's on me. I screwed up. The next time I take a girl to a dance like this I'll know."

"That's the attitude. So what shirt and tie are you

planning to wear?"

I shrugged.

"Can I make a suggestion?"

"Sure, I guess."

"Let's see." She put her finger to her lips and got some flour on her face. She laughed. "Since your suit is charcoal gray, I think a blue shirt would look nice. And don't you have a red-and-blue striped tie somewhere?"

"Do I?"

"I'll look for it. So when are you leaving? I'll want to have ironed those for you before you go."

"I don't have to pick her up until seven-forty-five. I'll probably leave here about seven-twenty."

"Will they be feeding you at the dance?"

"I have no idea. I've never done this before."

"Well, maybe you should eat a light dinner before you go, just in case they don't. I'll whip up something by six. That should give you enough time to shower and get dressed." She smiled. "Are you excited?"

"To tell you the truth, Mom, I'm a little nervous."

She chuckled. Then she had this wistful look on her face.

"I remember my first homecoming dance. It wasn't very romantic. But it was exciting. It was 1944. The war was still going on. All my date could talk about was enlisting when he was old enough. We spent most of the night talking about the army, and how great it was going to be. I wanted to talk about other things. Like my new dress. Well, it wasn't really new. My mother had sewn it for me. I'm guessing you'll be talking about different things tonight."

"I'm not sure what we'll be talking about. She's not from Cermak. We don't have much in common."

"Tell me, Paulie, how did this all come about? Why would you take a girl you know nothing about to a dance?"

This was starting to get awkward. I couldn't very well tell my mother I had been lusting after this girl for the past two years. There were just certain topics that were off limits when it came to your parents. And girls were at the top of the list.

"Well, it's kind of funny. You see, Mickey kind of dared me to ask her."

"Why would he do that?"

"You know Mickey, he's a little goofy sometimes."

"Had you ever met her before?"

It was time to end this conversation. She was beginning to probe too deeply. "Just once." I took a step toward the stairs. "So if you don't need me for anything else, I've got some stuff to do upstairs."

My mom had a funny look on her face. Like she wanted to know more about this mystery girl, but she knew she'd never find out, not from me, at least.

"Okay," she said. "I guess that's all I need to know, and that's probably all I'm going to get out of you, isn't it?"

I shrugged and smiled.

"Do me a favor. Leave the shirt and tie you'll be wearing tonight at the bottom of the stairs."

"Okay," I said. And I was off. When I got to my room, I rummaged through my closet for the shirt and tie in question, ran them downstairs, and hung them on the railing. For the remainder of the afternoon, I thought about Andie and Violet. Andie, unfortunately, was someone I would never have as a girlfriend. When I told the authorities about Colton, my fate was sealed.

Violet, on the other hand, was kind of like my girlfriend for the night. That was what other kids at the dance would probably think. But we all knew this was a one-time-only proposition. After tonight I was just another one of the schmucks without a girlfriend and without a social life. It was no big deal. That had been my life for as long as I could remember. I was really good at underachieving.

As the time ticked away, I got serious. I jumped in the shower and brushed my teeth. I used a razor to shave a few pesky hairs from under my chin. I hadn't been blessed with full-blown beard yet, so it was just a little light maintenance. I had wanted to have enough facial hair to shave every day like a real man, but my dad had soured me on that one. He told me to avoid shaving for as long as humanly possible. He said once you start, you can never stop, and that shaving was completely overrated. In my dad's opinion, it was a complete pain in the ass. He loved being on vacation, when his razor collected dust for a week.

I looked out my bedroom window and saw my dad putting the car in the garage. I was worried he would give me more crap about how he couldn't use the car for his cousin's party because I was using it for a date. But I was willing to take the abuse for access to the vehicle. I buttoned up my shirt, including the top button. I was never a fan of buttoning the top button. It always felt like you were wearing a noose. Then it was time for my undoing—tying my tie. I had about as much success tying a tie as I did with girls. I never liked the way it looked. The knot always looked uneven. It wasn't this perfect triangle my dad was able to pull off. His ties always looked great. So why didn't

I just ask him for help? Well, tonight was not the night. He was still pissed about having to get picked up by a cousin and then owing him something.

I walked downstairs and into the kitchen in my suit and tie. My mom immediately starting applauding. Why did mothers have to do that? I was just a kid in a suit and tie, not some Saudi prince.

"You look great, Paulie," she said. "I wish I could be at that dance and watch the whole thing."

Oh, my God. I was about to puke.

"Peter, look at your handsome son."

My dad leaned in and disgustedly shook his head. "That tie looks like hell. You have to learn how to tie a Windsor knot." Then he ducked out.

I looked at my mom. "I don't know how to."

"Come with me," she said.

I followed her into the living room, where my dad was sitting on the couch reading the newspaper.

"Do you think you could get off that couch and show him how to tie a Windsor knot? Would it kill you?"

My dad set the paper on the coffee table. "He never asked me how to do it. I didn't think he was interested."

"Paulie?" she said.

"What?"

She motioned her head in my dad's direction. It was her way of saying, "Ask him."

I could hear the door from my grandfather's room opening. He came downstairs and into the living room. He took one look at me and cupped his hands around my face.

"Paulo, who died?"

"Pop, no one died," my dad said.

"But he's all dressed up for a funeral."

My mom laughed. "Dad, he's going to a dance—with a girl." She raised her eyebrows.

That was the exact reason why you should never tell your parents anything about your social life.

"I'm leaving," I said. I headed for the stairs.

"Do you want to learn or not?" my dad said.

Hell, yes, I wanted to learn. But I couldn't make him think I would be forever grateful for him teaching me. I knew it would cost me in yard work in the future. My mother walked over and started untying my tie. She slid it out from around my neck and handed it to me.

"He's willing to teach you, Paulie. Take advantage of it," she whispered.

I knew she was right. I needed to suck it up and do this. I turned to my dad. "I'd like to learn, if you'll show me."

He pointed to his bedroom. "We'll need the big mirror."

I followed him into the bedroom and up to my mom's dresser.

"Let me see that tie," he said. He stood in front of the mirror. "I have to be in front of a mirror or I can't tie it properly." He placed the tie around his neck. "Okay, first of all, the skinny end of the tie has to be short. It should be no lower than the middle of your rib cage." He walked into his closet and grabbed one of his ties. "Here, you tie yours, and I'll do one of mine."

I placed the tie around my neck with the skinny end somewhat short.

"Okay, then you cross the big end over the little end, and take it around the back. Okay?"

I nodded.

"Then you take the big end and put it through the front portion but to one side. And then you do the same thing with the other side. Can you see how the tie is now balanced on both sides?"

"Yeah."

"Then you take the big end and wrap it around the knot, and tuck it in from behind. Then pull it through the hole in the front portion of the knot and tighten it. Slide it up to your neck, and *voilá*."

I glanced at his tie. It was perfect. Mine was not so perfect. The skinny end was longer than the fat end.

"I did something wrong."

"The knot's pretty good for a first timer. You just made the skinny end too long when you started. All right, untie it. Let's try this again."

And we proceeded to tie and untie for the next ten minutes. But I had to admit—once I got the hang of it, my tie looked like a million bucks.

"There you go. Now, that's how you tie a tie."

Right then, I was expecting a real father-son moment. You know, a Kodak moment. Something worthy of a bear hug. All I got was a half-smile and a nod. But I was fine with that. It was as much of a bonding moment as we were going to get. One thing I have to tell you—from that moment on, I always had the best-looking tie in the room. Hands down. It might sound kind of superficial, but the Windsor knot was probably the best thing my dad ever taught me.

Chapter 17

I lay low until it was time to leave. I went downstairs, retrieved the corsage from the refrigerator (a little something I learned from my mom), and entered the living room to say goodbye to my parents and my grandfather. I decided to take the high road. Both my dad and mom had helped me out with this date business. I needed to seem appreciative and gracious.

"Well, I'm leaving. Thanks again for letting me use the car. I know you had to change your plans for me. I just wanted to tell you I appreciate it."

My mom got up from the couch and kissed me on the cheek. "You look very handsome. Doesn't he, Peter?"

"That tie looks a hell of a lot better," he said.

I just smiled. "Okay, I'm off. Have fun tonight."

"You look *bello*, Paulo."

"Thanks, Gramps." And with that, I was now on my own. I was entering uncharted waters. The times Guennie and I were together this past summer weren't really dates. This was, however. Whatever happened tonight, good or bad, I had a feeling I would always remember Violet Cassandra Kulick.

I backed out of the garage ever so carefully. We had a one-car garage, and it was a tight fit. I got out, closed the garage door, jumped back in, and headed out.

I drove the speed limit at all times. I didn't take chances on the road. One ticket or one accident and I'd lose driving privileges for God knows how long. I couldn't risk it.

I pulled up in front of Violet's house about twenty minutes later. I looked at the clock on the dashboard—seven forty. I was a little early. I decided to wait in the car for a few minutes. While I was sitting there, I glanced at Violet's house. There was a white picket fence in the front yard. Half of it was falling over, and the whole thing needed a coat of paint. The grass was really high, and most of it was weeds. There was a broken window on the second floor. The Ritz this was not. I wondered why her parents had let it get so run down. That could never have happened at our house. My dad was a real stickler for fresh paint and pristine landscaping.

At precisely seven forty-five, I hopped out of the car, grabbed the corsage, and made my way up the walk to Violet's house. When I reached the porch, I was just about to ring her bell when I noticed a sign that read *Out of order. Knock or go away* taped underneath the doorbell. Not very welcoming. I rapped a couple of times on the front door with my knuckles. When I had waited a good minute and no one had answered, I was starting to get nervous. Oh, no, had she stood me up? Was this some kind of cruel joke? I waited another minute and decided to knock again, this time a little more forcefully. If no one answered this time, I would know Violet had played me for a fool.

A moment later, the door opened. A tired-looking woman stood in the doorway. It had to be Violet's mom. She had a cigarette between her lips. Her hair was pulled back in a short ponytail. It was October, but she still had a deep, rich tan. Looking closer revealed a million tiny wrinkles on her face and neck. I leaned forward slightly and detected the smell of alcohol on her breath.

"Yeah," she said.

"I'm here to pick up Violet for the dance."

She motioned me inside with her finger. I immediately noticed the house had kind of an old-person smell to it. The living room was jammed with a couch, loveseat, recliner, coffee table, bookcase, and a TV. The woman motioned for me to sit.

I picked the loveseat, not for any particular reason. It was closest to me.

The woman walked over to the stairs and yelled, "Violet! He's here."

"One minute," Violet said.

The woman sat down on the couch and stared at me. I tried to keep my eyes off her, but they were just drawn to her for some strange reason.

I smiled nervously. I wasn't sure what to do in this situation. I had never experienced it before. Should I start up a conversation? Or should I wait for her to say something?

The woman took a long drag on her cigarette and immediately started coughing. It was what you'd call a real smoker's hack. It was loose and gross. And it lasted a good fifteen seconds.

What do you say when that happens? Not "God bless you." I wasn't sure what to do.

"I gotta start smoking with filters," she said.

I just smiled.

A moment later, Violet appeared on the steps. I

stood up as my heart skipped a beat. She looked sensational, in kind of a skanky way, but still sensational. She had on three- or four-inch heels, black fishnet stockings, an extremely short black skirt, and a white blouse with silver sequins all over it. The thing that caught my attention right away was how low-cut her blouse was. I'd never realized how well endowed Violet was. Two of the things girls at Cermak weren't allowed to do—wear short skirts and show cleavage. Violet had managed both in the same outfit. I wasn't sure if we'd get any guff from the chaperones tonight, but I was willing to take my chances. Over the years, the girls at school who had broken these rules had become legendary—and not in a good way. Violet's makeup, as usual, was thick. Her eyeliner made her eyes look deep set and enormous. They just jumped out of her head. Her hair was ratted in the typical way. One thing for sure—when we walked into the gym tonight, heads would turn. No Cermak girl would risk looking like this. Having Violet on my arm would do wonders for my social status.

"Have you met Paulie?" Violet said to her mom.

"Well, at least this one is more clean-cut than your usual boy callers," she said.

Violet rolled her eyes. She glanced at me and smiled. "Ready?"

"Yeah," I said. I started to walk to the door but stopped abruptly. I handed her the corsage. "This if for you."

"It's beautiful," she said. She took off the plastic top and lifted it out. There was a long hat pin on the back of it. She handed it to me. "Would you like to do the honors?"

The honors? What did she mean? What was I supposed to...and then it hit me. She wanted me to pin it on her dress. But where? There was no way to pin it without touching her skin. And it was the skin most boys would love to touch. But I wasn't ready for that. This was too soon. I pulled out the pin and held the corsage out toward her.

"Where would you like it?" I said.

She pointed to a spot at the top of her blouse over her left breast.

That was what I was afraid of. I reached out in that direction but never actually made contact with her blouse. My hands were suspended in midair for the longest time.

"Give me that damn thing," her mother said.

I handed her the corsage and the pin and stepped back. Her mother pinned it to Violet's blouse in a matter of seconds.

"This one's a little green," she whispered to Violet.

You're tellin' me. We walked to the front door.

"Don't wait up," Violet said.

"I'll probably be in this same spot, dead to the world, when you get home."

"Good night," Violet said.

"Good night...Mrs. Kulick," I said.

Violet's mom made a face. "Tell yer friend I ain't no Kulick. Got rid of that bastard's name the day he walked out on us."

Violet looked uncomfortable. "Really, Mom!"

I stepped back and let Violet lead the way to the car. She pointed to our brown Chevy and made a face.

"This is it?"

It wasn't what she said that bothered me. It was the

way she said it. And I wasn't upset with her little dig. Right at that moment, I was pissed at my parents for having bought such a loser car. I don't think I ever realized it until that point. Up until now I had been thankful whenever I'd gotten a chance to drive. But now I didn't want to be seen in it.

"Yeah, that's our second car. The Camaro's in the shop."

"Camaro, huh?"

I nodded in sort of a cocky fashion. I just hoped my nose hadn't started to grow. I walked around to the passenger side of the car to open her door. But it was locked. I fished in my pocket for the keys. And wouldn't you know it—they fell from my hand and landed under the car. Unbelievable. I knelt down on the street side of the car and reached under to retrieve them. I brushed off my knees, smiled nervously, and unlocked and opened the door. Violet was grinning, but it wasn't what you'd call a happy grin. It looked more like a what-a-buffoon grin. Things hadn't started off well. As Violet got in, her skirt slid up a few more inches. I looked away. I would need to go to confession after this date.

I ran around to the driver's side, got in, and started up the car. We drove in silence for a couple of miles. I didn't seem to have the courage to ask her the questions I had rehearsed earlier. A few minutes later, it had gotten so awkwardly quiet I knew I needed to go for it.

"So," I said, "what teacher do you hate the most?"

Violet burst out laughing. "Where did that come from?"

I dropped my head. We stopped at a red light. "Maybe you can tell—I'm a little nervous."

"Paulie, can I ask you something?"

"Sure."

"Is this your first date?"

I chuckled. "First date? Come on. Give me a little more credit than that."

Violet tapped her fingers on the seat. "Well?"

"Is it that obvious?" I said.

She smiled. "You just gotta relax and be yourself."

"Be myself? That's a good one. You'd be bored to tears. I'm not very interesting."

"Everybody's interesting if you just take the time to learn something about them."

Right at that moment, I saw a different Violet. Not some floozy who didn't bother to read the books she was assigned. I saw a person who really cared for other people. I would never have guessed it.

"I hope I don't disappoint," I said.

"I'm sure you won't."

I turned at the next light and pulled into the Cermak parking lot. I drove around to where there were a few open spaces.

I turned the car off. "You ready for this?"

"Let's do it."

I started to raise the door handle but then suddenly froze. "Wait!"

"What is it?"

A car had pulled into the lot directly behind us and now parked across from us. Colton and Andie stepped out of the car. I leaned down so they couldn't see me. I waited a few seconds and then slowly rose. I knew I might have to face them tonight, but I wasn't quite ready for that kind of encounter this soon.

"What are you doing?" Violet asked.

"Oh, I just dropped my keys and I was looking for them. That's all."

"You didn't drop your keys," she said. Her eyes were following Colton and Andie as they disappeared from view. "Who are those two?" she said.

"Just some kids from school.'

Violet made a face. "I know when someone's hiding from someone else. And you didn't want them to see you." Her eyes narrowed. "Or didn't you want them to see *me*?"

I put my hands up. "That is definitely not it. I want everyone to see you."

She cocked her head and smiled. "I should hope so. I didn't get all dolled up for nothing, you know."

"Oh, I know that," I said. "So are you ready?"

"Not until you tell me about those two kids you were hiding from."

I sat back in the seat and shook my head. "It's a long story, and I don't want to bother you with it."

"I'm not getting out of this car until you tell me. I don't want to be the only one who doesn't know what's going on."

I sighed. "Okay, her name is Andie Walker and his name is Colton Brand. They're boyfriend and girlfriend."

"And?"

"And…they kind of hate me."

"They hate you? Why, for God sakes?"

I didn't want Violet to think I was a rat. I didn't want to tell her I had fingered Colton. What would she think?

"I'm waiting," she said.

I began rubbing my forehead. I was dreading this.

Violet now had her arms crossed. She wasn't making this easy. She leaned over and motioned with her hand.

"Spill it."

For the next ten minutes, I told her the entire story—the part about me waiting for Andie at the tennis courts—the part about hearing something under the bleachers and going to look—the part about what Colton was doing to Carolyn—the part about his threats—the part about telling Mr. Drennan—the part about telling the principal—the part about the football team forming a blockade in front of school—the part about the school board deciding to give Colton a slap on the wrist. The only part I left out was the fact that this all started because I had this giant crush on Andie. But Violet had seemed to figure that out.

"So you like this girl, and this guy is standing in the way? Is that it?" she said.

"Well, kind of."

"And since you ratted out her boyfriend, she hates you?"

I nodded.

"Sorry, I didn't mean to use the word *ratted*. That wasn't fair to you."

"What difference does it make?" I said. "That's what everyone thinks."

Violet stared forward with this determined look on her face. "I know exactly what this Carolyn girl went through."

"You do?"

"Yeah, because it happened to me."

I glanced over at Violet, and then quickly looked away. I wasn't exactly sure what to say. Did I tell her I

180

was sorry? Or should I ask her more about it? I wasn't sure if she wanted to talk about it. I eventually decided to choose the latter.

"So what happened to the guy who attacked you? Did you tell the principal or something? Did he get expelled?"

She smiled. "Nope."

"You mean he just got away with it?"

"Not really. You see, I wasn't sure the school would do anything about it. I didn't have any proof. So I took matters into my own hands."

"What do you mean?"

Her eyes lit up. "I simply told one of my friends what this kid did to me, and he took care of the rest. Did I happen to mention my friend is six-six and weighs two-hundred-and-eighty-five pounds, and just happens to be captain of the wrestling team?"

I shook my head.

"One day after school, he waited for the bastard. And he kicked the living shit out of him. He broke his arm in two places, and knocked out three teeth. That prick never bothered me again. That's what your friend, Carolyn, needs. She needs a big, tall friend."

I stared at the floor. "That's not me, unfortunately."

"There are other ways to handle the situation." She opened her door. "C'mon, let's go have some fun."

Chapter 18

We walked through the parking lot and into the gym. The minute Violet walked through that doorway, heads began to turn. First, there were the guys working the check-in table. I told them my name and handed them a pair of tickets. They never looked at me or at the tickets. They couldn't take their eyes off my date. Mr. Feingold, the school disciplinarian, stood a few feet away. As we passed him, his jaw dropped. I smiled politely. I wasn't sure if he disapproved of the way Violet was dressed or if he just liked looking at her. I didn't wait to find out. I looked at the place card in my hand. It read *Table 16*.

I noticed how the gym had been decorated. They had actually done a pretty good job. Lots of streamers and balloons and signs. When we reached our table, there were only two seats left. I didn't know the kids we'd be sitting with very well. I knew them enough to say hi to them in the hallways, but that was about it. And like before, all eyes were on Violet.

"Hi, guys," I said. "Looks like we'll be sitting together. For those of you who don't know me, I'm Paulie Passero. And this is my date, Violet Kulick." I held Violet's seat for her and then sat down.

She was looking all around. "I was in this gym for a basketball game once," she said. "It seemed a lot bigger then."

The next thing I knew, Mr. Feingold was standing directly behind me. "Can I talk to you for a moment, Mr. Passero." He turned to Violet. "I need to borrow this gentleman. We won't be long."

I glanced at Violet and shrugged. I followed Mr. Feingold into the boys' locker room, which happened to be emitting a God-awful smell. When we were in here for PE, it didn't seem quite that bad. I guess when you smell really bad, and everyone around you reeks, apparently you don't notice it as much.

"Mr. Passero, I don't recognize your date. Is she from Cermak?"

"No." I decided not to offer any more information unless it was specifically asked for.

"Well, where's she from, young man?"

"She goes to Ridgeway."

Mr. Feingold smiled but not in a happy sort of way. It was more like a sinister smile.

"I should have known. It figures."

"What's that, sir?"

"Did you bother to tell the young woman that here at Cermak we have a strict code regarding attire? Girls are not permitted to dress in the fashion your date is dressed. Did that ever cross your mind?"

"Not really. I guess I didn't think the same rules applied to a social event held at school."

"Well, they do."

"I'm sorry to hear that."

Mr. Feingold grabbed his nose. It took him a while, but he had suddenly realized just how awful it smelled in here.

"The stench in here is insufferable," he said. He

shook his head. Then he refocused on me. "This is what I want you to do, young man. I want you to go back to your table and inform your date she has two choices if she intends on remaining at this affair: One, she must return home to find more suitable attire, or two, please tell her that she'll be forced to wear a long terrycloth robe we've been keeping in the office for situations just like this. Do you understand?"

I nodded.

He pointed at the door. "Be gone."

I left the locker room and headed back to my table. I had felt bad about leaving Violet with a bunch of strangers, but I soon discovered she had no problem fitting right in—with the boys, that is.

"So what kind of detentions do they have at Ridgeway?" Christopher Lundeen, a member of student government, asked her.

"Probably the same as you. Sit in the principal's office. Clean up the lunchroom. Do laps in the gym. You know, shit like that."

"Have you ever had detention?" Jeff Mikolas, head of the Audio-Visual Club, said.

By this time, I had rejoined the group.

"Detention? Little old me? Whatever makes you think that?"

All of the boys at the table laughed. Their dates just sneered. They were staring daggers at Violet.

"That's kind of a personal question, guys," I said. "Violet might want to plead the fifth."

"I don't mind," she said.

Two of the girls at the table crossed their arms and glared at their dates.

This appeared to be getting out of hand. I needed to

put this conversation to rest.

"So I wonder what's on the menu tonight," I said.

"Who cares?" Christopher said. "Violet, you were saying."

"Well, I don't know if I should tell you this or not..." she began.

"Please do," Jeremy Huff, a runner on the cross-country team, said.

"I was in the library with my *then* boyfriend when we decided to sneak off to the stacks on the third floor. No one ever goes up there."

The boys at the table were all ears.

"We just started messing around. Nothing heavy, mind you. Just some light petting..."

Jeremy leaned forward a little too far when his tie, of the clip-on variety, fell onto his dinner plate with a thud.

Violet laughed. "Oh, sorry. I just haven't seen a tie like that for a few years."

"Never mind," Jeremy said. "Please finish." He was too invested in Violet's story to care about a simple social gaffe.

"Maybe she's finished," Pam Contini, Jeremy's date, said.

"And maybe she's not." He turned to Violet. "Was there more?"

"Well, Mr. Hopkins, the vice principal, just happened to be walking by," she said. "Can you believe that? He just *happened* to be walking by. What a perv. 'Please, button up your blouse, Miss Kulick,' he said. It was no big deal. I got three weeks of lunchroom duty for that one." She put her finger to her lips. "Now, let me see, oh, yeah. There was this other time when..."

I had turned multiple shades of red during Violet's story. I knew then she and I would never be an item, not that it would ever happen anyway. Violet was a little too rough around the edges for me. The more time I spent with her, the more I knew we came from two different worlds. Make that two different universes. But it was still nice being seen with her.

Jeremy leaned over. "Passero, you are one lucky son of a bitch."

I smiled.

Mr. Feingold had now wandered over. He was staring right at me and pointing his finger. He nodded a couple of times and walked away.

"What's with him?" Violet asked.

I leaned over to her and whispered. "He seems to have a problem with the way you're dressed."

"What's wrong with the way I'm dressed?" she blurted out for all to hear.

Everyone at the table was now staring at us.

"Nothing. You look great," I said. "But he thinks your blouse is too low-cut and your skirt is too short."

"What an asshole," she said. "Where'd he go? I'd like to tell him that to his face."

Violet was getting really upset now. I needed to calm her down. Even though I didn't think giving her Mr. Feingold's ultimatums would help things much, I needed to let her know what the consequences were.

"Um, he wants you to go home and change, or you'll have to wear this long, white terrycloth robe they keep in the principal's office."

"Oh, my God," she said. "You're shitting me!"

"No, I'm afraid not."

"Well, I'm not doing either. And I'd like to see him

make me."

Oh, boy. It was looking as if this would be a short night. If Violet wasn't willing to follow Mr. Feingold's orders, we would certainly be escorted out of here in no time. I was hoping this incident wouldn't reflect badly on me. Since there was no way I could make her change or wear a robe, then I shouldn't be punished, right? At least, that was the way I saw it.

A moment later, someone bumped into my chair and nearly knocked me over. When I looked up, I was staring into the bloodshot eyes of Tom Webster from the football team. I could smell alcohol on his breath.

"I am soooo sorry," he said. "How could I be so clumsy?"

Violet was following the exchange.

Tom leaned in and whispered, "You've got a lot of nerve showing up here like this after ratting out Colton." He was slurring his words. "But he showed you. You tried to get his ass thrown out of here, but nobody believed your lies. I got a little advice for you. Watch your back, little man."

Before I could respond, as if I even had the guts to, Violet was out of her chair and staring down Tom.

"I heard about this Colton character," she said. "I heard what he did. I just wanted to tell you that any friend of Colton's is an *enemy* of mine. You got it?"

Tom laughed. "So what's going on, Passero? You got a broad fighting your battles for you?"

With that, Violet raised her leg and stomped her five-inch heel onto Tom's foot.

"Ow, God damn it! If you weren't a broad, I'd kick your ass right here."

Violet smiled at Tom. "It was nice meeting you."

Tom huffed and limped away.

"That's how you handle the big ones," she said. "Don't be afraid. Sure, they might tower over you, but most of them are just talk. And if they get physical, then just mix it up with them. They might get the better of you, but you have to let them know they were in a fight. Make them sorry they tangled with you. Let 'em know you can't be pushed around."

She nodded, picked up her fork, and dove into her salad.

What the heck had just happened? It had all taken place so fast I was getting dizzy. I needed to retrace the last sixty seconds. Okay, now, Tom had bumped into me. He had threatened me. Violet had showed him up. And then it was over just as quickly as it had started. It all could have ended right there, but it hadn't. The best was yet to come—the pep talk Violet had given me. It was easy for her to stand up to bullies because very few of them would ever touch a girl. But she had made a great point. The last thing these no-neck jocks would expect from a kid like me would be for someone to stand up to them. They'd never expect it. And if you played your cards right, you might even be able to catch them off guard. Land the first punch maybe. *Wait a minute, Paulie. You're getting ahead of yourself.* Let's face it—I wasn't the type who spent a lot of time mixing it up with a thug. I needed to back up. First, I had to learn to stand up for myself. Second, I had to be prepared to get physical if necessary. And third, I would need to simply accept the consequences. They might not be pretty. I might walk away with a few bruises, but at least I would be able to hold up my head because I hadn't run from a confrontation.

I watched Violet shovel a cherry tomato and a cucumber slice into her mouth. It wasn't very dainty, but what difference did it make? Could a girl like Violet actually teach me something? I had always thought of her as so superficial. I'd thought she was a knockout but with little upstairs. That wasn't the case. It wasn't the case at all. She had real street smarts. They may not have helped her in her English composition class, but it was nonetheless an admirable trait. *Maybe I should pay more attention to what comes out of her mouth. I might just learn something.*

I felt a tap on my shoulder. It was Mr. Drennan. When I turned around, he was standing there with a woman who had to be his wife. She wasn't a raving beauty, but she was at least streetable. You know—you wouldn't be embarrassed to be seen with her on the street.

"I'm so glad to see you here, Paulie. I'd like you to meet my wife, Annette."

"Hi," I said.

She leaned in and whispered, "Bill's told me so much about you. You're such a brave young man. I really admire you."

I didn't know quite how to respond. "Thanks," was the only thing that came out of my mouth.

"Who's your date? I don't think I recognize her," Mr. Drennan said.

"Oh, this is Violet Kulick. She goes to Ridgeway."

"It's very nice to meet you, Violet," Mrs. Drennan said.

Violet smiled and nodded.

"If you run into any trouble here tonight, you let me know," Mr. Drennan said.

Trouble? Maybe he could be of help. I wondered if he would be willing to run interference for me.

"There is one thing," I said. "It has to do with Mr. Feingold."

"What's that?" he said.

I lowered my voice and proceeded to tell him about how Mr. Feingold had pulled me aside regarding Violet's outfit. I told him about the ultimatum he had given us. And I asked him if he could talk to him about the matter. During my explanation, I could see him glancing at Violet to see how she was dressed.

"You leave everything up to me," he said. "I'll get Feingold off your back. He's living in the 1950s."

"Gee, thanks," I said. "That would be great."

I watched as he approached Mr. Feingold a minute later. Mr. Drennan was talking to him in what seemed like a civil manner when Feingold suddenly made a face and placed his hands on his hips. He said something back to Mr. Drennan. Then the two appeared to be in the midst of a heated exchange. I was too far away to hear what they were saying, but I kept praying Mr. Drennan would win the argument and get Feingold off our backs. After another minute had passed, I could see Mr. Feingold's shoulders slump. He looked defeated. Had Mr. Drennan actually convinced him to back off? This would be so great. I watched as Mr. Feingold spun around and walked away. Mr. Drennan waved to me and gave a thumbs-up. Fantastic!

Mr. Drennan was so cool. I could see why everybody loved him. I remembered last year when a handful of upperclassmen had figured out where he lived. So they went over to his house at midnight on the day of his birthday and sang *Happy Birthday* to him standing on his front porch. Mr. Drennan ran downstairs in his pajamas, opened the door, and when he saw who it was, he applauded the unlikely men's chorus. His address was common knowledge after that, but no one, to my knowledge, ever bothered him again.

So Violet could remain in her current outfit, and we didn't have to leave. It was nice to finally have all the drama behind me. Or at least so I thought.

Chapter 19

The remainder of the dinner was fairly uneventful. The waitresses brought out plates of roasted potatoes, fried chicken, and string beans. We asked for seconds of the chicken, and we needed extra napkins. The chicken was really greasy, just the way kids like it.

Before the program began, Violet got up to visit the little girls' room. While she was away from the table, Jeremy punched me in the shoulder.

"What was that for?" I said.

"You are one lucky son of a bitch."

"You already said that."

"So what are you doing after the dance?" he asked.

I shrugged. "Just taking her home, I guess."

"Taking her home? Are you crazy, Passero? You gotta go park somewhere. I'm sure you'll be able to get a little…if you know what I mean?"

Right at that moment, I wasn't sure how to respond. Did I want to seem cool and agree with him? Or did I want to defend Violet's reputation and seem outraged by the suggestion? While I was thinking about which road to take, I felt the presence of someone standing directly behind me. I turned to see Mr. Feingold. He had that sinister smile again.

"You're a very lucky young man, Mr. Passero. You're fortunate Mr. Drennan has taken a liking to you."

I didn't say a word.

"Well, since I can't punish your inappropriately attired date, I've decided to make you pay the price. Be at my office at eight-thirty Monday morning. And don't be late." He displayed a fake grin and disappeared.

Oh, shit. What did Feingold have waiting for me? Apparently, I had celebrated too soon.

When I looked up, Violet was standing there. I jumped from my seat and pulled out her chair for her.

Violet leaned over and lowered her voice. "While I was in the ladies' room, I think I ran into that girl who hates you," she said.

"Andie?"

"She looked a lot like the girl we saw in the parking lot. I think it was her."

Oh, God. What did she say to Andie? "You didn't talk to her, did you?"

"Why, should I have?"

"No, no, that's not necessary."

She smiled. "I didn't say anything."

And then I started to get curious. "Did she…talk to you?"

"She was telling another girl about how glad she was the school board threw out her boyfriend's suspension and let him come to the dance."

"That had to be Andie."

"I watched what table she went to." Violet stood and pointed across the room. "She's sitting right over there at table number five."

I grabbed Violet's arm and pulled her back down.

"Paulie, relax. She won't bite. But somebody ought to tell her that her boyfriend is a real loser. If this creep assaulted one girl, he'll do it again. Even to his own girlfriend. You can book it."

"Can I have your attention, please," a voice from the front of the room called out. It was the principal, Mr. Payne. "I would like to welcome all of you to our official homecoming dance. And I'd like to congratulate our football team for a resounding victory over Oak Grove High." There were cheers from the crowd. "It was so good to have Colton Brand back on the field. He was a real force out there."

There were cheers as Colton raised his arms in victory.

Violet looked at me and stuck her tongue out in disapproval.

I nodded my agreement.

"I hope you enjoyed your dinner," Mr. Payne said. "It's now time for the entertainment portion of the evening to begin. I am happy to introduce the Mike Faynor Band." He turned to the band members. "Gentlemen, it's all yours." And with that, the music began. It was loud, really loud, ear-piercing at times.

I watched as groups of kids got up and proceeded to the dance floor. Colton and Andie were the first ones out there. I found myself staring at her. It was weird. With all that had happened between me and Andie in the past few weeks, I still really wanted to be with her. I tried to imagine myself holding her during a slow dance. I wanted to feel her skin next to mine. I glanced at Violet. She looked great and everything—really sexy, to be exact. But she just wasn't my type. I had already figured that out. It was fun to be seen with her and all, but this was a one-time-only event. She knew it and I knew it. I sighed. And so I had come to the painful realization that Andie Walker and I would never be an item. She wasn't about to dump Colton. And even if she did, what were the chances she and I would ever get together? Slim to none. The girl hated me, for Pete's sake. There was no getting around that. I guessed I would need to set my sights on other fish in the sea. There had to be someone out there for a kid like me. The only problem was I had no interest in any girl but Andie. I didn't want to be with anyone else. It seemed I was destined to be a loner in the dating department. Oh, that didn't mean I wouldn't try to ask out a girl, but I'd just be doing it for appearances' sake, not because I really cared for her.

"So are you ready to get out there?" Violet said.

Okay, here was the problem. I probably had no business asking a girl to a dance…since I couldn't dance. I had never been to an event like this before. Sure, I had gone to a few sock-hops at school, but since I never had the courage to ask a girl to dance, I never had to learn how to. I only went to sock-hops to be seen by other kids. I didn't want people to think I was some kind of social outcast. I had asked Violet to this dance on a dare. I never really thought she would say *yes*. And then I decided it would help my image to be seen with her. But I never stopped to think about the fact that I'd actually be expected to dance.

"Well….um…"

"What's the problem?"

"I'm…not…a very good dancer. I don't want to embarrass myself."

She smiled and grabbed my hand. "Come on, it's easy. I'll show you."

"I don't know."

"There's nothing to dancing fast," she said. "You just throw your arms and legs all around like your hair's on fire. Nobody'll care what kind of moves you have. They won't be paying attention to you. They'll be too concerned about their own style." She sighed. "And if you can't do that, then just copy what you see other people doing."

"I'm still not sure."

Her eyes narrowed. "Listen, Paulie, I didn't come here to sit on my ass and talk about the weather. I came here to dance." She put her hands on her hips. "When you ask a girl to a dance, you dance with her. Period. Now, let's get out there."

I could tell she was serious. I swallowed hard and followed her onto the dance floor. Once we got out there, Violet was like a wild animal. Her head bobbed, her arms flailed, and her feet sailed in all directions. I'd never be able to keep up with her, but I knew I had to do something. I started to sway to the music. I was waiting for it to speak to me. A minute later, I still hadn't felt any magic. I wanted to go sit down in the worst way, but I knew I couldn't abandon Violet. I looked at how some of the other guys around me were dancing. Some seemed to know what they were doing. Others seemed really awkward, but at least they were trying. That was more than I could say for myself.

Violet grabbed my arms and tried to make me do something. At first, I resisted, but then I decided to give it the old college try. I began to borrow various moves from each of the guys I had observed. Then I threw them all together. I was sure it looked pretty disjointed, but to tell you the truth, I really didn't care. Violet was right. No one was watching me...because everyone was watching Violet. As I looked around, I could see all the boys had their eyes on my date. The girls too, but for a different reason.

Then, just as I was beginning to feel more comfortable, I spotted Andie and Colton out of the corner of my eye. It seemed as if they were moving closer and closer to us. At one point they were right next to us. Violet hadn't realized how close they were at first, but a minute later she had her eyes on Colton. The expression on her face changed suddenly. She was glaring at him. I was praying for the music to end so we could go sit down. I avoided making eye contact with either Colton or Andie.

Then, as if strategically planned, Colton leaned over and threw a shoulder into me. I sailed a few yards but managed to stay on my feet. When I walked back to where Violet was standing, Colton was whispering something to her.

She pulled away and crossed her arms. "You wish, creep. You'll never get your hands on this." She caressed her sides.

Colton moved closer. This time I was within earshot.

"You need a real man. Not this twerp."

She reached over and put her hands around my waist. "He's more man than you'll ever be."

"You're dreaming, sweetheart."

I was watching the expression on Andie's face. She looked disgusted. And why not? Who'd be excited about your date hitting on another girl...right in front of you?

Violet pulled her hand away and approached Colton. "Listen, asshole. Real men don't beat up girls.

They don't assault them." She was poking her finger into his chest. With each poke, Colton took a step backward.

The music had stopped. Everyone was now watching us.

"I know all about what happened under those bleachers. You should have been expelled. But since your wussy school board cares more about winning football games than protecting innocent girls, they let you off easy. If you were ever to try anything like that with me, I'd castrate you right on the spot." She pulled her arm back. "This is for that girl you tried to rape." And with that Violet, with a closed fist, hit Colton right in the gut. He bent over and backed up a few steps.

"You bitch!" he yelled out. "I'm gonna teach you a lesson." Colton ran right at Violet.

I don't know what made me do it, but something inside me kicked in. I suddenly had no fear. Before Colton collided with Violet, I slipped in between them, and threw a bear hug around him. I held him as tightly as I could until he broke free.

By this time, Mr. Drennan had arrived. He stepped in between us and raised his arms.

"Now stop it, both of you."

Mr. Feingold and Principal Payne had appeared.

"Who started this?" the principal said angrily.

"She did," Colton said. He was pointing at Violet.

"I should have known," Mr. Feingold said.

"Gentlemen, you got it all wrong," Violet said. She nodded at Colton. "That jerk put a shoulder into Paulie and nearly knocked him down. That's what started this."

"All right, all right. Let's just calm down," Mr.

Payne said. He waved to the band. "Play something!"

When the music resumed, everyone was still staring at us. Then, slowly, kids started to dance.

"Colton, you and Andie, please return to your table," he said.

He looked at me and Violet. "You two, follow Mr. Feingold to his office."

This was bad. Very bad. Feingold was going to kill us. But what had I done? I just brought Violet. I wasn't responsible for her actions. She was her own person.

Violet glanced at me. She shook her head and rolled her eyes. "This is bullshit."

We followed Mr. Feingold out of the gym, down two hallways, and into his office. He pointed to a couple of chairs facing the desk. We slipped into them while he sat down, folded his hands, and rested them on the desktop.

"Your evening has come to an end," he said.

"You're kickin' us out?" Violet said. "We can't go back and dance?"

"Yes and no," he said. "Yes, you're being kicked out. And, no, you cannot return to the dance."

Violet sat back in her chair, crossed her legs, and shook her head. "I told you. It's bullshit."

Mr. Feingold leaned forward. "Young lady, I don't appreciate your tone or your language. That may be the way you and your friends talk at Ridgeway, but at Cermak, our students act more like proper ladies and gentleman."

"You call that Colton kid a gentleman?" Violet said. "You know what happened to that girl under the bleachers, don't you?"

"Young lady, I'm doing the interrogating here, not

you," Feingold snapped. "The actions of Cermak students are no concern of yours." He opened the top desk drawer, pulled out a pad, and tore a sheet off the top. "I'm issuing you a No Trespass violation. You are no longer welcome on this campus." He looked up. "Your full name, please."

Violet sat back and smiled. "Shirley Temple."

He looked at me. "Mr. Passero, what is this young woman's name?"

I glanced at Violet. She shrugged. I guess that was her way of telling me it was okay to answer the question.

"Um...Violet...Kulick."

Violet sighed and crossed her arms. "How long is this going to take?"

Mr. Feingold glared at her, then looked in my direction. "Spell the last name, please."

"K-u-l-i-c-k."

"Her address?"

"3113 North Neva Avenue here in Chicago."

He continued writing, then handed Violet the slip.

"You know what you can do with this, don't you?" she said.

It was time for me to run some interference. The angrier Feingold got at Violet, the more he would take it out on me. I desperately needed to diffuse the situation.

"I'll make sure she doesn't come back here," I said.

Violet turned and looked at me as if I were some kind of traitor. "I'll come back here any time I want," she said. "You got that?"

"Let's just finish this up so I can get you home." It was time to cut my losses. I knew it. The more I defended Violet's actions, the worse it would be for me. I needed to distance myself from her, and the sooner the better. It wasn't that I didn't appreciate her support. She was the only one who had the guts to say and do to Colton what I had fantasized about doing myself. She had also made me an instant hit with the guys. Just being seen with her gave me a reputation with girls I had always dreamed of. So I had gotten about as much out of this situation as I was going to get. Time to move on.

"If you're finished with Miss Kulick, Mr. Feingold, I'd like to take her home," I said.

"That's the most intelligent thing that's come out of your mouth all night, young man."

I just nodded.

"Young lady, we're done here. I think it's safe to say we won't be seeing each other ever again."

"Don't be so sure about that, Pops. I was thinking about transferring to this dump next year."

Feingold's eyes widened. "I am very tight with the admissions people here at Cermak. I can guarantee that would never happen."

Violet stood up and winked. "I just wanted to give you a scare, old man." She turned to me. "Let's go, Paulie."

"Not so fast, Mr. Passero. I've done about all I can do to your date. But I've just begun to deal with you. Remember—eight-thirty Monday morning—right here." He grinned. "Now I'm going to personally escort the two of you out of the building." He stood and motioned for us to follow him.

We walked down a long hallway until we reached the exit. He held open the door for us. Violet walked through the doorway first. I followed. Then the door slammed behind us.

"Well, Paulie, I'm sorry and I'm not sorry. I'm sorry about getting you into trouble. But I'm not sorry about giving your friend Colton a little taste of his own medicine."

"I did enjoy watching you clobber him."

She laughed. "Let me see." She started counting on her fingers. "He's like the sixth boy I've slugged over the years."

As we got into the car and drove to Violet's house, she proceeded to tell me the circumstances surrounding each of the other guys she had gut-punched. Each was more interesting than the one before him. And all of them made me want to tread very lightly around this girl. You never knew when she would have had enough of me and would let me have it.

When we pulled up in front of her house, we could see a light on in the living room. I glanced at the clock on the dashboard. It was nine-forty-five.

"I'm sorry the night ended so early," I said. "We can still do something, if you want."

"No, I think I've had enough excitement for one evening." She grabbed the handle to open the door.

"Let me get that." I got out, ran around to the passenger side, and opened her door.

"Thank you, kind sir," she said.

We walked slowly up to the front porch and climbed the stairs. She turned to face me.

"Well, Paulie Passero, we're even," she said.

"Even?" I asked. Although I knew exactly what she meant.

"You know. You helped me with that book thing.

What book was it again?"

"*Lost Horizon.*"

"Oh, yeah. And I returned the favor by going to the dance tonight with you."

There was a momentary period of awkward silence.

"Oh, well, maybe I'll see you on the bus."

"I don't think so. One of my girlfriends is getting a car this weekend, so I'll probably be riding with her from now on."

"I see. Okay, then. I just wanted to thank you for going to the dance with me. I know you may not have wanted to, but I appreciate it."

"It was fun." She smiled. "Well, see you around."

And then the strangest—and greatest—thing happened. Violet cupped her hands around my face and gave me the wettest, sloppiest kiss on the mouth I had ever experienced. It was long and it was hard.

When she finally came up for air, she smiled and winked. Then she opened her front door and she was gone.

I wiped her saliva off my mouth, and I floated to the car. I didn't even remember going down the porch steps, but somehow I had managed to negotiate them safely. I took one, long, last look at Violet's house. I was pretty sure I would never go down this street or come upon this house ever again. It was one for the ages. And it had come to an end. With her new transportation arrangement, I was fairly certain I would never again lay eyes on Violet. And that was okay. It really was. I knew she and I would never be an item, and I wasn't so sure I even wanted us to be. She was too much to handle for one guy. I wished her next boyfriend good luck.

Whenever I find myself thinking about Violet Cassandra Kulick, I don't think about getting into trouble with the school disciplinarian. Instead, I remember that awesome kiss on her front porch. I could still feel her lips pressed against mine. I could feel the wet around my mouth. I wasn't sure I would ever be able to get that feeling out of my head. And I didn't really want to. For some reason, I wasn't concerned about what Mr. Feingold had waiting for me on Monday morning. Whatever it was, it would definitely be worth it. And so, as the Violet chapter closed, I wasn't quite sure what would await me tomorrow, or the next day. As I drove home, I started thinking about Andie again. She had to be even more pissed at me for bringing the girl who laid out Colton. Move on, Paulie. Get this girl out of your head. It will never happen.

Then I got to thinking. A month ago, if you had asked me if I would ever go on a date with Violet, I would have laughed. Violet would never agree to go out with me. I just wasn't cool enough. And she was completely unattainable. The only way I could see myself going on a date with Violet was in my dreams. But I just did. We did go out. And she kissed me. All of that had been an impossible feat, yet somehow I managed to pull it off. If I was able to go out with Violet, then why couldn't I win over Andie? It was equally impossible. But I had done it once. There was no reason I couldn't do it again. Yeah. I *could* do this. And no matter what immovable force I needed to overcome, I *would* do this. I *would*.

Chapter 20

The next morning I ran over to Mickey's house. I had to tell him what had happened at the dance the night before. And I was dying to share the news about the whopper of a kiss Violet had laid on me. Knowing Mickey, however, he would undoubtedly have a hard time believing the kiss part. If I really sold it, though, maybe, just maybe he would buy it. The problem was there was no one to vouch for me—no one to tell him she had actually kissed me. We'd probably never see her again, and even if we did, there was no way either of us would have the guts to ask her about the kiss. That moment might live forever between Violet and me— and no one else.

When I got to Mickey's, I ran up the front porch stairs and rang the bell. To my delight, Judy, his older sister, answered the door. I might have had a crush on Judy for years, but that was all it would ever be, just a crush. Judy was three years older than us. Definitely not in my ball park.

"Hi, Paulie, how are you?"

"Good. I was wondering if Mickey was home."

"He's down in the basement. I'll call him. Come on in and sit down." She walked over to the basement door and yelled, "Mickey, come on up. There's someone here to see you." She turned to me and smiled. "He should be up soon."

"Okay, thanks."

"Would you excuse me for a minute?" she said.

"Oh, sure."

I followed her with my eyes as she left the living room, walked through the dining room, and entered the kitchen. I had always liked watching Judy from behind. She had a great figure. For just a moment there, I had actually forgotten about Andie. That didn't happen too often.

A minute later, Mickey appeared in the basement doorway. "Paulie, my man, what are you doing here?"

"I wanted to tell you about last night."

"Oh, yeah. The dance." He looked around. "Come on down."

I followed the Mick down the stairs into his basement. Mickey's basement was like probably all the other bungalows on the block—cinderblock walls and a cement floor. On one side, you'd find the washer and dryer. On the other side there was a floor-to-ceiling tool cabinet and a woodworking station. Mickey's dad, Big John, was a carpenter, plumber, electrician…you name it. The man could build anything. And right in the middle of the basement, on the north wall, partially hidden by a clothesline full of ladies' underwear, was a dartboard—English darts on one side and baseball on the other. We sat down on an old couch.

"Okay, let's have it. What's Violet like? How did she look? What was she wearing? Was it skanky? What did you guys talk about? Did you make out in the parking lot?" He chuckled. He threw in the last question for yuks. He never expected to hear our lips had actually met.

"Well, she looked pretty good…in kind of a skanky way."

"I knew it," Mickey said. "How skanky, exactly?"

"She had on a really short skirt, fishnet stockings, and a low-cut blouse."

Mickey smiled. "You're killing me. How low cut?"

"Can you say—cleavage?"

"Holy shit. How I would have loved to have been there." He thought to himself. "Of course, I could have been there if I'd wanted to…but I chose not to."

Whatever. Mickey didn't want to see me get the upper hand with the ladies. When you got down to it, we were pretty much even—we both sucked at dating.

"So…what else happened?"

I proceeded to tell him the whole story: about Violet's sorry excuse for a mother; about our conversations in the car; about not wanting to be seen by Colton and Andie in the school parking lot; about Violet's thoughts on Colton and Carolyn; about Mr. Feingold's reaction to Violet's wardrobe; about how interested the boys at our table were in Violet; about Tom Webster's threats; about Violet's attack on Tom; about how Mr. Drennan ran interference for me with Mr. Feingold; about how I have to be in Feingold's office bright and early on Monday morning; about how Violet ran into Andie in the girls' bathroom; about how Violet told me I had to dance with her; about how I made a fool of myself on the dance floor but really didn't care; about how Colton was talking trash to Violet; about how she accused him of attacking Carolyn under the bleachers; about how she punched him right in the gut; about how I intercepted him before he could get to her; about how we had to go to Feingold's office after the fisticuffs; about how we got kicked out of the dance; and about Violet's unforgettable kiss.

Mickey sat there with his mouth open. "Oh, my God. I can't believe it. All that shit happened in one night?"

"I guess so."

"I believe everything except the parts about you fighting off Colton, and Violet's French kiss."

"I didn't really fight him off. I just got in his way so he couldn't hurt Violet. And she didn't French kiss me. No tongue. All lips. Very wet lips."

"Were there any witnesses?" he said.

"To what? The Colton thing or the kiss?"

"Both."

I knew the Mick would have a hard time buying this story. "Well, there were dozens of kids who saw me block Colton. You can ask anyone who was at the dance. As far as the kiss thing, I'm afraid there weren't any witnesses. You're just gonna have to believe me."

He walked over and grabbed me by the shoulders. He stared at me. "Paulie, I can always tell when you're bullshitting me. I can see it in your eyes."

I smiled. "So what do you see?" I asked.

"I see a guy who likes to stretch the truth a little to impress people."

Before I could respond, Mickey was qualifying his comment.

"Now, listen, Paulie, I'm your best friend. You don't have to exaggerate the truth for my benefit. I'd be your friend no matter what."

I wasn't sure if I should hug him or slug him. I took the high road.

"Mick, everything I told you is what actually

happened. I can't help it if you don't believe me."

He leaned over and got right into my face. Our noses were only millimeters apart. He seemed to be studying my eyes. The Mick considered himself to be a human lie detector. He was determined to sniff out the truth.

I couldn't help but smile as he scrutinized every blemish on my face. The smile eventually turned into laughter—for both of us.

"Shit, I don't care if you are making it all up," he said. "It's a great story no matter what."

"Well, that's nice to hear."

"So what do you think Feingold has cooked up for you on Monday?"

"I have no idea. He's such a jerk. I'm sure it's gotta be some kind of bullshit busywork."

"I don't know about that. If he was as upset as you make out, I'll bet he's got a real doozy waiting for you."

"I could care less. Whatever he can dish out, I can take."

"Famous last words." Mickey glanced at the clock on the tool chest. "Well, we'll both find out in about forty-six hours." He smiled.

****

And forty-six hours later, we were hopping off the bus and speeding for the front door of school.

"Of all days for the bus to be late, it had to be today," I said.

"Here, gimme your books," Mickey said. "I'll jam 'em in your locker. You got one minute to make it to Feingold's office."

I handed him my books and took off. As I passed

Mr. Drennan's office, I couldn't help but notice that someone else was sitting behind his desk. I stopped momentarily and peered in. Was it a sub? Maybe Mr. Drennan was sick or something. I couldn't wait to find out. I pinballed my way through the hallway and made it to the administrative offices in record time. When I entered Mr. Feingold's office, he was seated at his desk sipping a cup of coffee. When he made eye contact, he immediately glanced at the clock on the wall. It read 8:31.

"You're late," Mr. Passero."

"The bus was behind schedule today. A bunch of people are probably gonna be late to class."

"And how is that my problem?"

I didn't answer.

He pointed to a chair opposite his desk.

I plopped down into it. I was about to find out exactly what kind of mindless busywork he had planned for me.

"I hope you enjoyed the little fun you had on Friday night at my expense," he said. He pretended to be looking around. "I don't seem to see your fairy godfather here this morning. Looks like there's no one to bail you out of this jam."

I wasn't sure what he was talking about. I must have had a confused look on my face.

"I'm referring to your old bud, good old Mr. Drennan. I'm afraid he can't help you out anymore."

"What do you mean?"

"I had a little talk with Principal Payne following the dance. I shared with him some of the antics Mr. Drennan engaged in on Friday night. They were completely inappropriate. In fact, Mr. Drennan was guilty of insubordination."

"I don't understand. He didn't do anything," I said.

"Oh, so that's how you see it." Mr. Feingold shook his head. "Anything to protect your sorry ass, is that it?"

"I…I…"

"Quit your stammering. This is now a matter for the school board. Mr. Drennan has been suspended. The board will decide his fate at an emergency meeting tomorrow night. And I plan to be there. It promises to be quite a show."

"This isn't right."

Mr. Feingold leaned across the desk. "You let me worry about what's right and what's wrong, understand?"

I sighed and stared at my shoes. I was feeling awful about Mr. Drennan. It was all my fault. If I hadn't gone to the dance, or if I hadn't brought Violet, none of this would have happened. He was only defending me. He didn't deserve any of this.

Mr. Feingold folded his hands and smiled. "Now, let's get down to business."

I was waiting for him to announce I had been suspended as well. If he had managed to get Mr. Drennan booted, it wouldn't take much for me to get slapped with the same sentence.

"We considered suspending you too, but that would be too good for you. Why should you be able to sit at home twiddling your thumbs when we could inflict some real pain?"

I wished he would have just spit it out. I didn't appreciate the theatrics.

"You'll be spending a little time in the penalty box

after school for the next week—which just so happens to be the last week of the season. You, Mr. Passero, will be working locker room detail after the football team returns from practice each day. You'll be cleaning up the place—picking up dirty uniforms, wet towels, and those disgusting jock straps. And you won't leave until the place is spic 'n' span."

This was the absolute worst punishment possible. It had nothing to do with cleaning up after a bunch of pigs. It had everything to do with being in the middle of a hornets' nest. Most of the guys on the football team hated my guts for speaking up about Colton. This was their chance to kick my ass each day with no witnesses around. Mr. Feingold knew exactly what he was doing. He had given this a lot of thought—and by the expression on his face, it appeared he was very proud of himself.

"Why the long face, young man? You should be thanking me. You'll have a chance to spend some quality time with all your buddies on the team. Won't that be nice?"

I didn't say a word. I refused to give him the satisfaction of knowing what I was thinking. Then I thought for a minute. Maybe I should say something—something to take the wind out of his sails.

"We're done here," he said. "You're free to go."

I reached over the desk to shake his hand.

He didn't reciprocate.

"Thank you very much, Mr. Feingold. I was worried you'd pick some horrible job for me. Cleaning up the locker room? I can handle that. No problem. Thanks." I got up to leave.

He stood up. "Listen, you little snot. You don't

fool me. You're shittin' your pants, and you know it. I'm sure the guys on the team will be oh-so-happy to see you after the lies you told about their star linebacker." He smiled. "And don't think about ditching. I'll be there each day to sign you in, and sign you out. Be there by five p.m."

I took a deep breath. "Is that it?"

He nodded. "Get out."

I was halfway out of the office when I heard his voice.

"See you after school, Mr. Passero." He chuckled.

After everything I had been through lately, I didn't think things could get much worse. But they had managed to. I walked down an empty hallway to my locker, grabbed books for morning classes, and headed to Mr. Drennan's room.

Chapter 21

I wasn't sure how I pulled it off, but somehow I had managed to suffer though English, Spanish, and math without getting called on. If I had, it would have been a disaster. I hadn't been paying attention in a single class. In fact, I couldn't tell you two words spoken by any of the teachers. My thoughts were elsewhere. How was I ever going to survive the week from hell? Feingold had turned out to be the devil incarnate. Though I'd never let him know it, he had devised the ultimate punishment.

When I got to the cafeteria for lunch, I was faced with my usual dilemma—where to sit. My old spot across from Andie was now strictly *verboten*. I looked for the table where Carolyn Mancuso was sitting. I had gotten kind of friendly with her during the whole Colton thing. Maybe I could join her again. But when I finally spotted her, something unexpected had occurred. She was now sitting with Brian Lambert. They were talking and smiling. Something had changed. Something dramatic. Ever since the incident under the bleachers, Carolyn had been a virtual outcast. No one from Andie's group, or especially the football team, would be seen with her. And now, the team's starting fullback was sitting at her table. Either people were starting to believe Carolyn, or Brian was one of the bravest guys at school. I took it as a good sign—one of the few I had experienced lately.

It appeared I was destined to join Mickey and the nerds. They weren't really bad guys—they were just different—you know, math and physics geeks. And how the Mick ever befriended any of them was beyond me, other than they were guys from his neighborhood. They had started sitting together freshmen year. When you start a new school, and you have no one to sit with at lunch, you tend to do stupid things. Mickey saw a group of familiar faces the first day and decided to join them. He had been sitting with these goofs for the last two years. He'd be the first one to tell you he had nothing in common with any of them, but he felt bad just abandoning them. They had, after all, welcomed him into their little group when he had nowhere else to go. I had been after him for months to break away from nerd city and start our own little lunch club, but Mickey, who was nothing if not loyal, refused. When he saw me walking in his direction, he waved me over.

"Hey, Paulie, pull up a seat." He pointed at his lunch mates. "You know the guys, right?" The *guys* had apparently been doing something with a slide rule and couldn't be bothered to look up.

I rolled my eyes and sat down.

"I've been thinking about you all morning," Mickey said. "So what did Feingold have up his sleeve?"

I exhaled and dropped my head. "I can't even talk about it."

"Hell, now you gotta tell me."

I sighed. "I have to clean up the locker room after the football team comes back from practice every day."

Mickey looked concerned. "That's not too safe, pal. Those guys put a bounty on your head."

"No shit!"

"Feingold wants you to go into the lion's den alone? You could get messed up."

"That's why he's such a bastard. He knows what's likely to happen in there, and he doesn't care."

Mickey shook his head. "How long you gotta do it?"

"A week."

"Well, that's good, at least."

"That's good? Okay. Mick, can I ask you a favor?"

"Sure, anything, buddy."

"Would you do the eulogy at my funeral?"

He laughed. "I don't think they're gonna kill you."

"Don't be so sure." Out of the corner of my eye, I saw this kid coming right at us. When he got closer, I recognized him. It was Jeremy Huff, the cross-country jock who was sitting at my table at the dance on Friday night.

"Hey, Passero, are your ears burning?" he said.

"Should they be?" I asked.

"Duh…yeah. Man, you're the talk of the school."

Wait a minute. Had he—had everyone—heard about Feingold's punishment? What was going on? I decided to play dumb.

"I don't know what you're talking about."

He laughed. "That babe you brought to the dance? Have you forgotten already?"

"Oh, you mean Violet."

"Man, she was smokin'."

"She did look pretty good, didn't she?"

"*Pretty* good? Are you kidding? She was the

hottest girl there."

I suddenly started to feel a little better about myself. "So people are talking about it, huh?"

"I'll say. Guys *and* girls. Anyone who was there. Of course, they have differing opinions on things."

"What do you mean?"

"Well, the guys are all drooling. They want to know the next time you'll be bringing her around. But the girls—now that's another story. They never want to lay eyes on Violet again." He leaned in. "Too much competition, if you ask me." He slapped me on the back. "You hit a homer Friday night, Passero. Time to bask in the glory."

Mickey appeared impressed. "Well, look at you," he said. "Romeo, Don Juan, and Casanova all rolled up into one."

It made me feel good to hear those things. A week ago, I was Mr. Nobody when it came to the opposite sex. Now these guys were making me out to be a legend of some kind. Yeah, right. Paulie Passero, a real ladies' man. A real ladies' man? I knew that was the farthest thing from the truth, but I sure wasn't going to let them think any differently. In time, they would all know it was just a fluke. At the next dance, I'd either show up stag or not show up at all. Then they'd realize Paulie Passero had returned to his old pathetic ways.

"I wish there was something I could do to help you with this Feingold thing," Mickey said. "Hey, do you want me to go with you to the locker room? Maybe those guys would be less likely to kick your ass if there was a witness."

"I appreciate the support, Mick, but then you'd be getting in the middle of this mess. And you haven't done anything to deserve that. This is my problem, and I'm gonna have to deal with it myself. Like you said, they probably won't kill me."

"Didn't you say Brian Lambert was on your side? Maybe you should hang around him while you're in there."

"Yeah, but what can one guy do against forty others? It's hopeless." For the remainder of the lunch period, I tried to change the topic, but no matter what subject we were discussing, we kept coming back to the impending torture in the locker room.

After lunch I paid about as much attention in my afternoon classes as I had in the morning ones—which wasn't a lot. During chemistry and PE, I just went through the motions. The calisthenics in PE class, as bad as they were, helped keep my mind off things. I had something else to hate. The last period of the day, study hall, couldn't have come at a worse time. Usually those forty minutes afforded me an opportunity to get a head start on my homework, but today I just sat on my ass and felt sorry for myself.

I wasn't sure what I was supposed to do while the team practiced. I decided to kill time in the library. I hoped I'd be able to concentrate on other things and maybe get some work done, but no such luck. At one point, I found myself dozing off. The next thing I remembered was Mrs. Tompkins, the school librarian, tapping me on the shoulder.

"The library is closing in five minutes, son."

"Okay, thanks." I glanced at the clock overhead. It was time to go—time to meet my maker. I grabbed my backpack, threw it over my shoulder, and headed for the gym. When I got there, I looked for the boys' locker room. Standing in front of the door with his arms folded was Mr. Feingold.

"I thought for a minute there that you were going to stand me up," he said.

I decided not to respond. I couldn't think of anything clever to say.

"I'll be back in an hour or so," he said. "Don't leave without seeing me."

"Will there be anyone else helping me?" I said.

Feingold smiled. "I gave my last lackey the week off. So, no, it's just you."

I pushed open the door and was immediately greeted by an overwhelming stench. I had forgotten just how bad this place smelled. I put my backpack in a corner, sat down on a bench, and waited for the onslaught. Before long I heard voices. I could tell it was them. A moment later, the outside door flew open and the team filed in. I got up and stood against one of the walls. As the guys filed past me, some didn't make eye contact, but the majority of them sneered at me. They apparently knew who I was. I considered myself lucky I had survived the first minute or so without any physical abuse. That soon changed.

"Well, look what we have here." It was Colton. "Hey, guys, look who decided to pay us a visit."

I avoided looking directly at Colton. I was praying he would just go away.

"What are you doing here, Passero?"

I sighed. I wasn't sure if I should respond.

"Hey, dumbass, I asked you a question."

"Feingold is making me clean up the locker room this week."

"Why now?" Colton said.

"It's because—"

"Wait a minute. Wait just a minute. This is because of the other night, isn't it? Why, sure. This is because you brought that whore to the dance."

"She's not a whore," I said.

"Trust me, anybody who dresses like that is a whore."

I wanted to continue my defense of Violet, but I didn't want to piss him off.

"So did you get in her pants?" a voice yelled from across the room.

"I doubt if a pussy like Passero could have managed that," Colton said. "Give me five minutes with that slut, and I would have nailed her."

"Unless she kicked your ass first, Colton," another player yelled out.

Colton turned in the direction of the voice. "Who said that?" No one spoke up.

He walked up to me and stuck his finger in my chest. "Listen, asshole, I owe you and your little girlfriend. Since she's not here, you're gonna have to pay." He stepped back and looked around. "But not now. I'm gonna make you sweat. On Friday, after practice, right here, you and me are gonna have it out, once and for all. And there's nobody who can help you. You got it?"

I nodded.

"Good. This should be fun. You and me—Friday."

"I can't wait to see it," Tom Webster said. There were cheers from the rest of the group.

I walked back to the corner. I would just wait until the guys returned from the showers. Then I'd start collecting uniforms, towels, and—oh, God—jock straps. I kept my head down. I didn't want to make direct eye contact with anyone. I didn't want to set them off. A few minutes later, a few of the guys returned from the showers. I grabbed a large bucket on wheels and rolled it toward the lockers. I reached down to pick up a towel on the floor but stopped.

"Are you done with this?" I asked.

The player smiled. He grabbed the towel from my hands and proceeded to wipe his ass with it.

"Now I'm done." He laughed.

I decided at that point to employ a new strategy. I didn't want to confront any more of these guys. I would wait until they all left. That would be safer. I returned to the corner, pulled a book from my backpack and pretended to be reading. One by one the players got dressed and headed out. A few minutes later, it appeared the locker room was empty. I dragged the bucket back and got to work. I soon knew why the room always smelled so bad. Every item I tossed into the bucket reeked of body odor. I tried not to touch the jock straps. I picked them up with a towel whenever possible.

Then out of nowhere I felt someone slide something onto my head. When I looked up, I saw a smiling Colton standing there. I grabbed at the item and ripped it off. I should have known. It was his jock.

"Friday. It's a date." He laughed as he exited.

I walked the length of the locker room to make sure there were no more surprises. After an inspection, I was certain it was empty. I ran around and picked up all the smelly, discarded items and tossed them into the bucket. It took me about twenty minutes to clean up everything. I slid the bucket back to where I had found it and headed for the exit. When I opened the door to the gym, I found Mr. Feingold standing there.

"So how'd it go, Passero?"

I knew he was just baiting me. He had to know it couldn't have been a pleasant experience. He wanted to hear me bitch about how awful it was. I decided to give him just the opposite.

"Good," I said. "All the guys were really nice. I'm looking forward to coming back tomorrow." I smiled and waved. "See you."

He was speechless. It was great. But that feeling of satisfaction soon faded. I began thinking about what was awaiting me on Friday. I found myself imagining the worst—black eyes, knocked-out teeth, and more. I was no match for Colton, and he knew it. I was just hoping it would only be him versus me. If I somehow had to defend myself against multiple combatants, there'd be little left of me. I found myself breathing heavily. I felt like I was about to hyperventilate. Was there nothing I could do about the Colton threat? Was there anyone I could tell? My immediate thoughts went to Mr. Drennan. But he was in no position to help me. He had to be more worried about saving his own can. Then I thought back to what my dad had told me when I was a freshman. He told me to *face the problem head on...learn to battle through it...fight the good fight...and never, never let them see me cry.*

Chapter 22

At school the next day, I tried—I really tried—to concentrate in class. I had to overcome feelings of fear. Why should I lose an entire week of my life, I thought, because of some silly threats? Who knew, maybe Colton was just trying to scare me with words. Maybe he was just messing with my mind. Maybe he never intended to harm me at all. Maybe I was imagining something that would never happen. I could only hope.

I did manage to apply myself more in class the next day. I actually participated in discussion in English and Spanish. I was starting to feel better about things. At lunch that day, I exited the cafeteria line and began looking for a place to sit. As I walked around, with tray in hand, I guess I wasn't really looking where I was going, and I collided with Andie Walker. The French fries flew from my tray and spilled onto the floor.

"Oh, I'm really sor—" she started to say—until she saw who it was. The smile on her face disappeared. I had to give her credit, though. She did help clean up the mess. Then she left without saying a word.

I stood there momentarily. I wasn't really upset about losing the fries. But I realized I was heartbroken about losing Andie's friendship. I missed sitting across from her. I missed talking to her. I wondered what might have happened if she *had* given me a tennis lesson that day—a day that now seemed eons ago. I might have been able to win her over. It wasn't an impossibility, I told myself. Stranger things had happened.

Back to reality. Andie was gone. Not only would we never be boyfriend and girlfriend, but we would never even be friends. That was hard to accept.

I returned to the locker room after school on Tuesday. The day turned out to be rather uneventful if you don't count getting shoved and knocked down more than once while I waited for the team to shower and leave. On Wednesday, Tom Webster described for me the way in which Colton was going to kick my ass.

"First, he's gonna land a heater right to the chops," Tom said. "Then he'll nail you with a hard right to the breadbasket. You won't know what hit you."

The picture he was painting wasn't particularly pleasant. I listened but chose not to speak, which seemed to make Tom even more upset.

"I can't wait for Friday," he said. "It's gonna be great."

As I walked away, he was still yelling.

"You're a dead man, Passero."

I waited for Tom to leave before getting to work. I discovered that waiting for the entire team to finish up was clearly the most opportune way of handling this job. By late Wednesday afternoon, I had become even more efficient. I cleaned things up in fifteen minutes. As I was leaving the locker room, I bumped into Mr. Feingold standing in the hallway.

"Done already?" he said.

"Yes."

"See you tomorrow," he said.

I kept walking.

"Oh, Passero," he called out.

I stopped and turned around.

"I thought you'd be interested in knowing what happened at the emergency school board meeting last night."

Why in God's name would I give a good crap about the school board meeting? I continued on my way.

"Oh, so you're not interested in finding out about how your buddy, Mr. Drennan, fared last night?"

I stopped and spun around. I had completely forgotten about that.

"I thought you might want to know," he said. "It seems the board extended Mr. Drennan's suspension until the end of the semester. They'll review the matter in December. If he's permitted to return to Cermak, he may be back in the classroom in January. Or maybe not at all. If you want to know my opinion, I'm betting on the latter."

By the time Thursday rolled around, my stomach was in knots. I was having chest pains, and my breathing was labored. I was pretty sure this was what they called a panic attack. When I met up with the team on Thursday, I could tell some of the guys were licking their chops. They couldn't wait to see me taken apart by one of their star players on Friday. There were some less than endearing comments directed at me as I stood in the corner waiting for them to finish up. As the players filed out of the locker room one by one, each brushed up against me, every one more physical than the next. Some of the guys stepped on my toes. Others conveniently elbowed me in the ribs as they exited. No

225

one ever made eye contact. It was hit and run. And I never fought back. There were just too many of them. This wasn't the time to be a hero.

That night when I got home, I apparently wasn't hiding my emotions. My mom stopped what she was doing and seemed to study me.

"Paulie, what's wrong? What's bothering you?"

"Nothing," I said.

"You look so down—so distraught."

"I just have a lot of homework, and I'm not looking forward to doing it. That's all."

She dropped the dish towel she'd been holding and put her arms around me. "I don't like seeing you look so sad. It bothers me." After a few moments, she released me and took a step back. "Are you absolutely sure nothing is wrong?"

I feigned a laugh. "Mom, how many times do I have to tell you? I'm fine. Nothing's wrong." I sighed. "Do you mind if I go upstairs now?"

"Sure."

I headed up the stairs.

She walked over to the railing. "I'm available if you ever want to talk. Okay?"

I turned back. "Okay, thanks." I continued on my way up the stairs and entered my bedroom. I dropped my backpack on the floor and fell into bed. I just wanted to go to sleep and wake up three or four years from now—long after high school had ended. I didn't like the way I was feeling. I felt like a coward. Maybe I could convince my mom to let me stay home tomorrow. I'd been known to fake an illness pretty well. But what would that do? It would only delay the inevitable. Colton was going to get his shot at me no matter what.

And there was nothing I could do about it.

I just lay there for what seemed like an eternity. The next thing I knew, my mom was waking me up for dinner. An hour or so later, I had a vague memory of a conversation I had had with my grandfather at the dinner table, but for the life of me I couldn't tell you what it was about. I just hoped I hadn't said anything inappropriate. I assumed I'd know by that time, if I had. My dad would have been all over me.

I spent the remainder of the evening on homework. I didn't even go back downstairs to say good night to anyone. I knew it was kind of rude, but I was in no mood for a discussion about anything. My mind was elsewhere. At about ten-thirty, I loaded up my backpack and went into the bathroom to brush my teeth. I stopped momentarily and stared into the mirror. I wondered what my face would look like in twenty-four hours. I sighed, washed up, brushed, and hit the sack.

When the alarm went off the next morning, I was in no hurry to get out of bed. Today was to be my moment of truth. Whatever happened in the locker room a few hours from now would probably come to define me. I wasn't sure how I felt about that. And the more I thought about it, the more unfair it seemed. How would I ever be able to hold my own versus an athlete who easily had thirty pounds on me? There was no way this would be a fair fight, but what could I do? I had to go through with it. If I didn't, it would be all over school I was some kind of pansy. When I took the time to think things through, it actually seemed it would be better to get roughed up physically than have to deal with the backlash of being labeled a coward for the next two years. For better or worse, this thing had to happen.

When I met up with Mickey at the bus stop, I wasn't in much of a talkative mood. He, on the other hand, was all upbeat.

"So why the long face?" he said. "You should be ecstatic. This is the last day of Feingold's torture chamber. In a few hours, you'll be a free man."

As you may have guessed, I hadn't shared with Mickey what was waiting for me later that day. I just hadn't felt like talking about it. I suppose it wouldn't have mattered anyway. There was nothing the Mick could have done to undo the whole thing. This problem was solely in my lap, and mine alone. When he saw the condition of my face the next day, he would undoubtedly find out.

"You're right," I said. "It'll all be over later today."

"Then you can get back to living your life and just being you. That has a nice ring to it. Don't you think?"

I nodded.

The bus ride to school was quiet. Mickey talked. I nodded and smiled. But, please, don't ask me to repeat a single thing he said. There was no way I could do that. My attention was elsewhere. When I got off the bus, there was a welcoming committee waiting for me at the front door of school—Colton, Tom Webster, and five or six other members on the football team.

"This is your big day, loser," Tom said. "Right, Colt?"

"You got it, pal," Colton replied. He leaned over and got right in my face. "I owe you, Passero. For lying about what happened with that broad under the bleachers. And for the gut punch your little whore friend laid on me Saturday night at the dance."

"I keep trying to tell you," I said, "she's not a

whore." I was surprised those words had come out of my mouth. I knew I'd be pissing him off even more, so why did I say that? I guess, deep inside of me, I felt this need to defend Violet's honor.

"Don't talk back to me, you piece of shit. You got it?"

I smiled and walked into school. He's gonna kill me, I thought. The day dragged on. Normally, that would have made me crazy, but today I was in no hurry for what was to come. I met up with the Mick at lunch. As much as I had wanted to keep this whole thing between me and Colton, I thought it best to let someone in on the secret, just in case things got out of hand.

"Say that again," Mickey said.

"Colton told me he plans to beat the crap out of me after practice today."

"So what are you gonna do about it?"

"Nothing. Just take it and get it over with."

"Paulie, you gotta tell someone. You could get really messed up."

"Who am I gonna tell? The principal? And if I did, how is that gonna look? It's gonna look like I'm a chicken. How would you like that hanging over your head for the rest of your high school career?"

"I get it, man. But this is different. If I knew someone was out to get me, I'd sure speak up."

"Who would you tell?" I asked.

"Other kids, maybe. You know, they might be able to put pressure on the guy to back off."

"If you haven't noticed, I'm not the most popular guy at school these days. After I outed Colton, most kids think I'm a rat. If we told other kids about what was going to happen, all they'd probably do is come out for the show." I shook my head. "I'm not planning to tell anybody."

"This is when you really gotta miss Mr. Drennan," Mickey said.

"You know, I'm not so sure I'd even tell him. It's because of me he got suspended. I'm bad luck for the man."

For the remainder of the lunch period, Mickey kept trying to convince me to speak up about Colton's threats. But I would have none of it. I'd just have to suck it up.

When the bell rang a couple of hours later, I headed for the library. I sat there and stared at the walls until I got booted out some ninety minutes later. As I made my way to the locker room, it felt a lot like walking the plank. Instead of trying to muster up enough courage to defend myself against Colton, I was feeling sorry for myself. With such a piss-poor attitude, I was sure to be a victim. I began to wonder what kinds of stories kids would tell in the aftermath of the slaughter. It would probably go down in the annals of Cermak school history as the day the rat got what was coming to him in the boys' locker room.

When I got to the gym, Mr. Feingold was standing at the locker room door. His arms were folded, and he looked kind of disgusted.

"I'm beginning to think I was too easy on you, Passero. I would have thought you would have appealed this punishment to the principal. The fact you didn't suggests it wasn't severe enough."

Wait a few minutes, Mr. Asshole, and you'll end up getting your wish, I thought. Not severe enough? Yeah, right. In an hour or so, after they carry me to the nurse's office for first aid treatment, then you'll feel better about things.

I didn't know what he wanted me to say. Did he expect me to agree with him, or argue it was an awful punishment? I said nothing.

"Well, at least you'll think twice about bringing that kind of girl to another school dance."

"What kind of girl is that, sir?" Oh, no. Me and my big mouth. I had managed to do it again. For all I knew, Feingold might get pissed off and give me another detention. There was just something about defaming Violet that really bothered me. I would probably never see her again, but no one, and I mean no one, would get away with dragging her down as long as I was around.

"Our paths will definitely cross again, Mr. Passero, and when they do, I guarantee I'll come up with a punishment that will break you once and for all. Now get your ass in that locker room and get to work."

I decided not to tempt fate again. I pushed the door open and entered the gates of hell.

Chapter 23

A few minutes later, team members began to appear. Most just filed past me and smirked. Others chuckled.

"I really didn't expect to see you here today," Tom Webster said. "But I sure am glad you decided to come. It wouldn't be a party without the guest of honor."

I faked a smile and dropped my eyes. I was just hoping this would be over soon. When Colton entered the room, he leaned over and whispered, "I'll be right with you as soon as I change into something more fitting for an execution." Then he let out a belly laugh.

As I waited for the players to shower and change, I could hear rumblings going on. Someone would whisper something. Someone else would look in my direction and smile. As the minutes passed, I could feel my heart begin to race. It was beating faster and faster. I allowed myself to imagine the worst possible outcome. I knew that was a defeatist attitude, but if things didn't turn out as badly as I had imagined, then I'd feel better about things. A moment later, the locker room got eerily silent. I knew this was it.

Colton suddenly appeared from behind a locker. He walked right up to me. The entire team fell in behind him. "It's that time, Passero," he said. He motioned for me to follow him. "Let's go."

"Um…no, I'd rather not," I said.

"Well, I don't particularly care what you'd *rather* do. I told you to follow me." He moved in the direction of the door that led out to the football field.

I stood my ground. I wasn't leaving. At least I wasn't leaving under my own power.

Colton nodded to some of the other players. "Bring him out here."

Four players approached me. One grabbed my left leg—another my right leg. And two others grabbed my arms. Before I realized what was happening, I was airborne. They were carrying me out of the locker room and out the door. I didn't fight it. What was the use? It appeared we were headed to the practice field. It was starting to get dark, and there were no lights out there.

"Tom," Colton yelled out. "Get your car. Point it over there and turn on the headlights. We gotta make sure everyone can see the show."

The players continued to carry me to the middle of the field.

"Dump him right there," Colton said.

And they did precisely that. They dropped me onto the ground. The rest of the group began to form a circle around me and Colton. A car engine could be heard in the background. A 1965 Dodge Monaco pulled up a few feet from where the team was standing. Out popped Tom Webster. He reached back into the car through the driver's side window and flipped on the headlights. They were blinding.

I looked around. There was no means of escape— not that I planned on trying to do so.

"You have no idea how long I've been waiting for this moment," Colton said. "It's payback time,

Passero." He motioned for me to come closer, but I didn't budge.

If he wanted a piece of me, he'd have to come and get me.

Colton began walking toward me. I lifted my arms from my sides and moved them up in front of my face in a stance a boxer might take. I had watched boxing matches with my dad before, on TV, so I had a vague idea of what to do, but since I had little experience with fisticuffs myself, I was only guessing. I remembered my dad telling me you had to protect your face at all times or you wouldn't stay on your feet for long.

"Well, look at you," Colton said. "You're all ready for a fight. Isn't he, boys?"

Laughs and catcalls followed.

Colton approached me with two large, menacing fists. He started circling me. The entire time he was smiling. I spun around and kept my eyes on his. Before I knew what had happened, he swung wildly at me. He hit one of my fists, and it banged into the side of my head. It hurt, but it wasn't a fatal blow. I kept spinning around, waiting for the eventual onslaught. At one point, I decided to take a chance and throw a punch. I did, but he managed to knock it away.

"That's the best you got?" he said.

"C'mon, Colton," a voice called out. "Tear him apart."

He smiled. "That's just what I had in mind." A second later, he swung low and hit the buckle on my belt.

I had backed away just enough to soften the blow.

He opened his hand, knuckles up, and stared at it. His hand was bleeding. "Why, you son of a bitch. Now you're gonna get it." He moved in for the kill, but I kept backing up. "You running away from me, prick?" He ran right at me, swinging wildly. I held my fists high to protect my face. Seeing that, he punched me right in the gut. I dropped to my knees. Colton stood over me. He backed away a few feet. "Get up, pansy." His teammates were cheering him on.

I held my stomach. I wanted to cry, but I knew I'd never live it down.

"What are you gonna do?" he said. "That whore's not around to protect you."

Again with the whore comment. I was getting pretty tired of it. I began to think about Violet, and something she had told me Saturday night at the dance. We had been talking about how to handle bullies. She had some great advice: *"Don't be afraid. Sure, the big ones might tower over you, but most of them are just talk. And if they get physical, then just mix it up with them. They might get the better of you, but you have to let them know they were in a fight. Make them sorry they tangled with you."*

After I remembered what Violet had said, something inside me snapped. I was suddenly filled with rage. Colton couldn't get away with saying what he did about Violet. She was a nice girl, and I needed to defend her. I looked up at Colton. He was motioning with his hands for me to get up. Despite the worst stomach ache in my life, I managed to get to my feet. I gritted my teeth. I clenched my jaw. I ran as fast as I could in his direction, and right before impact, I lowered my head and buried it in his chest. The collision knocked both of us off our feet. I was lying on my side, waiting for Colton's next move. He rubbed his chest and stood up.

"You son of a bitch," he yelled.

Colton was running full speed right at me. But he wasn't running like a boxer. His hands were out like he was playing linebacker. He was sprinting at me as if I were an opposing quarterback. I had little to no time to react. At a millisecond before impact, I could see his face was exposed. That was where I would do my damage. At the last moment, I swung in the direction of his head. Crash! The collision had leveled me. I was on my back several feet from where I had been standing. Colton was on his knees holding his mouth. He pulled his hands away to see the blood dripping from them. Go for the kill, I thought. It was my only chance to survive this. I got up and stumbled to where he was kneeling. When he looked up at me, I reared back and slugged him squarely in the nose. He fell over. Blood now covered his face.

"Get up, Colt," someone yelled out. "Get up. You can't let him get away with that."

Colton slowly climbed to his feet. "Grab him!" he yelled to his teammates. "Hold him down."

A handful of players came to Colton's aid. They pushed me down onto my stomach and held me down. One of them grabbed me by the hair and lifted my head up.

It was hard to get the words out but I managed to. "Wait a minute," I said. "This is just supposed to be between you and me. This isn't fair."

A voice from the crowd of players could be heard. "What's up, Colton? You mean you can't handle this kid alone? You need help?"

"Fuck you!" Colton replied. He looked at the guys

holding me down. "Keep him right there." He smiled. "Hey, you know what—I think it's time for a little placekicking practice. Is it me or does Passero's head look like a football?"

"It kinda does," Tom Webster yelled out.

Colton walked over to me. He pulled his leg back.

I closed my eyes. I braced myself. This was gonna hurt. Really bad. I knew it. He might knock out a few teeth, or worse, break my jaw. I waited a few seconds, but nothing happened. When I opened my eyes and looked up, Brian Lambert had Colton in a headlock. He was gripping him so tightly, Colton couldn't speak.

"This ends right here," Brian said. "Let the kid go. He didn't do anything to you." Brian released his grip on Colton.

"I should have known," Colton said. "It's the traitor. Yeah, we've all seen you sitting with that lying bitch at lunch."

"Don't call her that!" Brian said. He grabbed Colton by the collar. "You know, the more I talk to Carolyn, the more I believe her side of the story. You *did* try to rape her. You should have gotten expelled for what you did. Hell, you should have been arrested. And you definitely should have been kicked off the team." He released his prey. "Do you just hate everybody? How could you do that to a girl? Are you that screwed up?"

"Maybe he's not getting enough from Andie Walker," a voice called out.

"Who said that?" Colton screamed. "I get anything I want from Andie—anytime I want it. You got that?" He turned to Lambert. "Why'd you have to stick your nose into this? I wasn't done teaching this kid a lesson."

"Well, you're done now," Brian said. "If you want to get to him, you're gonna have to go through me." Lambert was a good four inches taller than Colton, and at least twenty-five pounds heavier.

"You're a killjoy, Lambert. Anyone ever tell you that?" Colton said.

Brian looked out at the group of players. "Listen, guys, the show is over. It's time to head out."

But Colton wasn't finished. "Don't leave, any of you. If we have to, we'll go *through* Lambert to finish off Passero. What do you say?"

Todd Michaels, the team quarterback, chimed in. "This is all wrong. I, for one, have no beef with Lambert—or with Passero, for that matter. I don't know about the rest of you, but I'm leaving." He turned to the group. "Let's get out of here." One by one, the players started to disperse.

"Where are you going?" Colton said. "We're not done here." But apparently the rest of the team *was* done. The players who had been holding me down let go of me and left with the others. Colton turned to Lambert. "Thanks for nothing, asshole. You ruined a perfectly good evening." Colton huffed and walked away.

A minute later, it was just Brian and me.

"Are you okay?" Brian said.

"I'm okay—thanks to you. If you hadn't stepped in when you did, I would have gotten really messed up. I owe you big time, Brian."

"You don't owe me anything. When you stuck your neck out for Carolyn, you did everybody in this school a favor. The problem is—they didn't realize it."

"It took me a while to step up. I'm not proud of

that."

Brian lifted me up off the ground. "But you did it, man. And you had to know that big jerk would be coming after you. That took a lot of guts. I just don't know why some of the kids can't see that."

"I feel awfully lucky you did."

"Well, it's not just me. I've been talking to a lot of people. They're starting to come around. They finally realize what really happened under those bleachers that day."

"So everybody doesn't hate me anymore?"

"Hell, no. You know what I think, Paulie? I think a lot of kids, in their hearts, know what happened to Carolyn that day. They knew she didn't make up the story. But since it didn't happen to them, it was easy to look the other way. Most of those kids would never have had the balls to do what you did. None of them would have been able to point the finger at one of the stars on the football team. You see, it was easier for them to pretend it didn't happen than to admit it really did and have to take sides."

I was starting to feel better—physically *and* emotionally. Listening to Brian gave me hope things would work out in the long run. My gut was still a little sore, but at least I wasn't hunched over anymore. I was confident I would start to feel better relatively soon. Brian and I talked for a few more minutes before returning to the locker room to get our stuff. When I walked out into the gym, Mr. Feingold was waiting for me.

"What took you so long? I went in there looking for you. Did you think you could sneak out early?" He stopped for a moment and seemed to be studying me with his eyes. "What happened to you? You're filthy and you look like hell."

At that moment I was feeling confident and a little cocky. "You got your wish, Mr. Feingold. After practice, Colton took me out onto the field, and roughed me up."

"What do you mean—*I got my wish*? Do you think I put him up to it? Is that what you're suggesting?"

"I don't think you put him up to it, but you had to know something like this was bound to happen. You fed me to the lions. It wasn't right, and people should know about it."

"What people?" He put his hands on his sides. "Are you threatening me, young man?"

"I'm not threatening anybody." I turned to leave. "Goodbye, Mr. Feingold."

"Don't turn your back on me, Mr. Passero."

I kept walking.

"This isn't over—not by a long shot."

Feingold was still ranting when I left the building. I could hear his voice trail off as the door closed behind me. I looked back at the school. This would be a day I would never forget. Not ever. I was guessing that, when I was old and gray, this memory would still be as vivid in my mind as it was today. It was awful—yes—but, in the end, it had all turned out okay. I was on the road to recovery. If Brian was right, people might look at me differently from now on. I wouldn't have to hang my head any longer. Colton would probably still occasionally get in my face, but he wouldn't have the legions behind him the way he did before. Just knowing that would make those confrontations easier to handle.

As I stood on the corner waiting for the bus, I felt

as though I wanted to tell somebody about what had just happened. I knew I would eventually tell Mickey the entire story, but I wanted to tell someone else. But who? Carolyn? Mr. Drennan? My parents? And then all at once I had it. Of course, that would be perfect.

About ten minutes later, the bus pulled up. I hopped on and began rehearsing the story in my head. I didn't want to leave out any details. I kept my eyes on the street signs as we passed them. I had to make sure I got off at the right stop. When I heard the bus driver yell out, "Next stop, Neva Avenue," I got up and pulled the cord. I was starting to wonder if this was a really bad idea. A few minutes ago, it had seemed perfect, but now I wasn't sure.

I jumped down when the bus stopped, crossed Belmont, and headed in the direction of 3113 N. Neva Avenue. I walked slowly past the rows of bungalows until I reached my destination. The house looked the same as it had a week ago—picket fence falling over, peeling paint, and so on. I climbed the front steps and hesitated before knocking.

Will she be upset with me? Will she think I'm bothering her? There was only one way to find out. I closed my eyes, swallowed hard, and knocked. Oh, please, don't let it be her mother, I thought. A few seconds later, the door opened, and standing before me with a confused look on her face was Violet.

Chapter 24

"Paulie? What are you doing here?"

"I just had to talk to you. I'm sorry. I know I shouldn't be here, but I wanted to tell you something. I hope it's okay."

Violet smiled. "Sure."

"Who is it?" her mother yelled from inside.

"Nobody," she answered. "I'll be on the front porch for a few minutes."

I didn't take the "nobody" comment to heart. It was just Violet's way of keeping her mother on a strict need-to-know basis.

She stepped out onto the porch, closed the door behind her, climbed down a couple of stairs, and sat. She was in a sweatshirt and tight jeans. It was the first time I had seen her without all the eye makeup. Actually, she looked even better. Violet may not have known it, but she possessed a natural beauty. She didn't need all the makeup. She looked great the way she was. She patted the step next to where she was sitting, for me to join her.

"So what's up?" she said.

"I just wanted you to know I was thinking about something you said last Saturday, and I put it into motion with really good results."

"What was that?"

"You know, the part about if you ever get into a scrape with somebody bigger, *make them sorry they tangled with you.*"

She smiled. "I remember. So what happened? Did you mix it up with Colton?"

I nodded.

"What happened?"

I sat there and told her the whole story—Feingold's punishment, Colton's threats, being carried limb by limb out onto the practice field, the initial slugfest, my bull rush into Colton's chest, punches to his nose and mouth, being held down by the other players, and Brian Lambert's heroic appearance. As I continued, I could see the smile on her face growing wider and wider.

"I love it," she said. "See, you knocked him on his ass. That'll make him think twice about messing with you in the future."

"But he almost used my head as a football."

"He couldn't beat you by himself, Paulie. He had to cheat. He needed other guys to help him. You should feel good about that."

"I feel good *and* lucky."

"Well, sometimes we all need a little luck." She grinned. "So do you still have it bad for that Andie girl?"

"Yeah, but that'll never happen."

"Things are already happening," she said. "Once this Andie sees a lot of people think her boyfriend really attacked that girl, she'll start to think twice about things. You wait and see."

"I hope you're right."

"I think you two are going to end up together. I just have a feeling." Violet glanced over her shoulder. "My

mom's gonna be on my case any minute. I better go in."
We stood.

"Well, thanks for taking the time to talk with me,"
I said. "I appreciate it."

"Anytime, Paulie." She put her arms around me
and kissed me on the cheek. "You take care now,
okay?"

"I will. Thanks again."

She winked, climbed the stairs, and disappeared
behind the front door.

I headed back in the direction of the bus stop. I
thought about that peck on the cheek. Even though it
wasn't a sloppy kiss on the lips, it was still pretty good.
I reached Belmont Avenue just as the bus was arriving.
I ran across the street to catch it. On the ride home, I
had time to think about everything that had happened
today. I still couldn't believe it. I fought a guy. I
actually fought a guy. And I took his best shots—and I
survived. I rubbed my stomach. It was still a little
tender. I might have a bruise there, but that was okay. It
would be my badge of honor.

When I walked in the front door, my mom took one
look at me and covered her mouth with her hands.

"Oh, my God, Paulie, what happened?"

I decided to give them a little info but without the
details. "I got into a little scrape at school with a guy."

"About what?"

"To tell you the truth, I don't really know. I guess I
rubbed him the wrong way. He just went off on me."

"Well, did you tell the principal?"

I smiled. "Mom, you can't go running to the
principal every time someone looks at you cross-eyed.
Stuff happens. What can I tell you?"

"How did it end? Is he going to come after you again?"

"No, it's over. We had it out, and it's done."

My mom sighed. "It's not like you to get into fistfights."

"I don't like it any more than you do," I said. "If you don't mind, I'm going to go upstairs and get cleaned up. Okay?"

"Okay," she said. "I don't like to think about you getting into fights. It worries me."

"Well, don't worry. It won't happen again. I promise."

"And so you never found out why this other boy was mad at you?"

I had a feeling I needed to give my mom something or she'd be bugging me about this incident for the rest of my life.

"Apparently, I was talking to this girl who this other guy likes, and he wasn't happy about it. So I'll just avoid both of them in the future, and everything will be fine."

"Boys are so possessive. It's silly."

"What are you gonna do?" I said. "It's life."

She walked over and hugged me. She kissed me on the forehead. "You're right to stay away from them." She smiled. "Dinner's almost ready."

I smiled and nodded. I headed upstairs, then stopped in my tracks. "Mom, do you mind if Mickey comes over tonight?"

"That's fine. Do you want to invite him for dinner?"

"I'll find out." I scooted past my mom, walked into the hallway, and grabbed the phone. I quickly dialed his number. I waited a moment, and Mickey answered.

"Hello."

"Mick?"

"Yeah. Paulie? What the hell happened? Did you get into a fight with Colton?"

"I'll tell you all about it tonight. You wanna come over for dinner?"

"Maybe, let me check something."

I could tell he was cupping the receiver with his hand, but I was able to make out, "Hey, Mom, what are we having for dinner?" There was a pause, and then, "Ugh."

"What's your mom making?" he asked.

"Wait a sec." I set the phone down. "Hey, Mom, what's for dinner?"

"Lasagna," she said.

I picked up the receiver. "Lasagna," I told him.

"I'll be there in twenty minutes. That sure beats meatloaf."

Ten minutes later, the doorbell rang. Mick had to have run the entire way. He was anxious to hear the dirt. We went upstairs to my bedroom.

"I want every sordid detail," he said.

I plopped down on the bed and told him the entire story. I didn't leave out a thing. His jaw dropped when I described the fight with Colton. His eyebrows raised when I explained how Brian Lambert stepped up and saved the day. Then a little smile appeared on his face when I told him about stopping at Violet's house on the way home. I made sure to include the peck on the cheek. I think the only reason Mickey believed me was because I wasn't claiming another kiss on the mouth.

He squeezed the sides of his head. "Oh, my God,

Paulie! You aren't shitting me, I hope?"

"Scout's honor. It's all true."

"Oh, man. So what's gonna happen when you bump into Colton on Monday?"

"Your guess is as good as mine. He might ignore me. He might come after me again. I just don't know what to expect."

"Are you worried he might freak out at you again?"

"Sure, but what can I do about it? At least, my week in the locker room is over. He can't get at me there."

"I have to ask. Is Brian Lambert your new best friend?"

I smiled. "No one can replace you, Mick. You know that."

"I was just checking."

We shot the breeze for a few more minutes before my mom called us down for dinner. You should have seen the serving size of lasagna Mickey heaped onto his plate. But he was a big kid, you have to remember, who would easily burn it off the next time we played fast pitching in the playground of the grammar school across from his house.

After Mickey headed home, I had time to do some deep thinking. So much had happened in the last few hours, I was wondering if I had dreamed it all. But when I glanced at my puss in the mirror and saw the bruises, I knew it was real. I had been in a real fight, and I had survived. Not only had I survived but, for all intents and purposes, I had come out of it as the victor. You wouldn't have thought so if you had seen me sprawled out on the practice field about to be kicked in the head.

But fortunately that didn't happen. And that didn't diminish my victory over Colton. He knew I had bested him. The entire team knew. That was good enough for me. If he had stuck with boxing instead of tackling, the story might have had to be rewritten. But he had gotten so angry he lost his perspective. He must have thought he was still wearing a football helmet, because he forgot to protect his face. That oversight saved my ass.

I was wondering what things would be like on Monday. I hoped Brian had been able to recruit more believers of Carolyn's story. He appeared to be a pretty influential guy—someone people would trust. I'm not sure what version of the story Andie would hear. I doubted if it would feature me as the hero. I was wondering if she would ever speak to me again. I wanted so badly for her to do so. So many times I would imagine a scenario where she would finally see the error of her ways and come running to me. But I knew things like that only happened in the movies.

My weekend was pretty much spoken for. I had to stock shelves at the High-Low all day Saturday, and my dad had asked me to rake up the leaves in the yard on Sunday. Both went pretty much to form. The store was having a big sale on Monday, so before we left on Saturday we had to have the shelves jammed. I didn't get home until nearly seven p.m. On Sunday, as I raked, my mind relived Friday night over and over again. The more I thought about it, the more upbeat I became. Things were actually working out in a positive manner. It had been so long since something like that had happened.

And then suddenly I was feeling sad again. I found myself thinking about Mr. Drennan. He had been forced out by Feingold. It just wasn't right. I remembered telling Feingold on Friday that someone should be told about how he put me in harm's way by assigning me to the football locker room. He knew what might happen, and he was probably hoping for it. This wasn't the kind of thing a responsible adult should have done. If Feingold could bring down Mr. Drennan, then I could bring down Feingold. I decided I would tell Mr. Drennan about what he had done. But when? How? Mr. Drennan wasn't at school anymore, and I didn't have his home phone number. But...I did know where he lived, thanks to the birthday songsters last year.

I hurriedly finished up raking the leaves, and then I asked my parents if I could use the car. I didn't want to tell them I was going over to a teacher's house, and I sure didn't want to have to explain anything about how Mr. Drennan had gotten suspended. All my parents needed to hear was how Violet was dressed at the dance. Who knew how they would have reacted. I decided to tell a little fib about needing to meet up with classmates, and how we were working on a group presentation. How could they turn me down? Heck, it was all about academics. And fortunately, they bought it.

Minutes later I was sailing down Harlem Avenue on my way to Mr. Drennan's house. It took about ten minutes to get there. During the ride I started feeling funny about just popping in on him unannounced. I didn't know if I would be disturbing him or not. What if he was having company or something? That would be really awkward. When I pulled up in front of his house, I started to get cold feet, so I drove down a few more houses and parked. I kept thinking about all the reasons *not* to go in. Then I started to consider the good reasons—maybe he'd be happy to see me; maybe he was lonely and might appreciate some company; maybe he'd love to hear the juicy tidbits about Feingold and my tussle with Colton. Maybe...maybe...maybe. What to do? I sat in the car a few more minutes trying to work up the courage to do this. Right or wrong—I had to.

I got out of the car and walked slowly to Mr. Drennan's house. I tried to see if he might be out in the back yard. He didn't appear to be. I looked in the windows, hoping to make eye contact with him. Nothing. I climbed the front porch, rang the bell, and crossed my fingers. A moment later, a woman answered the door. It was his wife.

"Can I help you?" she said. "Oh, it's you, Paulie."

"Hi, I was wondering if Mr. Drennan is in."

"Wait right here."

Within a few seconds, Mr. Drennan appeared in the doorway. "Paulie, I was just thinking about you. Come on in."

"You sure it's okay?"

"It's fine."

I followed him through the living room to a stairway that led to the basement.

"Annette, I'll be downstairs if you need me."

"Okay," she replied. "Would you guys like something to drink?"

Mr. Drennan looked to me.

"No, thanks. I'm fine."

"No, we're good," he called out to his wife. We walked downstairs to a nicely decorated, finished basement. The walls were filled with sports memorabilia. He pointed to a couch for me to sit. "So, Paulie, what brings you here?"

I tried to collect my thoughts. I knew what I wanted to tell him, but I felt kind of uncomfortable being in his house and everything. I think he could tell I was nervous.

"Just relax. We're friends here."

"Okay." I exhaled. "First of all, I want to tell you how sorry I am about what they did to you. If I hadn't brought Violet to the dance, none of this would have happened. It's all my fault."

He smiled. "It's not your fault. Violet was perfectly welcome at the dance. Mr. Feingold was the one who overreacted. You did nothing wrong."

"But I want to fix this for you."

"Don't worry," he said. "It'll all work out. And if it doesn't, I'm sure I can find another teaching job somewhere else."

Boy, I sure didn't want to hear that. I wanted him teaching at Cermak—and nowhere else.

"So is that all you wanted to tell me? Because I have some news to share with you."

"Well, actually there's more."

"Okay, let's hear it."

For the next several minutes, I proceeded to tell him everything that had happened since his suspension. I told him about Feingold's punishment, how I survived the first few days in the locker room, and I concluded with the real doozy—what had happened Friday out on the practice field.

Mr. Drennan was now sitting on the edge of the couch. "Are you okay?"

"Yeah, I'm fine. I have a bruise on my stomach,

but other than that, I'm okay."

He grinned. "I can't believe you decked Colton."

"Me neither. I got real lucky."

"Well, it sounds like you used your head—in more ways than one."

I laughed.

"And I am so glad to hear about how Brian Lambert stepped up," he said. "I always considered him to be a high-character young man. It sounds like my instincts were right."

"Brian was a life saver," I said.

He stood up and folded his arms. "I can't believe Feingold put you in such a dangerous environment. People are going to hear about this."

"Good."

"Now I have some news for you," he said. "It's not very pleasant."

"Oh, really?"

Mr. Drennan got up and began pacing. "Well, let me just come out with it. Andie Walker was attacked last night."

"Oh, God! Is she all right?"

"She's in the hospital. She's pretty well bruised up." He paused momentarily. "And one more thing. It appears she was sexually assaulted."

"That's terrible! Do they know who did it?"

He sighed. "That's the shocker. Or maybe not so shocking. It was Colton Brand."

"But they're like boyfriend and girlfriend. I don't get it."

"Well, just because you're someone's boyfriend doesn't give you the right to have your way with someone. He wanted her to do things she didn't want to do. And when she refused, he made her pay for it."

I just sat there and thought about Andie lying in a hospital bed.

"Paulie, you can't speak a word of this to anyone. I shouldn't even have told you. But since you saw Colton trying to do the same thing to Carolyn Mancuso, I thought you should know. And you're probably going to be a witness at a hearing."

"Again? The school board didn't believe me the first time."

"This isn't with the school board. I got a call this morning from the superintendent. He's in charge of all of the schools in our district. He was naturally informed when the assault on Andie took place. But it wasn't until now he learned about the attack on Carolyn. He didn't appear too pleased at how the school board handled that matter. He wants to speak with everyone involved."

"Will he be able to help you get your job back?"

"That's what I'm hoping."

"I'd be happy to tell him everything I saw."

"Good. That's what I told him."

"Mr. Drennan, where is Colton now?"

"Jail. He was arrested last night and charged with rape. The judge set a hefty bail. It's doubtful his parents will be able to raise that kind of cash. He's going to be there for quite some time."

"Do you think he'll get expelled this time?"

"I think you can count on it."

"Do you know what hospital Andie is in?"

"St. Anne's on North Avenue."

I looked up at the clock on the wall.

"I think you'll make it before visiting hours are

up."

He knew exactly what I was thinking. I talked with Mr. Drennan a few more minutes before leaving. I jumped in the car and headed to the hospital. I wasn't sure if Andie would want to see me, or if she was even allowed visitors. Things hadn't been on very good terms with her lately. But I had to see her. I just had to.

Chapter 25

I walked into the lobby of St. Anne's about twenty minutes later. It was late on a Sunday afternoon. I wasn't sure when visiting hours ended. I walked up to the front desk and tried to get the attention of a lady on the phone. She held up one finger when she saw me. A couple of minutes later, she hung up.

"How can I help you, young man?"

"I was wondering if you could tell me what room Andie Walker is in?"

"Visiting hours end at six p.m. sharp. You only have about twenty-five minutes."

"I understand."

She glanced at her chart for a moment. "Miss Walker is in room three-eleven." She pointed to the right. "The elevators are over there."

"Okay, thank you."

As I walked in the direction of the elevators, I noticed the hospital gift shop on my left. I checked my wallet—thirteen dollars. That should be enough, I thought. I walked in and made my way to a large refrigerated case containing flowers. I found a bouquet that looked good. The price tag read twelve-ninety-five. Perfect. I brought them up to the counter and took out my wallet. The clerk began wrapping them. She punched in some numbers on the cash register.

"That'll be thirteen-twenty-four with tax."

Oh, no, I forgot about tax. I wasn't sure what to do. Then something popped into my head.

"Uh…I only seem to have thirteen dollars with me. Do you suppose we could take out a flower to get the price down?"

"Son, that's not how it works," the clerk said.

"Okay, I'll have to go back and look for something cheaper." I picked up the bouquet and was in the process of returning it when the clerk called out.

"Who are the flowers for?"

"This girl from school. She was attacked last night."

The clerk waved me back. "Thirteen dollars is fine."

"Really?"

She nodded as she wrapped up the flowers.

I handed her the money. "Thanks a lot. I really appreciate it."

The clerk smiled. "This girl? Is she the one?"

I grinned. I was embarrassed.

"She'll love them. Now hurry up. Visiting hours are ending soon."

I scooted to a bank of elevators and entered the first one that opened. I pushed number three. I got out and began checking room numbers. They started at three-twenty-six. The closer I got, the less confident I became this was a good idea. I knew Andie had probably been visited by family members and close friends. To be perfectly honest, I wasn't in either category. Would she be upset I came? Would she ask me to leave? She didn't have to worry. I wouldn't stay long. I just had to know if she was all right. Maybe it would be best if she was sleeping. Then I'd be able to see if she was okay or not, and she would never even know I had stopped by.

When I reached room three-eleven, I immediately noticed the door was open. That had to be a good sign. I stopped when I reached the doorway. I could see a man and a woman sitting in chairs, but I couldn't see Andie. When the woman saw me, she smiled. She turned away and seemed to be speaking to someone else.

"Well, it looks like there's someone here to see you, honey," she said. She and the man disappeared for a moment. When they reappeared, they waved. "We'll be back first thing in the morning."

"Okay, bye," a voice said. "Love you." It sounded like Andie's voice.

"Love you, sweetie," the man said. They then walked past me, smiled, and abruptly stopped. "Excuse me, son, do we know you?" the man said.

"I'm Paulie Passero. I go to Cermak with Andie."

"Okay, but don't stay long. She needs her rest."

"Oh, don't worry," I said. "I'll be quick."

As they left the room, the man turned to his wife. "She's probably going to miss a whole week of practice because of this. She's gotta be back on her feet for the next match."

His wife shook her head. "Tennis is the last thing you should be worried about right now."

The man grunted.

I watched as her parents made their way to the elevators. I just stood in the doorway for what seemed like an eternity. I couldn't muster the courage to walk in.

"Is there someone out there?" Andie said.

257

"Yeah, coming," I said. I swallowed hard and entered the room.

When our eyes met, Andie immediately covered her face with her hands and began crying.

"Paulie, I don't want you to see me like this."

"Like what?" I said. "You look fine. You look perfect."

"No, I don't. I look hideous."

I just stood there. I wasn't sure if she would ever uncover her face.

"I'm not leaving until I see you, so you might as well take your hands down."

"No."

"Okay, I can wait."

Andie slowly began to slide her hands down. The first thing I noticed was her left eye. It was discolored and swollen shut. It was a little hard to maintain a smile, but I forced myself to. When she revealed her mouth, I could see her bottom lip was puffy. It also appeared to be split.

"Well, go ahead and say it," she said.

"Say what?" I asked.

"Just say it, Paulie."

"I don't understand. Say what?"

"Say *I told you so*."

"I would never say that."

Andie managed a half smile, then immediately held her mouth. "It hurts when I smile."

"I'm sorry."

"Are you just going to stand there, or are you going to sit down?" she said.

I pulled up a chair and slid it closer to the bed.

"What's that you're holding?" she said.

"Oh…these are for you." I unwrapped the flowers and handed them to Andie.

"They're nice. Thank you." She set them down on a tray.

I wasn't sure how to get the conversation started. "So how are you feeling?"

"I look like I feel—awful."

"You look outstanding. You always look outstanding."

She appeared embarrassed. She looked the other way.

"He turned out to be a monster, you know," she said.

I nodded.

"You were so right about everything. He did attack Carolyn, didn't he?"

"Yes."

"Why didn't I listen to you? I was so stubborn. I was so stupid."

"How were you supposed to know he would hurt you?"

"I should have known," she said. "You tried to tell me." She seemed angry at herself.

"I had a feeling Colton would show his true colors someday," I said. "I'm just sorry it had to happen to you."

"I hope he stays in jail for the rest of his life. I never want to see him again." She sighed and folded her arms. "But if this goes to trial, I'll have to look at him every day in court. I don't think I can do it."

"You *can* do it," I said. "And I'll be right there with you."

"You would do that for me?"

"Andie, I'd do just about anything for you."

She raised her eyes. "Why couldn't I have met someone like you...instead of Colton?"

"Well, I'm here now—if that helps."

She reached over and held my hands. "It does help. It really does."

An announcement over the PA interrupted our conversation. "Visiting hours will end in ten minutes. At that time, all visitors must leave patient rooms."

I glanced at the clock over Andie's bed. "I wish I had gotten here earlier."

"Don't leave. I don't want you to."

"I have no plans to leave. They're gonna have to kick me out."

For the next twenty minutes, we talked and we laughed. It was as if we had been friends for years. She was so easy to talk to. I did eventually get booted out, but the nurse was pretty nice about it. Before I left, Andie made me promise to come back to visit her tomorrow. That was going to happen with or without a promise.

On my way home, I swung by Mickey's house. I had to update him on my impromptu meeting with Mr. Drennan and my visit to the hospital. He told me I should write a book about the last forty-eight hours of my life. I laughed. If I did, no one would believe me, I told him. We talked about the reception I might get at school tomorrow from the football guys. I wasn't sure if they'd still be pissed at me, or if maybe Brian Lambert had managed to twist a few arms and had changed their minds about me and Colton. I could only hope for the best.

At school the next morning, it seemed as though

the news about Colton's attack on Andie had spread throughout the entire junior class. People I had never met or spoken to were smiling at me in the hallways. Football players were nodding at me. A few of them patted me on the ass. Apparently things had changed, literally overnight. I had suddenly become popular. I wasn't this outcast I had been for the last few weeks. It felt good. Actually, it felt great. At lunch, I had more offers than I knew what to do with. Andie's friends had waved me over and asked me to sit with them. Brian and Carolyn did the same. Mickey's bunch was too busy with their slide rule to care. I opted to sit with Brian. I figured I owed him.

"Paulie, Brian and I were just talking about something," Carolyn said. "I've decided not to transfer. Things are getting better." She looked at Brian and smiled.

"Well, that's outstanding news," I said.

A moment later, Mr. Feingold came up to us.

"Paul Passero, Carolyn Mancuso, can you be here tonight at eight p.m. for a meeting with the school superintendent?"

"Yes, I think so," Carolyn said.

"I can make it," I said. "Where will it be held?"

"In the principal's conference room," Mr. Feingold said. "I think you know where that is, Mr. Passero."

"Can I ask what this is about?" Carolyn said.

"That's not any of your concern," he said. "Just be there." He exited as quickly as he had appeared.

I turned to Brian and Carolyn. "A prince of a fellow, don't you think?"

They both laughed.

After school, on our bus ride home, the Mick and I

chatted about the upcoming meeting with the superintendent. Mick was wishing he could be there. I told him I'd call him later tonight with the lowdown of what went on.

I had to wait until my dad got home from work to borrow the car to visit Andie in the hospital. When I got there, I noticed the eye that had been swollen shut was now open. She was thankful for that. One of her friends from the tennis team had applied some makeup to her swollen eye. It looked a lot better.

"You look great," I said.

"I know you're lying, but don't stop."

"I won't be able to stay as late as I did last night," I said. "I have to be at a meeting tonight at school with the superintendent."

"I know," she said.

"How?"

"The superintendent was here today. We talked for about an hour. He had a secretary who was taking notes the entire time."

"Wow, this guy doesn't mess around."

"He seemed to believe me. He never once made me feel uncomfortable. He wasn't happy about the fact his office wasn't notified following the attack on Carolyn."

"Finally, we have someone who really listens," I said. "I have a good feeling this is all going to work out."

"Me too."

I left the hospital at seven-thirty and headed to school. When I arrived at the principal's conference room, Carolyn was already there. She was seated outside the room talking to Mr. Drennan. I sat down with them. While we were waiting, the principal, Mr.

Payne, and Mr. Feingold arrived. At precisely eight p.m., a man in a suit emerged from the conference room.

"The school board is already inside," he said. "Principal Payne, please join us."

The rest of us waited our turn. Twenty minutes later, Principal Payne, looking very grim, exited the conference room, and Mr. Feingold was called in. When he came out several minutes later, he gruffly brushed past us without saying a word. Then Mr. Drennan and Carolyn were called in, one by one. Mr. Drennan winked at me when he came out. Carolyn smiled at me when she emerged. Their expressions were definitely different from those of the principal and Mr. Feingold.

The door opened. "Paul Passero?" the man said.

"Yes."

"Come on in."

The superintendent sat at the head of the table with school board members on either side. Unlike my last interrogation, this one was conducted by one person—the superintendent. He asked me about the incident under the bleachers. I answered to the best of my ability. Then he asked about the punishment from Mr. Feingold following the homecoming dance. I hadn't expected that, but I told him about how uncomfortable I was being in a room with a bunch of guys who supposedly hated me. Then he asked about what took place on the practice football field with Colton and the team this past Friday. He seemed to be bothered by my account of the story. The whole interview took about twenty-five minutes. When I left the conference room, there was no one waiting in the hallway.

I drove home and thought about what had just taken place. I was hopeful this mess would all be worked out. When I walked in the door, I immediately ran to the telephone and called Mickey. I told him everything that had happened at school with the superintendent, and about my visit to see Andie. I just talked and talked. He was speechless during the entire call. When I hung up, I ran upstairs to do some homework. It was late—nine-forty-five. I wouldn't be getting as much sleep as I usually got, but fortunately I wasn't tired. I was so amped up following the meeting that I was wide awake. I eventually turned off the light at midnight, and even though it was hard to fall asleep, I managed to, because the next thing I knew, the alarm was going off.

I fell back asleep and didn't wake up until my mom called out from the bottom of the stairs. When I glanced at the clock, I was in a panic. I threw on the same clothes I had worn the day before, shoved down two pieces of cinnamon toast, and ran to the bus stop. Mickey wasn't there. He had to have taken the most recent bus. Another bus didn't come by for ten minutes. If we made the majority of the lights, I would be on time. I glanced at my watch the entire ride. When we pulled up in front of school, I had thirty seconds to get to my locker and make it to English. I was still at my locker when the bell rang. I didn't know how strict the sub in Mr. Drennan's class would be. But when I got there, I was pleasantly surprised. Sitting behind the desk was Mr. Drennan himself. He was back. This was amazing. When he saw me, he grinned.

He stood up and faced the group. "Class, I need you to do me a favor. I want you to study quietly by

yourselves for about five minutes. And remember—
quietly." He turned to me. "Paulie, can I see you for a
moment?"

What was up? Was he actually going to nail me for
being tardy? He knew how late we got out last night. I
followed him into the hallway.

"I was only like ten seconds late," I said.

"Don't worry about that. I wanted to tell you about
some of the decisions the superintendent made."

I pointed to him. "I see one already. You're back."

"He called me at six a.m. this morning to welcome
me back. I never like early morning phone calls before
I'm awake, but this one was more than fine."

"I'm so glad to have you back," I said.

"Me too. Well, let me tell you about the other
changes. Assistant Principal Ken Thomas is now acting
principal. Mr. Payne was given his walking papers late
last night. As was Mr. Feingold. He won't be back.
Good riddance."

This was amazing news. I had a hard time hiding
my excitement.

"Two members of the school board have been
asked to submit their letters of resignation. The
superintendent was especially bothered by the fact that
some of our administrators seemed more concerned
about winning football games than protecting our
students." He paused. "And the last item—Colton
Brand has been expelled. He won't be welcome in any
of the district schools. But since he may be facing some
lengthy prison time, it may all be moot. I thought you'd
like to know."

"I can't believe any of this. So the good guys won
this time?"

He put his hand on my shoulder. "The good guys won. Let's get back to class."

Could things have gotten any better? You bet. I visited Andie in the hospital for the next two days. Then she was released. She came back to school the following Monday. Everyone made a big deal about it. You should have seen the kids who came by to greet her at lunch. It was like Grand Central Station. And since I had been welcomed back to her lunch table, many of them were very cordial to me—even the football players.

I continued to talk to Andie every chance I had— before school, in the hallways, at lunch, after school. It took me another week to build up the courage to ask her out. I fumbled through it, but thankfully she said yes. I took her to see *Funny Girl* at the Golf Mill Theater in Niles. And then it was a visit to Johnnie's Beef in Elmwood Park. After that we sat in the car and talked and laughed. And—are you ready for this?—I actually asked her out the next two Saturday nights, and she accepted. It wasn't until I was saying goodbye on our third date that I had the nerve to kiss her. I had planned it out all day. When the time came, I rattled on and on about something trivial, trying to build up enough courage to make my move. At one point when things were about to get awkward, it was do or die. I used the same technique Violet had used on me, minus the moistness. I cupped her face with my hands and pressed my lips against hers. It was unbelievable. And if that weren't good enough, after my move, she smiled and kissed me back. I floated all the way home.

We had been dating for about a month when Andie finally made things official. At lunch one day, she was talking to a new student, and she introduced me as her boyfriend. I was speechless. I had considered myself her boyfriend the day I first visited her in the hospital, but I was so glad she now felt the same way. I could not remember ever being happier.

Then there was the matter regarding Colton. With pretty strong accusations from two victims, and eyewitness testimony from yours truly, Colton's attorney encouraged him to accept a plea of first-degree sexual assault. He agreed to it. His sentence was no less than two, and no more than four years in prison. So I guess it was possible Colton would resurface in a couple of years. But by then both Andie and I would be in college, miles away. I can't see how he will have an opportunity to bother us in the future.

So where does that leave things? Well, I'm still putting in ten to twelve hours a week at High-Low. And that cash really comes in handy now, because movies and restaurants and concerts and miniature golf dates can be costly. I've gotten busier at the school newspaper. I'm cranking out, on average, one to two articles a week. I'm prioritizing my studies. I'm spending two or three hours a night doing homework. Dating Andie has made me a better student, a better journalist, and a better person. I couldn't ask for more.

What will the future hold? Well, what would you say if I told you, at the ripe old age of seventeen, that I know who I'm going to marry? You'd probably think I was crazy. Most high school romances fizzle after a few months. But not this one. It's going to last forever.

You probably think I'm acting a little naïve. But I'm dead serious about it. Think about this for a minute. If I had told you two months ago that I would take

Violet out on a date, beat Colton Brand in a fist fight, and go steady with Andie Walker, you would think I was crazy. But they all happened. So why can't Andie and I stay together for eternity?

I've beaten the odds before. I can do them again. You'd better stay tuned.

A word about the author...

John Madormo, Chicago area screenwriter, author, and college professor, has created a body of work that has attracted the attention of motion picture producers and publishers. John sold a family comedy screenplay to a Los Angeles production company, signed a contract for a three-book deal with a major New York publisher, and was named the Grand Prize winner of a national writing competition. The book series has been embraced by educators on a national scale.

John has placed well in many screenwriting competitions, including as Grand Prize winner in the Reno Film Festival Best Synopsis Contest, First Place for Best Family Film Synopsis ("Paulie Perkins, P.I."), and First Place winner for Best Family Film Synopsis at the Reno Film Festival Best Synopsis Contest ("Dream Machine"). He has also entered into option agreements with several motion picture production companies.

http://www.johnmadormo.com

Thank you for purchasing
this publication of The Wild Rose Press, Inc.

For questions or more information
contact us at
info@thewildrosepress.com.

The Wild Rose Press, Inc.
www.thewildrosepress.com